BLACKHILL

CW00853384

THE
MISSING
GRIMOIRE

CLAIRE HASTIE

CRANTHORPE
MILLNER

First published by Cranthorpe Millner Publishers (2022)

ISBN 978-1-80378-061-0 (Paperback)

www.cranthorpemillner.com

Cranthorpe Millner Publishers

To Barry Junior

Magic – to create an illusion to con the observer.

Magick – to channel our energy and that of the elements in order to manifest our desires and outcomes with intention and will.

Chapter 1

☽ Many Moons Later ☾

A blanket of white enveloped the sculptures, creating a pillowy artefact of their previous shapes, as giant snowflakes sprinkled from the overhanging branches to land on top of the unsuspecting unicorn's head. Theodore shook his mane of white fur, the snow tickling his nose. Ambling around the manor's gardens, he desperately tried to nibble some winter berries from the trees, but every time he reached for some, the branches would sprinkle him with tiny avalanches. He could easily go to Illuminos to feed on the fresh berries available, but he wanted to be here at the manor for Luna Green. The unicorn gazed up towards a window on the first floor of the manor, as though sensing his friend's presence beyond the brick and mortar.

"Oh my, you look beautiful." Bell Tilly clapped her hands together as Luna twirled before a long mirror.

"Don't you think it's a little over the top?" Luna asked, turning to the young teacher.

"Not at all! This is an important event. Especially for us witches." Bell smoothed her hands along her purple gown.

Luna turned back to the mirror. "But I'm not a witch."

Bell clicked her tongue as she made her way over to stand by Luna's side. "Your mother was a witch, and don't you ever forget that, miss!" She pointed a finger at Luna, pretending to be angry. "Anyway, the Winter Solstice ball is a tradition here. Every year we celebrate it." The young witch glanced down. "Unfortunately, we haven't had one since Edward Blackhill passed. We had no children here apart from the Edgar twins."

"Why is that?" asked Luna, turning to face her.

"The next generation of crystal children were still too young," explained Bell.

"There must be more than just eleven children who possess gifts."

"Eh, twelve actually."

The two turned around to see Lily Jackson glide into the room.

"Oh, sorry Lily, I didn't mean to offend."

Lily laughed. Since she had helped to recover the onyx crystal from the clutches of the shapeshifter, Amadan, they had appointed her as a new guardian of the athame. Luna had not even contemplated that her best friend from back home in Scotland might in fact be a ghost. That is, until she had arrived here at the manor.

"Wow, you look terrific!" Lily floated in circles around her friend, grinning as Luna's pale cheeks tinged a slight pink. "It goes perfectly with your hair and eyes."

Luna turned to the mirror. She felt dressed for a prom. The silver dress twinkled in the overhead light, the silky fabric skimming just above her ankles, and silver glitter court shoes peeped out from the underskirt. Bell had plaited her long, white hair, threading silver ribbons through the knots, and it now cascaded down to her lower back like a shimmering river. Lily was also dressed up, but in a metallic grey trouser suit. She had always been a tomboy, thought Luna.

"How do I look?" Bell twirled in her long, fitted purple dress, styled with a daring low-cut heart shape at the bust. She had matched it with a purple chiffon scarf, which she wore wrapped around her shoulders to save her blushes.

"Stunning, Miss Tilly," announced the girls.

Deep down, Luna knew that Bell had a crush on Augustus the fairy. They had recently found out that he was in fact royalty, being the son of King Engogabal, but despite this, the fairy preferred not to be referred to by his title, Prince Augustus. He felt it was far too formal. This of course made Bell admire him even more for his chivalry. Luna, however, thought otherwise. Augustus still disliked witches, after the warlock Jonas Schmidt had tricked his brother, Cassieus, into handing over the magickal athame and the first missing crystal, before trapping Cassieus inside a glass jar until Edward Blackhill found him by chance, setting him free.

Luna looked at the young teacher. She hoped Augustus would look at Bell differently, and not as just another witch to be disliked. Maybe once he saw her in this dress, instead of her normal boring attire of blouses and long skirts, he would see her for who she was… maybe, just maybe, he would see beyond the fact that she was a witch, and fall in love.

"Come on, we have people waiting." Bell tugged at Luna's arm.

Luna followed the other two along the corridor towards the spiral staircase, pausing as they passed the tall window that overlooked the gardens. She could not help but marvel at how beautiful, how magical everything looked, covered in sparkling fresh snow. She was about to turn away when movement caught her eye. After a moment of panic, she sighed with relief, realising it was only Theodore. She waved down to him. Ever since she had gone into a trance and channelled the evil Jonas Schmidt last year, she had been constantly jumpy. Everyone had assumed he was dead, but it seemed he had survived the attack over seventy years ago by Cassieus and Edward Blackhill, when he had attempted to open the darker realms with the athame. It was strange… Luna knew he should be a frail old man by now, but when he had taken over her body, she had sensed a powerful presence from him, not one of weakness.

Shaking off these thoughts, Luna put on a brave smile and turned towards the staircase. As she reached the first step, she was delighted to see Magnus Scully waiting at the bottom. She smiled down at him. He looked so handsome, with his dark blonde hair swept into a side pattern. He wore a deep red blazer with black tailored trousers, and a black shirt poked out from underneath a waistcoat.

Luna noticed him smile from ear to ear as he watched her descend the stairs. She knew he was still not accustomed to her appearance, since she had transformed into her true Celestian self, but he had assured her that he thought it made her look more grown up. And more beautiful, he had told Lily in secret, though being a faithful friend, Lily had not been able to keep this to herself and had told Luna when they were alone. 'If the other boys found out, he would be in for an ear ribbing for a long time', she had told Luna, after repeating the boy's words to her.

"You look… different," said Luna, when she reached Magnus.

Magnus stuck a finger beneath his collar, pulling it away from his neck. "Thanks," he groaned. "I feel like I'm being choked."

"Where's your tie," said Bell, gliding past them.

The boy's face reddened. "I er…"

Bell giggled. "I'm only joking. But next year, please

invest in one. This is a formal ball."

Looking Magnus up and down, Luna shrugged, hooking an arm through his as they made their way towards the large conservatory at the back of the manor. The children had never been in this part of the manor before; Agnes Guthrie had informed them – after some of the children had been caught trying to sneak in – that it was unsafe as the roof was leaking. But when it was decided that a Winter Solstice ball would finally be held after so many years, Agnes had arranged for it to be fixed. Luna knew they had used magick, but Bell always insisted that they did not cheat on such matters. It was Urus the oxman's job to fix things. He was, after all, the odd-job man.

In days gone by, the ball had always been held a few days before Christmas, but given the state of the conservatory and the mandatory school holidays, Agnes had decided to wait until the week after New Year's Eve, when all the children had returned to the manor. It made more sense, she had informed them, to hold a ball in the new year, as a celebration of their reunion for the new term.

As they entered through the double doors, an array of colourful outfits outshone one another. All the children and teachers were already there. Hattie Bordeaux greeted them in her usual bright, cheery manner as she swept past in an azure blue dress with a matching headscarf. Luna noticed Tamara Hobbs and Angelica

Lawson lingering beside the Edgar twins. Tamara had chosen a fitted gold dress, while her taller friend was dressed in white. The Mexican twins looked handsome in their black suits, the dark silk enhancing their olive-toned skin and black hair.

Luna scanned her eyes over the long table at the back, where silverware filled with food and drink had been laid out. A tall, ominous figure hunched over the punch bowl, and Luna once again had to do a double take, swiftly realising, with a certain degree of relief, that the figure was Belinda Dobson, dressed in her standard outfit of black trousers and a black top. Only her bright green hair differentiated her from her shadow. Usually, her hair hung from her shoulders, but it seemed she had made some effort tonight, scraping it back into a neat ponytail. If it had not been for the green hair, or Belinda's tendency to wear thick black eyeliner and black lipstick, she would easily pass as 'normal'. But Luna loved her for being different. In fact, she admired her for her confidence to stand out. Luna had to use spells to change her appearance so that she could fit in with the 'norm', whereas Belinda did everything she could not to look normal.

Magnus let go of Luna's arm as a gangly redhead jumped goofily in front of them.

"Isaac, nice suit," mocked Magnus, as he took in the boy's matching purple velvet trousers and blazer.

The New Zealander rolled his blue eyes. "Yeah,

7

yeah. Just say it. I look like a magician trying too hard."

Luna cupped a hand over her mouth, stifling a giggle.

Isaac eyed her suspiciously. "Hey, how's it going, Ice Queen?"

Luna dropped her hand and glared sternly at his freckled face. "Say that again, Mr Bojangles!"

Magnus stepped in between them. "Hey, cut it out."

Isaac smirked. "Take a joke, or you'll freeze us all with that glare."

Magnus and Luna exchanged glances.

Isaac shrugged his shoulders. "You've got to admit, Ice Queen is a good nickname."

Magnus patted his friend on the shoulder as he wandered over towards the food table. "Whatever you say…"

Feeling awkward, Luna stepped away from Isaac, pretending to look for someone. When she turned around, she was glad to see him talking to someone else.

"Ah, Miss Luna."

Luna looked down to see Murdoch. Even the tiny imp was dressed for the occasion, sporting a miniature tartan waistcoat.

"Think I will wear something like this from noo on, whit d'ya think?" His cherubic face looked proud as punch.

"Yes, I think you should. Definitely much better than that oversized shirt you normally wear."

Murdoch frowned up at her. "And whit's wrong with

that?" he demanded.

Luna sighed. She should have known better than to insult the moody Scottish imp. Fortunately, she spotted Aengus the leprechaun, and quickly waved for him to come over and join them. Anything to distract Murdoch.

"Why, you look wonderful Miss Green," announced Aengus.

She mouthed 'thank you' back to him. She could have said the same back, but the leprechaun was wearing the same emerald-green attire he always wore. The thought of at least a dozen of the same outfits hanging up in a tiny wardrobe suddenly crossed her mind.

"Have you tried our magickal fruit punch yet?" asked Aengus.

Luna shook her head.

"Whit's magickal aboot fruit?" grumbled Murdoch.

Luna laughed. "Come on, let's see, shall we?" She made her way over to the food table, leaving Aengus and Murdoch to scurry after her.

☾

Agnes Guthrie pulled the collar of her wool coat up around her ears as the icy wind blew circles around her.

"They passed through the oak tree," boomed Urus, standing by her side.

The half man, half ox made his way over to the gates.

Agnes shuddered. She hoped she was doing the right thing by inviting the Chavrons to the manor. Her skin prickled whenever she heard horses' hooves coming in their direction. Following the gatekeeper, she walked over to stand in front of the security gates. Sure enough, two huge black horses came into view. White plumes of air snorted from their nostrils as they pulled the black carriage behind them. It looked like a funeral procession, with the horses wearing a plumage of black feathers sticking out from their bridles. They came to a halt just before the gates. Agnes chanted her spell, and the padlock and chain appeared, before falling to the ground. The gates creaked slowly inwards. Urus walked beyond the gates to check the carriage's occupants, before allowing them to pass on through.

Agnes continued to shiver as she watched the horses trot towards her. When the carriage finally stopped by her side, she glanced through the small window. A pair of glowing, amber eyes stared out at her from inside the darkness.

"Monsieur Chavron," she announced. "Welcome to Blackhill Manor."

Chapter 2

Augustus paced up and down the manor's foyer, stopping every once in a while to stare at the arched doorway. His eyes narrowed, boring holes into the aged oak wood.

"You're wearing the tiles down."

Augustus swung around in his shiny brogues as Bell gracefully stepped towards the fairy. Augustus' cheeks reddened slightly at the sight of her, and he quickly twisted away. But it was too late; Bell had already witnessed his admiration, as fleeting as it had been.

Concealing a smug grin, Bell walked over to stand next to him, the chiffon and taffeta of her dress rustling softly with every movement.

"They should be here by now," said Augustus.

Bell tilted her head to look up at the tall fairy. He was busy fidgeting with the collar of his white shirt and tie. He looked nervous. Sensing her watching him, he pulled his hand away and smoothed down his long silver mane of hair instead.

Bell opened her mouth to speak when the arched door suddenly flung inwards, causing a barrage of wind and snow to exhale into the foyer. On instinct, Bell grabbed hold of Augustus' arm as she felt herself being pushed backwards by the strong wind. The fairy quickly withdrew his arm from her grasp as the arched doorway slammed closed. Before them stood four figures, covered in fresh snow.

"Ah, Augustus, it has been a while." A dark figure emerged from the centre of the group, making his way towards the fairy.

"Frances," Augustus greeted him, not without a hint of sarcasm.

The stranger held a gloved hand out towards him. The fairy flinched as he accepted it.

"Where's Jeannie Gibbs?" barked Agnes. She shook her heavy coat off, creating a puddle of melted snow at her feet.

"Shall I fetch her?" boomed Urus by her side.

"I'm here!"

The group turned to see a short, stout woman bustling into the foyer. Instead of her usual grey uniform and apron, Jeannie wore a sparkly blue dress. Her enormous feet were bare, but being a hoglin – half human and half hobgoblin – this was not unusual, given that both her hands and feet were too big for normal garments, and were ridiculously clad in thick dark hair. Tutting at the state of them, the four-foot hoglin danced around the group, taking their soggy coats from them.

Bell smiled nervously at the new arrivals. "Please,

come and join the festivities," she beamed.

The two strangers followed the young witch through the foyer towards the sound of music.

When they were out of sight, Augustus turned to Agnes Guthrie. "Are you sure you know what you are doing?"

Agnes smoothed her pale blue hair back, checking it was still sitting perfectly in its chignon. "I know what I'm doing!" She took a step towards the fairy, her lilac eyes glinting in the light of the overhead chandelier. "I trust the Chavrons and so should you."

"B-but they are—"

Agnes held a hand up to shush him. "Come, we have a party to host."

Augustus' mouth clamped over as he watched the headmistress of Blackhill Manor glide in the direction their visitors had just gone.

☾

Luna Green and Lily Jackson watched the others dance to the melody of the music. They did not know the band, nor could they find out without asking someone; they did not have Wi-Fi or phone signal inside the manor. Hidden within the vast forests of Glenariff in Northern Ireland, inside a secret forest called Araig, Blackhill Manor was almost entirely detached from the 'real' world. Not only that, but the manor was also surrounded by a powerful magickal barrier, protecting its inhabitants from the dangers of the Dead Forest.

There was a break in the music as Agnes Guthrie waltzed into the room with two strangers, both of whom were wearing top hats. The older, taller one, the man whom Augustus had referred to as Frances, carried a black cane. When they reached the centre of the room, Frances stepped forward and removed his hat, before bowing to his audience. His dark, shoulder-length hair hung over his face, but as he straightened back up, Luna noticed that his eyes were an unusual bright amber. His attire was dated; designed and made in a bygone era. His tailored trousers were black, but his blazer was of a deep red velvet, short at the front and longer at the back. A black silk scarf adorned his neck over a collarless black shirt. His eyes seemed to lock onto Luna's and she exhaled sharply when she realised that they were, in fact, luminous. Frances' top lip curled as he drew his eyes away from the girl.

"Everyone, please welcome Monsieur Frances Chavron and his son, Sebastian Chavron," announced Agnes to the silent room.

Luna's gaze shifted to the boy standing behind his father. He wore the same attire, except his blazer was of royal blue. He smiled over at Luna, and just like the Edgar twins, he too exposed a pair of perfect white fangs.

"Vampires," Magnus whispered into her ear, making

Luna jump.

Isaac Newman sidled up to them. "Okay, I am totally freaked out now," he hissed.

Agnes Guthrie signalled to the band to play again, and as the music filled the air, the children's excited chatter soared above the din.

"Oh no, don't look, but it seems like the vamp is heading our way," murmured Isaac.

Luna turned to the New Zealander, but he was off like a shot. She turned her head to say something to Magnus, but now he too was scuttling after his friend.

"Ah, Luna Green." Luna spun on her heel, coming face to face with the two strangers. Pain seared through her right ankle.

"I see you have met our student, Luna Green." Agnes Guthrie smiled as she approached the group.

"Yes, I was about to introduce myself and Sebastian," said Frances smoothly. He locked his eyes onto the young girl. His amber irises twinkled. "We have heard so much about you."

Luna took a step back as the stranger held his cane out towards her. The handle featured a round, blood-red ruby. A thought flashed through her mind: could this be the next missing crystal from the magickal athame?

Agnes stepped forward to stand next to Luna. "Unfortunately, Luna's short time here at Blackhill Manor has been somewhat tragic, what with the fateful bite from Amadan. Though it has helped to move things along a little quicker with regards to her transformation into her true Celestian self."

"Mm… interesting." Frances inched closer to Luna. "The only one left of her kind, I hear?"

Luna quickly averted her eyes. She did not want to give away her father's identity. As the only other surviving Celestian, Jack Green had to remain anonymous, for Luna's sake.

Fortunately, Agnes saved Luna from answering. "Yes, so unfortunate what happened to the Celestian beings, but to have Luna Green here is such a blessing. She really is coming on with her powers."

"Is it true that she still has Amadan's poison flowing through her blood?"

Luna noticed how the man licked his lips when he mentioned blood.

Agnes nodded her head gravely. "Yes. Sadly, we have yet to find a cure. We are still searching. Luna, do you mind if we show Monsieur Chavron your wound?"

Frances' son, Sebastian, suddenly shifted his gaze to Luna's feet.

Luna hesitantly pulled up the hem of her dress, just enough for the visitors to see the mottled black bruise on her right ankle. She did not dare look at it herself. It was a constant reminder of her fate; of what would happen to her if they did not find a cure fast enough.

Frances Chavron bent his knees slightly to get a better look, making a clicking sound with his tongue as he stretched back up. "Such tragedy for a young girl."

There was a moment of awkward silence until Agnes piped up. "Come, Monsieur Chavron, I would like to introduce you to our talented teachers."

Luna let out a sigh as Agnes guided the man away from her.

"I really like the Illusionists, do you?"

Luna flinched in surprise. The boy had remained.

"Sebastian Chavron." He held out a pale white hand.

Luna noticed that the boy wore a ruby ring, similar to his father's cane. She looked into the boy's pale copper eyes, noticing that his were much softer and kinder than his father's.

"Although their sound takes a while to get into."

Luna stared at the boy with confusion, eventually realising that he was talking about the band that was playing.

"Yes, they are different." She absently stared over at the strange-looking group on the makeshift stage. With their long hair and hippie clothes, they looked like they had just stepped out of a time machine from the 1970s.

Turning her attention back onto the boy, she asked, "Are you staying here long?"

"I'm not sure. Your headmistress invited us."

Luna studied the boy. He looked to be around the same age as herself and the other children. But it was his accent that intrigued her the most.

"Where do you come from?" she asked.

"Paris, in France."

She was about to argue that she knew where Paris was, but so many questions were burning to come out that her curiosity got the better of her. "How old are you?"

The boy smirked. "One hundred and fifty years old."

Luna staggered backwards, but the boy grabbed hold of her hand, catching her before she could trip over the hem of her dress. She blushed a silent thank you.

Smoothing her dress down, she eyed the boy suspiciously. "Is it true you're a vampire?"

This time, the boy tipped his head back and roared with laughter. Luna stared wide eyed as she caught sight of two needle-sharp, pointed fangs, positioned on either side of his two front teeth.

He dropped his gaze back to hers. "Is it true you went into a trance and were possessed by the warlock Jonas Schmidt?"

The two children stared at each other, refusing to answer each other's questions.

"Hi!"

The voice of one of her fellow students saved Luna from her staring contest.

"It's so nice to meet you. I'm Ava Corsan, and this jerk here is my brother, Evan."

Relieved to be free of the strange vampire boy, Luna turned and disappeared through the groups of dancing children.

"Hey!"

Luna turned to apologise after stepping on someone's toes. Unfortunately, it happened to be Tamara Hobbs.

"What's the rush?" Tamara smirked. "Fang boy not up to your standards?"

Angelica Lawson giggled by her side.

Luna scowled at the two of them before marching away.

"Don't listen to her."

Luna looked up to see the Edgar twins.

"Yeah, she's just crazy cos me and Travis here are not interested in her bull crap."

Luna laughed along with them. She had feared the twins when she had first arrived at the manor, but knowing them now, even though they were in fact werewolves, she admired their courage and loyalty. She stood with them for a while, laughing and talking, mostly about Tamara's cringe worthy chat-up lines, when she spotted the new boy, Sebastian, staring over.

"Hey, you two have been here at the manor since you were little, have you met the Chavrons before?"

Leonard Edgar looked over his shoulder to where Sebastian was standing. "Nah, never even heard of them until tonight."

"Really?" This shocked Luna; she thought the twins knew everything and everyone.

"Although," Travis leaned in. "I overheard Agnes

discussing them with Salvador earlier." He sneaked a peek around them before continuing. "I heard them say that the Chavrons are in fact related to the vetalas."

Luna's eyes widened. "You mean the creatures who love to feed on children's blood?"

Travis nodded his head.

Luna felt her stomach drop. She stole a glance back at the strange boy. He was still staring at her.

Chapter 3

After the ball had finished, at one minute past midnight, Luna quickly made her way to the first floor towards her room. The last thing she wanted was to be stuck with the Chavrons again. It hadn't helped that Magnus and the other boys had spent most of the evening teasing her about Sebastian's persistent staring.

When she reached her room, it did not surprise her to find Belinda already there. The tall goth sat cross-legged in front of her small wooden altar, her eyes closed. A single black candle burned in the centre of the altar. The witch remained in silence as the flame flickered back and forth.

"Casting spells at this late hour?" asked Luna, surprised.

Belinda shushed her, keeping her eyes firmly shut.

Luna sniffed the air. "Great, burning more incense. One of these nights I'm going to choke on that stuff."

"Good, then maybe you'll shut up and let me finish

my protection spell!" snapped Belinda.

Luna pulled a face at the girl as she made her way over to her bed by the window. She stopped and gazed out at the gardens. It was still snowing heavily; everything was completely covered in pillowy whiteness. The garden statues were nothing but indistinguishable mounds of snow, making it look like an army of snowmen had replaced them.

Moving away from the window, Luna slumped down onto her bed, kicking off her silver pumps. Her right ankle was throbbing after standing for so many hours. She leaned over and rubbed at her wound. Ugly, black, spiderweb-like veins snaked around the scar where Amadan had not so long ago clenched his teeth.

She looked away to focus on something else. Her gaze drifted over to Belinda's bed across from her, and to the large black raven who was perched on top of the metal headboard.

"Hi Poe," she cooed. "Too cold for hunting tonight, huh?" Luna had read up on ravens and had been surprised to discover that they did not usually hunt at night. But Belinda had reassured her that Poe was no ordinary raven. After all, he was her familiar.

The raven's black beady eyes focused on hers, making Luna shiver. She was still getting used to sharing a room with the green-haired goth, let alone her large raven.

"He's more wary of you than you are of him."

Luna shifted her gaze over to her roommate, who was now on her feet, snuffing out the candle.

Luna rolled her eyes. "I doubt that very much."

Belinda trudged over to her bed, the bedsprings groaning as the taller girl sat on top of it.

"Yeah, well, that's what he told me." Belinda held her left arm out. The raven jumped from his perch and landed on her outstretched limb.

"Really? Poe told you that?" snorted Luna.

Belinda blew kisses to the raven. "Um, yeah. Have you not learnt anything yet about our animal guides?"

Luna shrugged. "I guess not."

"I must be more aware than the rest of you," shrugged Belinda. She continued to blow kisses to the raven.

Luna scowled. "I've only just learnt that I'm a Celestian, I've got loads to discover about my abilities."

"Alright, calm down." Belinda placed the raven gently back onto the headboard. "What I'm saying is that we can connect telepathically with our animals. I've had a head start I guess, cos I've known since I was a tiddler that I'm a witch."

Luna felt bad for snapping. She was warming to the witch. There had been a moment when all the other children had hated Belinda for casting a spell to crack the portal open in the Dead Forest. Jonas Schmidt had already damaged it all those years ago, but Belinda's powerful spell – which she had been taught by a coven of evil witches who had forced her to cast it – had opened the portal and allowed the deathly shadow walkers to escape. But Belinda had proved herself to be trustworthy, putting her own life at risk by casting a spell to freeze Amadan the shapeshifter mid-attack, saving the others.

Luna glanced over at her roommate's altar. "Why were you casting a protection spell?"

Belinda was changing into her pyjamas. Black ones, of course. "The moon is in its waning phase, so I thought it best to cast it now."

Luna shrugged off her own party outfit and reached for her pink pyjamas from under her pillow. "Did you feel evil coming from the Chavrons?"

Belinda shrugged, as she pulled her covers over her. "You mean the two vamps?"

Luna nodded.

"Not really. I didn't get so much of a vibe from them, but then again, I don't know who to trust in this place."

Luna watched her puff up her pillow before slamming her head of green hair down onto it. "Yeah, I guess so. And you were kind of staring at the lead singer of the Illusionists most of the night anyway."

"I was not. It's not even my kind of music," snorted Belinda.

Luna chuckled, "He was kind of cute though, if you're into guys with long hair."

"Hmph, I guess… though I'm more into death metal

fashion."

Luna placed her knuckle in her mouth to stifle her laughter. She was only teasing the witch, but she couldn't help herself.

"Are you laughing at me?"

Luna dropped her hand as Belinda bolted up from her bed.

"No… I was only trying to make conversation."

"Well, you just remember, Luna Green, that I am a year older than you!"

"What's that got to do with anything?"

"It means I know better."

"Well, I'm not the youngest here. Ava is months younger than me," said Luna matter-of-factly.

"Well, I am almost fifteen years old, and you're not even fourteen yet."

"I will be this June!"

"And I will be fifteen in May," snorted Belinda.

Luna sat up, resting against her headboard. "Okay fine, you are the wisest of the children here. Let's not fight over it, please?" She turned to Belinda, giving her the classic 'sad puppy eyes' look.

Belinda snorted, but gradually, a smile appeared on her normally solemn face. "Okay, I admit it, he was kind of cute, but nothing can compare to the way Magnus looks at you," said Belinda.

Luna felt her cheeks redden. "We're friends, that's all. Besides I don't want a boyfriend, I'm too young."

Belinda shrugged. "That means nothing. You can fancy someone at any age."

Luna held her hands up. "Change of subject, what do you really think of the Chavrons, and why do you think they are here?"

"I guess they are here to help, and that's a good thing."

Luna could feel a 'but' coming.

"But… should we trust them? They are vamps after all. They hunt at night. Might sneak into our rooms and suck our blood."

With that, Belinda reached over and switched the lamp off, leaving the room in complete darkness. Luna sighed, lying back on her pillows. Pulling the covers up to her ears, she stared ahead into the darkness. Every little creak or sound twitched at her nerves, until exhaustion finally took over and she fell into a restless sleep.

☾

At breakfast, it surprised the children to see the Chavrons sitting at the teachers' top table. Luna felt groggy as she played with the strawberries in her bowl, watching them float amongst the soggy cereal after having poured in too much almond milk.

"Cereal killer."

Luna glanced up. "Sorry?"

Magnus shrugged. "Doesn't matter." Then, in a brighter tone, he added, "Hey, do you think Frances is going to be our new teacher?"

Lucas Kane spat out a piece of bacon. "Seriously?"

Magnus shrugged. "Well, why else would he be sitting at the top table with the rest of them?" He nodded towards the teachers table.

Lucas and Isaac glanced over.

"What could they possibly teach us?" drawled Lucas, in his southern American accent.

"Oh, I don't know, how about how to catch your prey and drink their blood?" snapped Luna.

The three boys gawked at her.

"Really?" said Lucas, with a mouthful of more bacon.

Luna rolled her eyes. "Seriously, wise-up, guys. They are here to help us find out more about the vetalas. They're the real threat."

The three boys shrugged, just as Agnes Guthrie cleared her throat and asked everyone to pay attention.

"I realise it is the weekend, and we are off school duty—"

A low cheer erupted from somewhere in the room.

"But, as we have two new guests, it seems only polite to show them around."

The whoops turned to a groan.

Agnes ignored them a second time. "I realise most of you will still feel tired after the Winter Solstice ball, but

I thought a bit of fresh air would do us all good."

Luna and the rest of the children looked towards the window. It had stopped snowing, but from where they sat, everything was a blur of white.

Agnes held up her hand. "I know what you are all thinking. Yes, it is the middle of winter, and we are no doubt snowed in, but I'm afraid this cannot wait any longer—" Agnes paused as Frances Chavron tugged at her sleeve.

"May I?" he interrupted.

Agnes nodded her head, lowering herself down into her chair.

Frances stood up, clearing his throat. "Children, I would like to introduce myself and my son, Sebastian."

The boy by his side nodded his head to everyone in the room, but the children kept their eyes glued to the father.

"I understand you are all suspicious of us arriving here at your school, where you feel protected by the manor's enchantment, but let me reassure you, we are here as friends." He held both hands out towards them.

Luna noticed that he did not have his ruby cane, but then spotted it resting against the leg of the table.

"We came here to help, honoured to be invited by your headmistress, Mrs Guthrie. We have come to share our knowledge of the vetalas. But first, we need to investigate the Dead Forest."

Salvador jumped to his feet, startling everyone in the

room.

"That would be suicide!" he yelled.

Agnes ushered him to sit back down, but Salvador ignored her silent pleas.

"I cannot allow any of the children to enter the Dead Forest after what happened to Luna. As far as we know, Amadan is still out there, and Luna is a walking GPS for him!"

"We have been through this Salvador," said an exasperated Agnes. "The children have already been in a battle. They are fully aware of the dangers."

"I understand that, but do the children know what the vetalas actually are?"

"Vampires," offered Frances Chavron.

"Oh no, they are more than that!" shouted Salvador. "Go on, since you are the expert, explain to the children and the rest of the teachers here what exactly they are up against."

The room went eerily silent as the twelve children all looked at one another, wide eyed, expressions of fear etched on every face.

Chapter 4

Agnes Guthrie, her eyes glinting with anger, quietly informed Salvador that this conversation was to end now. Something in her tone clearly had the desired effect, for Salvador reluctantly returned to his seat, still scowling at Frances. After a moment's pause, Agnes informed the children that they would meet at the front doors of the manor shortly, before resuming her seat at the top table. The children quickly recovered from the shock of Salvador's outburst and resumed their conversations, the room once again filling with inane chatter. Meanwhile, Bell Tilly and Hattie Bordeaux bustled around the hall, asking the children if they wanted anything else to eat.

Luna craned her neck past Hattie and saw what looked like a heated conversation taking place between Frances Chavron and Salvador. She couldn't make out what they were saying, but the constant shakes of heads and animated hands suggested that it wasn't just a catch up on their local team's scores.

"Luna, do you want to come with me to the nurse's room so we can put some of my new cream on that wound of yours?" asked Bell. When Luna didn't answer, Bell snapped her fingers in front of the girl's face.

"I, uh, sorry?" mumbled Luna.

"I have made up a new potion for your ankle. Would you like to come along and try it now?"

Luna, still staring at the two men, nodded her head slowly. For all she knew, she could have just agreed to a slice of meatloaf, which would have been problematic given that she had now progressed from vegetarian to vegan. Fortunately, under the watchful eye of the head cook, Jeannie Gibbs, Aengus the leprechaun and the Scottish imp, Murdoch, ensured that she was well looked after. Murdoch liked to moan, a lot, but he assured Luna that he secretly enjoyed picking the fruit and vegetables from the gardens and creating new dishes.

Salvador bumped into Luna as he stormed away from Frances Chavron, muttering an apology under his breath as he sped away.

"I wonder what has got into him?" muttered Magnus, who had decided to accompany Luna to the nurse's office.

Luna shook her white mane of hair. "I really don't know, but something has irked him. And I'm guessing it's to do with our newcomers."

☾

Once Bell had treated Luna's ankle, the three of them joined the other children and teachers at the front of the manor, as they waited for Agnes Guthrie and the Chavrons to make an appearance. Bell Tilly chatted away to the young witch, Tamara Hobbs. Luna could just make out their conversation, as she stood behind the group with Magnus and the Edgar twins.

"Is it true, Miss Tilly, that there is a book of shadows, containing every powerful spell, hidden somewhere in the nearby forests?" asked Tamara.

The young teacher almost choked in surprise. "Well, er, I really don't think such a book exists," she replied. "Where did you hear about this?"

Tamara looked around, then in a hushed tone she said, "My mom told me before I arrived this summer. She said every witch in the world dreams of getting their hands on this book. It would make them the most powerful witch ever."

Bell placed a hand upon the girl's shoulder. "I think your mother has listened to too many fairy tales, for if such a book existed, Blackhill Manor would not be here, nor would we have a dark entity trying to attack us."

"B-but my grandmother was not lying when she told my mom." The young witch from Salem looked to be on the verge of tears.

Bell patted her back, then quickly turned and disappeared through the group back inside the manor.

"Did you get all of that?" Luna turned her head to the side.

Leonard Edgar leaned in towards her. "That rumour's been going around for centuries."

Luna frowned. "You mean about the book of shadows?"

Leonard nodded his head.

"What does it mean?" she asked.

"A book of shadows is a witch's personal book of spells, usually passed down generations of witches. They go back centuries, and this particular one is meant to be especially extensive. There has also been a rumour going round about the missing grimoire."

Luna wrinkled her face. "Grimoire?"

Leonard nodded. "It's a fancier term for a book of shadows, the difference being that a grimoire is written for all to read, whereas a book of shadows is more a witch's personal journal of their own craft."

Luna nodded out of politeness. The more she learnt about witches, the more complicated they seemed. She was glad she was a Celestian. Then again, she did not yet fully understand what a Celestian really was either.

Agnes Guthrie swept past the group to join Augustus and Salvador at the front, clapping her hands together to get everyone's attention.

"Children, once again I apologise for disrupting your weekend plans…"

"Yeah, like we had plans," snorted Lucas. "It's not

like we can just go to the cinema."

Agnes stopped mid-sentence and stared intensely at the boy. "I'm sorry, Lucas, did you want to share something with the group?"

Lucas lowered his head.

"Thought so," said Agnes. "I understand that those of you who have family abroad are not able to visit them at the weekends, unlike those of you who live closer. But the purpose of having you all here together is to protect our world. Ordinary children do not have this opportunity. You do. What we are about to do is urgent business, and once we return, you can spend the rest of the weekend playing on your game consoles or reading or doing whatever you like. But for now, we must go and investigate the forests."

The group remained silent as Agnes led them out towards the gardens, before speaking the spell to lift the invisible barrier, which would allow them to pass through.

"I stand before thy mighty wall, drop thy bricks and let them fall. Behold the powers that lie within, open your doors and let me in. Brick by brick, stone by stone, please be quick, let your secrets be known."

The ground beneath Luna's feet rumbled and the group took a step back. The familiar sounds of invisible glass shattering filled the silence. Luna could sense the glass bending inwards and outwards, expanding to its limit until it finally shattered. Of course, no glass shattered in their faces, but the knowledge that it had done so magickally was exciting all the same.

Salvador and Bell ushered the children through, while Agnes waited behind. The Chavrons rushed to join her, their pale skin reflecting the weak winter sun.

"I thought vampires couldn't come out in the daylight," said Isaac Newman.

Magnus looked over his shoulder towards the father and son. "Dunno, maybe they're special," he shrugged.

Travis Edgar laughed. "You really need to brush up on your knowledge of magickal creatures. I mean, you are the next generation of guardians."

Magnus and Isaac exchanged looks.

"I guess we'll learn next term," said Magnus.

Travis rolled his eyes. "Jeez, then we really are in trouble." He jogged on to catch up with his twin, leaving the two boys wondering what he had meant.

The large group walked through the gardens, their feet sloshing through the heavy snow. When Salvador got fed up with the children whining about getting wet feet, he turned to Augustus.

"Is there something you can do to get rid of the snow?"

The platinum-haired fairy glanced over his right shoulder, towards the children. "I am not sure, but I know how to get rid of the brats," he answered.

Luna, listening in, saw a brief glimmer of a smile form on both men's lips. An unusual sight. If only the other children had witnessed this rarity.

The tall fairy placed his left hand inside his navy suit jacket to retrieve his crystal wand. He slowed his pace and waved the wand in a circle above his head. The chatter of the group behind him hushed as they realised the snow was melting beneath their feet.

Salvador let out an inaudible sigh of relief. For a moment, he had been concerned that the fairy might actually carry out his suggestion of banishing the children.

Luna glanced down at her chunky white trainers. Only a moment ago, they had been trudging through thick, crispy snow. Now, a warmth crept through her trainers and into the soles of her feet. She was expecting to see flattened, soggy grass emerge from beneath the snow, but instead, the lawn before her sprung up lush and green like it was a warm summer's day. Even the flowerbeds sprouted early buds, as though spring had come early.

Agnes and Bell both clapped their hands together, delighted that they would not have to drag the dead weight of their sodden, ankle-grazing skirts around for the rest of their time outdoors.

"Hey."

Luna jolted as her ghostly best friend, Lily Jackson, appeared by her side. "Where did you just come from?" she asked, shaking her head as Lily giggled. "Sorry, that was a stupid question." She was still getting used to the fact that her best friend from her hometown in East Kilbride was in fact a ghost. She had only found out when she had arrived here at the manor that Lily had died instantly when she had been hit by a car as they were walking to school one morning.

"Don't worry," answered Lily. "I know it's a bit weird getting used to me just appearing and disappearing." Then in a hushed tone, she continued, "Remember when you asked me if I had seen your mum in the spirit world?"

Luna fixed her eyes on her friend. "Yes?"

"Well, that's where I've just been. I went to visit my grandparents, as I always do once a week, and got talking to this old man, Harry, who is an old friend of my Grandpa Robert. He mentioned there was something unusual going on."

Luna frowned. "What does that mean?"

Lily shrugged. "He said his brother, Thomas, overheard another spirit saying there was some cover-up going on. And he overheard the name Jocelyn Green."

Luna's eyes widened. "Really?"

Lily nodded.

"What could that possibly mean?"

"I asked him what he thought, and Harry told me it was top secret. He said that if I wanted to find out more, I would need to go to the Rainbow Gate."

"What's the Rainbow Gate?" asked Luna.

"It's where us spirits go for evaluation, after we leave our physical bodies."

Luna wrinkled her nose. "You've lost me."

Lily rolled her eyes. "Jeez, you human souls know nothing."

Agnes looked over and smiled when she saw that Lily had joined them.

Lily returned the gesture, then leaned in closer to Luna. "It's where our fate is decided, after we die."

Luna's eyes widened. "You mean the pearly gates?"

Lily chortled. "Yeah, something like that. Except it's called Rainbow Gate. It's the same concept though; it's where you find out which spirit realm you belong to."

"Okay, so how are you supposed to find out what happened to my mum at the Rainbow Gate?"

"I'm not sure, old Harry just said that's where I would find answers. But he also said travelling to the Ethers is where we would find the gate."

"The Ethers?" asked Luna.

Lily shrugged. "Yeah, it's the place in between both worlds. I never got the chance to visit – I just popped straight out of my body! That's why I'm stuck as a ghost, doomed to walk the Earth for eternity." She proceeded to walk with her arms stretched out, pretending to be a zombie.

Luna sniggered. "I think you're slightly over exaggerating. I mean, you can still visit your dead relatives."

"Yeah, but I get the feeling I've skipped that process regarding my fate at the Rainbow Gate. It makes me wonder if I can even visit the Ethers… or worse, if I do visit, I don't know whether I would be allowed back."

Luna thought about this as the group made their way along the winding path, past the many hedge carvings of mythical creatures, until the children in front, along with Salvador and Augustus, stopped before a five-foot gate. To outsiders, this gate would seem inappropriate as a security measure, but unbeknownst to most people, it was part of an invisible barrier, separating the manor grounds from the rest of the world.

Augustus let out an exasperated sigh as Salvador spoke to the space between them and the forest. The warlock stopped mid-sentence and looked at the fairy.

"What was that for?" he asked.

Augustus rolled his luminous silver eyes to the heavens. "This." He waved both arms out before him.

It was Salvador's turn to roll his eyes. "I know, I know, you are against having voice activated spells as security."

Augustus clicked his tongue. "We are not idiots, and neither are the creatures who lurk in our forests. After the spell was broken and the shadow walkers escaped the portal, you would think they would craft a more unorthodox charm of protection."

Agnes soon joined them, followed by the Chavrons. "Problem again, Augustus?" she remarked.

The fairy shook his head and motioned for the Spanish warlock to continue his enchantment. The surrounding air changed as a sudden gust of wind blew around them. A sound almost like an elastic band being stretched before being pinged resonated through the surrounding air. Luna and the other children had soon learnt that this meant the invisible barrier was opening, extending and creating a partition enabling them to enter the forest beyond.

Chapter 5

The large group drew closer together as they made their way through the dense foliage of the forest. The ground was rock solid beneath their feet, but they were thankful that the snow could not infiltrate through the thick branches overhead. Agnes instructed them to head north after entering the Araig Forest. Luna knew from experience that this was the route towards the Dead Forest; had they headed in the other direction, they would have reached Illuminos, where the light beings lived; where beautiful flowers in every colour grew. It was also where she would find her beloved unicorn, Theodore.

Luna thought back to her earlier conversation with Belinda Dobson. She had said something about telepathically communicating with their animal guides. The green-haired witch had scoffed that the rest of the children had not learnt this skill yet. But, now that Luna thought more about it, the day the shapeshifter, Amadan, had attacked her, Theodore had known she was in trouble and had come to rescue her from the dark creature. Subconsciously, Luna had connected telepathically with her animal guide. Perhaps it was not such a difficult skill to learn after all.

As the group made their way across broken twigs, pine needles and leaves, trying somewhat fruitlessly not to make too much noise, Luna pondered the events of the previous year. After Amadan had attacked her, Agnes and Augustus had taken Luna to meet King Engogabal, the king of the fairies, desperate to find a cure for Luna's injured ankle. It was then that he had suggested they call upon Lazarus, the giant indigo coloured dragon from the portal, Dracas. Once she had recovered from the shock of coming face to face with a twenty-foot dragon, she had realised she was able to talk to him telepathically, much to the surprise of Agnes and Augustus. Lazarus had informed her that this was one of her many Celestian abilities, though at the time she had yet to discover her true self. It was only once they had recovered her sacred crystal from the fiery mountains of Taragus that she had transformed into her Celestial form and had discovered that she was in fact from a destroyed land called Celestia.

Luna's thoughts dissolved when the group came to a sudden halt. Looking around, she discovered they were already in the Dead Forest. She had been so deep in thought that she hadn't noticed the sudden change in the air. The darkness enveloped them as they walked deeper into the woodland, a crushing feeling of doom and depression weighing down on them. The trees were devoid of life, their broken bark peeling back from their skin to reveal dark emptiness. Black leaves and debris littered the forest floor, crunching menacingly beneath their feet.

Salvador hushed the group, even though none of them were talking. Too scared to breathe, the children huddled closer together. Hattie Bordeaux sidled up next to Luna. The string of a leather pouch hung from her left wrist, like a small purse. Any unwanted visitors, and her voodoo hexes were on call.

Frances Chavron stepped forward, flicking the dead leaves aside with his cane. A look of disgust was clearly visible against his smooth, pale complexion. Salvador watched him with narrowing eyes as he entered the blackened circle, the same circle where the evil warlock Jonas Schmidt had attempted to open the portal to the darker realms over a century ago.

The group watched nervously as the vampire sniffed the stagnant air, before walking towards the only living thing in this part of the forest: the elm tree. Luna and the other children had learnt nothing yet of why it remained alive amongst its dead surroundings. The surreal image of the lone tree stood out against the dark background of death.

"The tree of the dead," said Frances. He continued to walk towards it.

Salvador seemed reluctant to enter the circle but

cautiously stepped over the line of burnt grass.

"Can you smell it?" asked Frances, turning to the warlock.

Salvador sniffed at the air. After a few moments, his black eyes widened. "This is the same scent I sensed months ago, when someone used dark magick to open the portal to the shadow walkers." He narrowed his eyes at the group of children, but there was only one of them he was referring to.

Belinda Dobson lowered her head. Last summer, she had confessed to using an ancient spell to open the already damaged portal, allowing the shadow walkers to escape and resulting in thousands of the horrific creatures attacking them all. But Belinda still insisted that it was the coven who had lured her in, after discovering that she would be attending Blackhill Manor. Being loyal followers of Jonas Schmidt, the evil coven talked her into helping them open the portal. In return, they had promised to make the young witch High Priestess of their coven.

Frances held up a gloved hand. "Yes, it is powerful."

Agnes Guthrie pushed through the group. She had been guarding the back along with Augustus. Lifting the hem of her skirt she stepped over the line into the circle.

"Has someone been casting dark magick again?" she asked.

Salvador shook his head. "It is not the magick we detect—"

"More like the blood of the black witches," interrupted Frances.

Belinda swayed. Fearing she might fall, Bell Tilly quickly grabbed hold of her arm to steady the girl.

"They're here," she murmured under her breath.

Everyone glanced around to look at the young witch.

"Who?" asked Bell. But she already knew the answer.

"The Jonas Schmidt followers. They must be here to come and take me back," wailed Belinda.

"This is preposterous," snapped Augustus. "She has led them here."

Agnes hurried over to stand before Belinda. The girl's head hung forwards, covering her face with strands of acid-green hair.

"Is this true?" demanded Agnes.

Belinda shook her head.

"Look at me, girl!"

The shock of hearing Agnes raise her voice startled the rest of the children, including Belinda. She snapped her head up, her black eyeliner smudged with fresh tears.

"N-no, Miss, I have nothing to do with them being here. I have had no contact with them, you have to believe me."

Agnes studied the girl for a few more seconds, before turning around abruptly. "I believe her," she addressed to Frances and Salvador, before making her way back inside the circle.

Augustus let out a loud snort. "Unbelievable! You witches are all the same."

Bell looked up at the fairy, anger spreading across her delicate features. "Us witches, huh?" With her fists clenched at her sides, she squared up to the tall fairy.

Augustus reared back. Luna tried not to giggle, for it was quite a comical scene. At last, someone was standing up to the pompous fairy prince.

"That is enough," demanded Agnes. "Do you honestly think 'us witches' are anything like those evil occultists? Do you really believe that we would go out of our way to undo all the hard work Edward Blackhill has done over the years?"

Augustus kept a straight face, before nodding his head.

A snigger escaped from one of the Edgar twins, prompting Augustus to snap his head towards them. Luna saw Leonard give the fairy an awkward smile in return. But she was sure she had seen a fang poke out from between his lips.

"Stop!" Frances Chavron held his cane up in the air.

Everyone turned their attention back to the vampire.

"I am afraid it is not only the smell of witches' blood... I can detect the faint odour of something more sinister."

Augustus snorted. "What could be more sinister than those ugly—" He stopped mid-sentence when he noticed Bell glaring back up at him.

"I know this scent too well," continued Frances. "It's the smell of an ancient creature… one that I fear the most."

Chapter 6

"We must search the forests," demanded Salvador.

After Frances Chavron had announced that a vetala was on the loose, Salvador had followed him around the circle while he continued to smell the air around the portal at the base of the elm tree.

Frances stopped his pacing and turned to face the warlock. "Yes, we should, but right now we have to make plans. We have a band of evil witches spying on us as well as one or more bloodthirsty creatures who have escaped from the Nocte Viventem portal."

Salvador opened his mouth to protest when Agnes placed a reassuring hand upon his shoulder. "Monsieur Chavron is right, Salvador. We need to head back to the manor and start making plans for our next move – finding the next crystal for the athame, for instance."

"And what about the witches? They could try to break into the manor and steal the athame!" said Salvador.

Agnes dropped her hand. "All the more reason for us to return to the manor. Don't worry, there is no way they can get through the manor's barrier."

"Yes, but they opened the portal." Salvador pushed past her. "Don't underestimate these witches, Agnes. This is powerful black magick we are dealing with."

Agnes watched him in despair as he hurried past the group, heading in the direction they had come from.

"Not to mention the bloodthirsty vetalas!" shouted Frances after him.

The rest of the group turned to stare at the vampire.

He shrugged his narrow shoulders. "It seems we have more to deal with than we thought."

Agnes turned away, leaving Frances to stand on his own in the circle. "Right children, let's head back to the manor."

The teachers immediately leapt into action, swiftly ushering the children back the way they had just come.

☾

Back at the manor, they gathered everyone into the dining room. Salvador appeared to have composed himself and was now sitting at the teachers table at the back of the room, but his worried expression was obvious to the others.

"I can't believe this is happening," whispered Magnus to Luna, as they took their seats at the food table.

Luna shrugged. "Yeah, but I guess it was always going to happen. May as well be now."

The sound of a knife hitting against glass alerted the children that something was about to happen, and they quickly shushed.

"Thank you all for remaining calm after today's discovery," announced Agnes to the room. "Once again, it seems we are not prepared for what is becoming a greater problem. As you are all aware, we have been expecting the vetalas to escape from the Nocte Viventem realm, but we were not expecting a band of witches to be hiding in our forests as well." She took a sip from her chalice. "With that said, I think it is time we taught you a little about the vetalas, and how they became the beasts they have now become."

Someone cleared their throat.

"I will allow our resident expert to explain what we are dealing with." Agnes nodded for Frances Chavron to take over as she took her seat.

The vampire nodded his head to the head teacher in acknowledgement, and stood up to face the room. He held a hand up to his mouth and coughed again. Luna noticed he had taken off his black leather gloves, but he still held onto his black cane. The ruby glistened atop its handle.

"Teachers, children, thank you again for inviting myself and my son, Sebastian, to your most precious sanctuary."

Salvador grunted at the end of the table, but if Frances Chavron heard it, he chose not to acknowledge the teacher's complaints.

"Sadly, the circumstances of our visit are less than fortunate. As you all know, we have received forewarning of the upcoming dangers." Frances gazed over at Luna.

The others turned and looked too. Luna suddenly felt like a rare treasure being displayed for all to see. It was not a comfortable feeling.

"When we were in the Dead Forest, we not only detected the scent of vetalas, but we also detected the smell of dark witchcraft. Now I do not know why these witches are here, and admittedly this is not my area of expertise, but you have gifted teachers who know how to track these perpetrators down. What I am most concerned about is the vetalas. We must catch the ones who have already escaped."

Wild chatter erupted, until Agnes clanged her knife against her chalice again, bringing order once more to the room.

Frances turned and gave her a slight nod in gratitude. "I must explain what these creatures are." Frances moved away from the table and walked to the centre of the room. "Many of you will have realised that my son and I are old vampires. I am three hundred and three years old, and my son, Sebastian, is now one hundred and fifty years old."

The room gasped.

"These creatures, the vetalas, are thousands of years older. But these ancient creatures did not begin as vetalas, no. When a human is turned into a vampire, or when we are born as a vampire, we have a choice: we can either drink human blood or use alternative methods to satiate our thirst. Sebastian and I use alternative methods; we started with animal blood, but now that synthetic blood is available, we no longer have any need to kill."

Luna could just imagine their animal guides sighing with relief.

"But if a vampire makes the choice to live off human blood, over time, they will change into the monsters they are."

Evan Corsan shot a hand into the air. Frances nodded his head towards him.

"Sir, er, what do these vetalas look like?"

Frances held up his walking stick to eye level and stared intently at the spherical ruby on the handle. "They are the most hideous creatures you could ever imagine; indescribable; grotesque; like something out of a nightmare. That is why I carry a replica of the magickal athame's ruby, to always remind myself of what I could become if I were to ever stray from my beliefs."

Evan Corsan mumbled a thank you and scribbled furiously inside his notepad.

Tamara Hobbs threw a hand up. "So, what you're saying is, if a vampire drinks too much human blood, they will become a vetala?"

Frances Chavron nodded his head.

Tamara thought about this for a moment, before adding, "So what is the difference between a vampire like yourself and a vetala?"

Frances walked around the room again, swinging his stick as he went. "Well, a normal vampire who no longer craves human blood can carry on as they did when in human form. Contrary to folklore, we can walk in the daylight, eat garlic and wear crosses." He laughed. "Well, we cannot wear crucifixes if made from silver, but I blame the rest on fictional tales, such as Count Dracula."

"So, he isn't real then?" piped up Isaac Newman.

Frances laughed, but then his demeanour changed. He stared at the boy, who squirmed under the vampire's glare. "He *is* real, very much so." Frances laughed out loud again. "But, on a more serious note…" He paced, walking in circles. "The vetalas are the myth of what a vampire should be. They cannot walk in daylight, nor would you see their image in a mirror's reflection. They cannot wear crosses or eat garlic. Yes, those old wives tales are true. But there is one thing that can change them back into the vampire they once were."

A chill ran down the length of Luna's spine.

"Children. The youth of your blood; the innocence of

your souls; the pureness of your very core that runs through your sweet, sweet blood."

Luna let out a gasp. It was as though the vampire was yearning to drink some himself.

Frances paused and stared into the ruby again, composing himself. "Young blood can take years off them, reversing the curse."

The air in the room suddenly felt stagnant.

Agnes shot to her feet. "Thank you, Monsieur Chavron, I think the children get the gist of it now." Her lilac irises gazed around the room. "If any of you have concerns or feel affected by anything that has been discussed today, please stay behind and I will talk more with you. Otherwise, please all carry on with your normal weekend plans and I will see you all at suppertime."

The sound of chairs scraping and children chattering erupted, breaking the awkward atmosphere. Luna noticed that all eleven of the other children, now that Lily Jackson had made an appearance too, had opted for the escape option, instead of hanging around to find out more.

"What do you guys think?" asked Magnus.

Luna shrugged. "I wouldn't believe any of this if I hadn't met other creatures already."

"Yeah," agreed Lily. "Nor would you be talking to your dead friend."

Luna and Magnus chuckled at this.

His face growing serious, Magnus continued. "What precautions do you think the teachers will take?"

Luna stopped in her tracks, causing Tamara and Angelica to bump straight into the back of her.

"Watch it weirdo!" snorted Tamara.

Luna mumbled sorry, even though she wasn't. Normally she would bite back, but this time she had too much on her mind. When a familiar streak of green sauntered past, Luna quickly grabbed at the black clothing that accompanied it.

"Ouch, that was my skin you idiot!"

Luna had to say sorry for the second time that day. "What are you doing now?" she asked the goth.

Belinda shrugged as she rubbed her arm.

"How do you fancy hanging out with us?"

Belinda's dark, eyeliner-smudged eyes shot up in surprise. It looked comical. But the girl's expression changed to a frown when she saw the smirk on Luna's face.

"What's going on?"

Luna looped an arm through the taller girl's and led her out into the foyer. A confused looking Lily and Magnus followed. Hoping that no one was in earshot, Luna let go of Belinda.

"I was wondering if you know any other powerful spells?" Luna finally asked, swinging around to face her friend.

Belinda looked down at her in disgust. "If this is a

trick to get me into trouble again, I mean it, I'll turn you into a dung beetle!"

"Yeah, Luna, this isn't funny," added Magnus.

Luna looked nervously around them. "I'm not joking, nor am I trying to trick you. I got thinking in there when Frances Chavron was talking about the vetalas… I knew what he was going to say before he said it."

The other three looked at her in confusion.

"I knew the vetalas craved children's blood. Jonas Schmidt told me… when he took over my body."

"Yeah, I remember you telling us about that. You went into a trance, and he warned you that they were coming," said Lily.

Luna nodded. "So, if he knew that they were coming, perhaps he also knows where they are…" She fixed her gaze on Belinda. "What if I can channel him through again, and he could tell us where the vetalas are?"

"Don't be daft!" Belinda exclaimed.

Luna hissed at her to keep it down.

"And even if you could, do you think he would tell you," Belinda hissed back at her.

Luna hung her head. "No, I guess not."

"What I don't understand is the whereabouts of Jonas Schmidt… is he dead or not?" asked Magnus.

"I haven't seen him around," said Lily.

Luna snapped her fingers, surprising the others. "That's it! We need to go to the Ethers and find the

Rainbow Gate and see if Jonas is dead, and while we're there, we can find out about my mum."

Belinda and Magnus looked at one another.

"I still don't know what any of this has got to do with me casting a powerful spell," said Belinda.

It was Lily's turn to get excited. "Can you concoct a necromancy spell?"

Belinda's pale face turned even paler. "You mean, to kill someone?"

Magnus held both hands up. "Whoa, time out guys. I don't like where this conversation is heading. We're not killing anyone."

Luna smiled. "Oh yes, we are. Me."

Chapter 7

Poe squawked at the sudden intrusion of his daytime nap as Belinda, Luna and Lily excitedly bustled into their shared room. Belinda jumped on top of her bed, making the headboard where the raven perched bang against the wall. Poe flapped his wings and screeched in protest.

"Moody chops," mumbled Belinda.

She leaned over the side of the bed and stuck a hand underneath her flimsy mattress. Seconds later, she pulled out an ancient-looking book. Luna recognised it straightaway.

"What's that?" asked Lily, drifting over to get a closer look.

Belinda quickly crossed both arms across the book, holding it protectively against her chest. "It's top secret. Unless you are part of my family or a descendant, you cannot touch my book of shadows."

Luna felt a pang of guilt. Only a few months had passed since she had sneaked a look. But that had only been because it was an emergency. She had needed to know whether Belinda was the traitor who had opened the portal. Unfortunately, it had been a pointless exercise, but the truth had come out anyway after the shadow walkers had escaped.

Confident that Lily would not sneak a peek, Belinda placed the hardback book on her lap. The spine of the black, worn, leather cover creaked as she opened it. The books pages were yellow with age, and Luna could just make out faint scribbled writing across the parchment.

Belinda studied the pages silently, slowly turning each one over to scan the next. Lily sat on the bed beside Luna. It was something Luna would never get used to, seeing her best friend as a ghost. She still couldn't get the image of that day out of her head. Thinking the car had only gently bumped her friend, they had carried on walking, after Lily had insisted that she was fine. But what neither of them had realised was that Lily had died; the car had pummelled straight into her, killing her instantly. Her spirit had risen from her lifeless body after impact, confusing them both, and since Luna had yet to recognise her psychic abilities, she had assumed Lily was still alive. It was not until Luna had arrived at Blackhill Manor that Lily had appeared and told her the truth.

"Have you found anything yet?" asked Lily.

Belinda let out a low snort in return and carried on flicking through the pages. Luna suddenly remembered the conversation she had overheard between Tamara Hobbs and Bell Tilly. Something to do with a missing book of shadows. She wondered if Belinda knew anything about this story.

"I overheard Tamara asking Miss Tilly if she knew anything about a missing book of shadows. Have you heard anything about this?"

Luna could see the girl's forehead wrinkle.

"You mean the missing grimoire?" she answered, without looking up.

"Er, yeah, I think so," stammered Luna. "What's the difference?"

"Well, if you had actually listened to the Edgar twins yesterday, you would know that a book of shadows is a witch's personal spell book, whereas a grimoire is written for all. Well, as long as you're a witch or a warlock."

Luna bit her lower lip. She had only asked to make sure she had heard right.

"So, what is the story behind it?" asked Lily.

Belinda eventually looked up and shrugged. "I guess with you two not being witches you would never have been told the story."

Luna held a feeble hand up. "I'm half witch."

Belinda rolled her eyes. "Yeah, yeah, forgot about that. But you never grew up knowing, so you wouldn't know anything about the history of witchcraft and the grimoire."

"Okay, so tell us," said Lily.

Belinda let out a vast sigh. "The story I got told growing up is that there is a grimoire which holds every spell, from good to evil, inside its ancient pages."

"So, what is so important about this book?" asked Lily.

Belinda shot her a look of utter disgust. "It's not just any book, it's the most powerful grimoire in the entire universe! The darker realms are in search of it, while the light creatures want it back to prevent the darker realms from ever getting their claws on it."

"So, it's lost?" asked Luna.

Belinda widened her eyes. "Are you two for real?" She closed her book of shadows and placed a hand protectively over its aged leather.

Luna and Lily exchanged confused glances.

"It's about time someone taught you two about the 'real' world." Shoving her Doc Martin boots against the edge of the bed, Belinda pushed herself back against the wall.

Luna copied her, knowing that this would be a long story, but one she was excited to hear. Poe, still perched at the top of her bed, opened his beak and let out a short caw. Then, turning his head, he buried it deep into his black feathered wings. He probably knew what Belinda was about to say off by heart. That or he was preparing for his bedtime story.

"As you both know, my family have been witches for

generations. We are not only related to the seventeenth century Pendle Hill witches, but our ancestry also goes far beyond, and can be traced to covens from the United Kingdom, Europe and America. Tamara wouldn't agree with this; she seems to think her Salem coven are the only witches to come out of America. But us Brits were the first to set foot on her land. Well, almost. But that's another history lesson for another time. Whether Tamara likes it or not, her ancestors are British. But don't tell her I said so," chuckled Belinda.

Luna nodded her head. "I know the history of Columbus discovering America."

"Well, that isn't strictly true. John Cabot was in fact the first, after being commissioned to go by King Henry VII," Belinda informed them. "But that is a discussion for another time. For now, I will tell you the history passed down by one of my ancestors to each generation of witches. It is the story of Elizabeth Drake. A young woman in her early twenties, who lived in a small village somewhere in the north of England."

Chapter 8

The North of England
1645

Elizabeth plucked at the spiky flowers from the lavender bush. She loved their scent. As well as being an excellent remedy for insomnia, she often dabbed lavender water on her wrists for luck. Hitching up her long underskirt, she bent over to reach the farthest flowers, when another scent captured her senses. Straightening up, she sniffed at the air. Smoke. Elizabeth's body went rigid as a fear crept into the depths of her soul. She sensed it before she even knew what was happening. Unfortunately, it was a gift passed down to her by her mother and her mother's mother. Foresight. Call it a curse or a blessing. This time, Elizabeth would call it the latter.

As she glanced up towards the sky, she could just make out black smoke billowing over the treetops. Pulling up the fabric of her skirt, Elizabeth rushed back the way she had come, stumbling along the trail in her haste, until she reached the edge of the rushing bourn.

She clutched onto her wicker basket – which unfortunately was not full of the wildflowers and herbs she had hoped to collect on her weekly journey into the forests – and leapt over the narrow bourn, landing precariously on the other side of the bank. A sludge of wet mud instantly seeped through the soles of her worn boots, but she took no notice of the dampness in her feet, running as fast as she could towards the gaps between the fir trees. When she made it through, the villagers who had been standing huddled in front of her tiny cottage, instantly came to meet her.

Her wide eyes took in the scene before her. The cottage had been in her family for generations, and as the straw roof burst into flame, she let out an almighty scream. She ran towards the man standing in front of her home, holding a lit torch, ready to hurl it into the mouth of the small cottage.

"Stop!" Elizabeth fell onto her knees before the man.

The man glowered down at her. "You cursed this village, and now you will pay for it!" he cried.

Elizabeth clasped her hands together, as though in prayer. "Please, Mr Aldworth, I have brought no curse to this village. I wish harm to no one."

"Then why is my daughter, Amelia, bedridden with smallpox?" he demanded.

Elizabeth looked up at the man. "I know of no such thing, but I can find a cure."

The man stood for a moment, looking hesitant. But

64

then he turned and barked at the other villagers. "Throw water over the fire, immediately!"

Elizabeth wanted to kiss his muddy boots as the rest of the villagers, already armed with buckets of water, threw them all at once, extinguishing the flames. Thankfully, the fire fizzled out as quickly as it had begun. Elizabeth remained on her knees, thanking them all profusely.

"Get up!" barked the man.

Elizabeth did as she was told, but as she struggled to stand, her long skirt got caught on the heel of her boot. She felt herself falling forwards, her hands sinking helplessly into the muddy earth. The man sneered down at her, relishing in her discomfort. Finally, she got her skirt free, and managed to push herself back up onto her feet. The man, Christopher Aldworth, wasn't much taller than Elizabeth. His red cheeks glistened with fury, and his steel-grey eyes fixed onto hers.

"Well? Are you not going to find a cure for my daughter?"

Elizabeth turned her head to look at the other villagers. The group consisted of mostly men, but a few of the women cowered behind their husbands. Afraid of being turned into a rodent or some other such nonsense. She caught them peering from under their bonnets, not daring to catch her eye. She knew they all called her a witch behind her back. But they remained on good terms, as long as she didn't interact with them or their children.

The only time she spoke to them was when they asked her to make a herbal remedy for their minor ailments. She also attended the church service every Sunday. She was far from religious, but she went along anyway, for fear of being labelled as a heathen and being burnt at the stake if she didn't. Apart from those few exchanges, she kept herself to herself. After her mother, Margaret, had passed away, she had carried on making the herbal medicines that had been passed down by their ancestors. Once a week, Elizabeth would travel into the forests and collect ingredients for her medicines. She was always searching for new plants to grow in the small patch at the back of her cottage. Thankfully, she lived by the edge of the forest, slightly apart from the other villagers. That was the way she liked it, and they were quite happy to leave her be most of the time.

"Can I see your daughter?" she eventually asked Mr Aldworth.

The man glowered at her, but after a moment, his features softened. "Very well. I suppose you will need to see what you are dealing with." His face hardened once more. "Unless it was you who cursed her."

Elizabeth shrank away from the man. "No, sir, I have no intention of harming anyone in this village, let alone a child. I am a healer, not a murderer."

He studied her for a moment longer before finally

turning on his heel. "Very well, follow me."

Elizabeth hung her head as she followed the man, passing all the other villagers. She felt their angry gazes burning down on her. It was then that she made a vow to herself that she would soon pack up and leave. But where? She sighed. She would worry about that at a later date.

They walked through a field of cattle and past a few small barns and huts until the man stopped outside a large, thatched cottage.

"This way," he barked.

Elizabeth followed him through the doorway, crouching so as not to hit her head on the low beams that separated the rooms. The man paused at an open doorway, removing his brimmed hat. He took a few steps forward, allowing room for Elizabeth to squeeze in behind him. Once the man had stepped aside she found herself looking at a small narrow bed in the middle of the room. A tiny figure lay in its centre. The man's wife, who kept a vigil beside the bed, looked horrified when she saw Elizabeth.

She shot up from her chair. "What is she doing here?" she demanded.

The man held both hands up. "Calm down, Anne, she is here to help." He gestured for Elizabeth to move closer to the bed.

Cautiously, she edged closer, but stalled when she glimpsed the frail figure. The young girl could be no older than six years old, and was laying with her eyes closed, her breathing shallow. Her innocent features were unrecognisable; every inch of skin was concealed by protruding, wart-like spots. It hurt Elizabeth to witness this tiny frail child suffering. She rushed towards the bed and placed a palm over the little girl's brow.

The mother looked taken aback. Why was she touching her? Wasn't the disease contagious after all?

"She has a high temperature." Elizabeth removed her hand. "I have some wheat germ in my cottage. I can fetch this and steep it in goat's milk to place over her forehead. This should take her temperature down and give some relief from the swollen spots."

Elizabeth moved towards the door but the man threw an arm out to stop her.

"And what about the spots? Will this wheat germ take those away?" he asked.

Elizabeth looked over her shoulder, back at the poor child. "I'm sorry. I do not have a cure for smallpox."

The man's face contorted in anger. "You will find a cure, or else I will burn your hut down for sure! And this time, you will be inside it!"

Elizabeth scurried from the cottage, inhaling deep breaths. Christopher Aldworth had demanded she go back to her cottage and fetch the wheat germ, then she was to return and concoct medicine for the disease.

Once she had collected her ingredients, Elizabeth

placed the wheat germ inside a piece of linen cloth, tying it together with a length of string. She stopped one villager on her way back to the child and asked for some goat's milk. They were reluctant at first, but when she explained who it was for, they obliged. After placing the pouch over the child's brow, Elizabeth could feel her temperature slowly dropping. But, as promised, the man now followed her back to her home to make sure she found a cure for the pox.

Elizabeth knew she had no such remedy within her belongings. But the man would not listen, threatening once again to burn down her house. Fearful for her life, she was suddenly struck by an idea.

"There is a flower, but I am afraid it grows deep inside the forest."

The man studied her for a moment. "Then you must go. Immediately!"

Elizabeth sighed with relief. Her plan to escape was working. She would gather her precious dairy cow and some of her late mother's belongings and flee into the night.

"But I am not taking any risks," the man continued. "Leave your cow with me, so I know you will come back."

Elizabeth almost collapsed. She had been so sure she had found a way out. Now she had to follow through with this plan. Thankfully, she knew of a plant that could heal the girl, and it was, in fact, deep within the forest. But if it didn't work, she would surely be burnt alive.

"I will leave first thing in the morning," she sighed.

"Time is of the essence, you will go now," demanded the man.

Elizabeth looked out of the small bevelled window, disheartened to see black clouds forming. "It's getting dark, I won't be able to see where I am going," she begged.

"You are the only one in this village who knows these forests. You must go."

Elizabeth knew she could not talk sense into this man, and with a heavy heart, she collected her basket and filled it with some bread and milk for the journey, before setting off towards the forest. The man watched her, holding the rope attached to her cow, his eyes cold and unforgiving.

☾

Elizabeth wrapped her cloak tighter around her hunched shoulders. The damp air clutched at her like icy fingers, trying to feast on her flesh. She glanced up towards the sky, but a canopy of thick branches grew overhead, blocking out any natural light. Elizabeth knew the day was nearing its end as the darkness dulled her senses. Mr Aldworth had been right about one thing: she knew this forest like the back of her hand, though that knowledge didn't stop her from tripping over the odd boulder or broken branch lying on the forest floor.

Elizabeth slumped against the rough bark of the nearest tree. Her feet ached, and the forest had become blanketed in darkness; even she did not understand where she was heading. For all she knew, she could be walking in circles. Sinking into the damp ground, she placed her basket down beside her and leaned over to rub at her aching feet. She could feel fresh blisters forming on her soles where there had never been blisters before.

Somewhere in the near distance, a twig snapped. Elizabeth froze. She listened out, holding her breath. It was then that she sensed it. Someone, or something, had been following her since she had entered the forest. She knew it was not one of the villagers, for none of them would dare enter these forests after dark. No, it felt more sinister.

A dark energy cloaked around her, suffocating her. She took a few deep breaths to ease her anxiety and focused all her senses, tuning in to the forest's heartbeat. She stayed like this, not daring to move, until her eyelids forced themselves closed and she drifted into a restless sleep, waking to the sound of birds announcing the new day ahead.

It took her a moment or two at first to realise where she was, but Elizabeth's bleary eyes soon adjusted to the sights and sounds around her. Her awareness restored, unfamiliar aches and those of old returned in double measures. She had fallen asleep sitting upright against the rough bark of a tree, her shoulders twisted in a crooked position that she knew she was going to regret for days to come. She rubbed at the back of her neck as she thought of the day's trek to find this rare plant. Her mouth was dry, reminding her she hadn't eaten or drunk anything since nightfall. Relieved to see her basket still beside her, she rummaged through its contents and brought out a flask of milk and chunk of crispy bread. She ate sparingly, so as to leave enough for the rest of her journey, knowing that it might be a long road ahead.

Satiated, she pulled herself up, taking a moment to gain her bearings. Although the trees and foliage looked the same in every direction, Elizabeth knew to head east. Setting off at a pace, she forced her way through the forest, fighting off thick bracken and overgrown foliage. She tried her best to block out the pain in her feet and the other aches that riddled her body, which throbbed each time she took a step. Now and again, sunlight would stream down through rare gaps in the overhead branches, bringing some warm relief to her shivering body.

Each time she felt the need to give up, she would think about the little girl who needed her help, as well as the threat to her own life if she failed. But what if she was wrong, and the Rosa Diaboli wasn't real? Her grandmother had told her a story when she was just a little girl, around the same age as Amelia Aldworth. Her grandmother had been the village's herbalist, and had often travelled into the depths of these forests in search of rare plants. On one particular occasion, she had travelled many days, until she came across a patch of black roses. On closer inspection, she had realised these must be the legendary Rosa Diaboli – the Devil's Rose – a rare black flower that had the strength to cure any ailment. It was even said that, if used in combination with dark spellcraft, these flowers could bring back the dead.

These thoughts urged Elizabeth onwards, giving her a new focus. She was so deep in thought she never noticed the shadow creeping behind her amongst the trees.

A patch of sunlight streamed through the canopy and Elizabeth eagerly stepped beneath it, tilting her chin towards the heat source. She basked in the delight of its warmth, the only comfort she had experienced since stepping inside the forest. Her eyelids suddenly became heavy and she staggered backwards into a tree. Grabbing the trunk for balance, Elizabeth focused on her whereabouts, when something to her right caught her eye.

She jerked her head to the side and saw a dark, hooded figure hunched before an old, gnarled oak tree, its face concealed by shadow. Elizabeth gasped. Slowly moving backwards to try and hide, she accidentally stepped onto a twig. The cracking sound echoed through the silence, reverberating back and forth between the trees.

To her dismay, the figure straightened, its hidden face instantly turning in her direction.

"Who goes there?" The voice belonged to a man, but the tone was guttural, like a wild animal.

Elizabeth knew she was cornered. She didn't have the strength to run. Instead, she stepped out of the shadow of the trees and faced the stranger.

"I'm sorry, sir, I didn't mean to intrude. I am only passing through."

The figure straightened its body, and Elizabeth was shocked by its height. The man, if it was a man, was at least seven feet tall.

"Don't be a frightened, child, come forward."

Elizabeth hesitated. "I am heading east, sir; I won't be any trouble."

The man held out an arm and used his index finger to beckon her. Elizabeth looked warily around her. There was no fast route for escape. Her only option was to approach this stranger, so she slowly made her way forwards.

As she approached, she still could not make out the stranger's features. He wore a long black cloak, the oversized hood making him appear sinister and foreboding. She stopped a few feet away. The stranger stepped closer, and to her amazement, he pulled his hood down. She was shocked to see a man not much older than herself. His features were sharp, but handsome all the same. His raven black hair sat upon his shoulders, and when he fixed his black eyes upon hers, he smiled warmly.

"So charmed to meet such a young and beautiful creature." He held his hand out towards her.

Elizabeth was unsure whether to accept; it was not normal for a lowly village woman such as herself to be treated in such a manner. Eventually, she relented, stepping forward and accepting the man's hand. His skin was hot to the touch, and she instantly noticed his fingernails were long and sharp, unlike those of any other man she had encountered before, although admittedly she had not met very many men, excluding the villagers. Lifting her hand, the man pressed it to his lips. Elizabeth blushed as he let go.

"What brings you out into these treacherous forests?"

Elizabeth averted her gaze. "I, um, I need to find a plant."

The man's eyes seemed to penetrate through to her very soul. "Hmm, a plant you say? What type of plant, maybe I can be of some help? I know these forests like I created them myself."

"Rosa Diaboli," murmured Elizabeth.

"Ah, the Devil's Rose, such a precious black flower. Such a rarity," said the stranger.

It shocked Elizabeth that the stranger knew what she

meant. She had been waiting for him to laugh at her; to tell her there was no such thing; that it was an old wives' tale.

"So, you have heard of it?" she asked.

The man let out a hearty laugh. "Why, of course. And I know exactly where you can find it."

Elizabeth's eyes lit up. "Really? Do you think you could show me?"

The man took a step closer to her. "I can do even better. I can bring it to you."

Elizabeth frowned, ready to ask what he meant, when the man reached inside his cloak and pulled out a flower. But it wasn't just any flower. He was holding the black stem of the Devil's Rose. Elizabeth stumbled backwards. Was she really witnessing this?

"Don't be alarmed, child. Is this not what you are seeking?"

"Y-yes," she stammered. She found her feet and slowly walked towards him. She focused directly on the rare flower. "How did you find this?"

The man laughed, "I can find anything I want."

Elizabeth held her hand out to take the flower, but the man snatched it away again, placing it back inside his cloak.

"There's plenty where that came from, but you must earn it."

Elizabeth dropped her arm. "I don't understand."

The man turned towards the oak tree where he had

been crouched only moments before. He held both hands out to touch its bark, chanting in a strange language. Elizabeth moved closer, drawn to the magick that was taking place before her. A circle of white light whizzed around the tree, then disappeared. The man stopped chanting and placed his hands inside the trunk, emerging with a large, worn leather book, with symbols embossed on its skin. He held it out in his open hands and turned towards Elizabeth. Her eyes widened with awe.

"I can grant you anything you wish."

Elizabeth looked up at the tall man, then her gaze fell back to the book. "What is it?" she asked.

The man laughed darkly. "It's a grimoire."

Elizabeth looked puzzled. "A grimoire?"

"Elizabeth."

She staggered backwards. "H-how do you know my name?"

The man's smile wavered this time. "I know more about you than you will ever know. In fact, I know more about you than you know about yourself." He paced around her, the book now clutched under his arm. "Elizabeth, you are more powerful than you will ever know. You are wasting your magick by allowing the spawn of a cowardly God to use you for their meaningless desires. Their greed for your misfortune is empowering their egos. You deserve more, and that is why I have followed you into these forests to reveal to you your true self." He stopped pacing and stood before her.

"I don't understand. Who are you?" she asked.

He placed his fingers under her chin and lifted her face to meet his gaze. The blackness in his eyes swirled like a whirlwind of shadows, and Elizabeth found herself sucked into their lifeless void. In that rare moment, Elizabeth witnessed the true horror of dark magick; the depths to which evil could make one sink. Screams of agonising pain tore through her mind as distorted bodies, devoid of limbs, scrambled towards her in the darkness. She could hear their tortured cries drawing ever closer. She fell to her knees, clutching her head in her hands, covering her ears in a desperate attempt to block out this waking nightmare.

When she dared to open them once more, Elizabeth looked down at the man's feet. She recoiled backwards, dragging her body along the forest floor. There, facing Elizabeth, where there should have been human feet, were two black hooves, poking out from beneath the stranger's cloak.

Chapter 9

Luna and Lily left their room, leaving Belinda to carry on searching for spells on reversing necromancy. Or, as she liked to put it, how to murder someone for a short while.

Walking down the corridor, Luna went over to the large ornate window on the upper floor and gazed down at the gardens below. Fresh snow was already replacing the snow they had melted earlier. Luna wondered if it would rain soon and wash away the rest for good. Although it looked pretty, she was more of a summer girl, perfectly content to sit outdoors all day with a good book. She couldn't wait for this year's summer solstice.

Turning around, she headed towards the left staircase.

"Where are you going?" asked Lily.

Luna shrugged. "I can't be with everyone else; they'll be in the games room."

"What about the library? We could see if we can find anything related to Elizabeth Drake?" suggested Lily.

"Good idea."

The two girls began their descent towards the foyer.

"I wonder what happened to Elizabeth after meeting the strange man?" pondered Lily.

"Yeah… personally, I think it was the devil himself she met," said Luna.

"You believe in all of that?"

Luna shrugged. "What is there not to believe?"

Lily nodded her head. "True." She thought for a moment. "So, what do you think happened after the stranger gave Elizabeth the grimoire?"

Luna shook her head. "He made her a more powerful witch, perhaps?"

"Maybe… I just think it's funny that we haven't been taught any of this in our history class. Perhaps we should ask Mr Brutt," suggested Lily.

Luna was about to reply that there were a lot of things they had not been taught, when she was interrupted.

"Wit ye up tae lassies?"

The girls looked down, smiling when they saw the little Scottish imp, Murdoch. His green-tinted cherub face was unusually pink looking, and the smattering of freckles that dotted his pug nose gave him a childlike appearance.

"Have you been out in the cold?" asked Luna.

Murdoch scowled. "Aye, an' it's bloody freezing! They got me oot grittin' the steps. If ye ask me, I'd have done it better wi' a defrosting spell!"

"Why didn't you use one then?" asked Luna.

Murdoch stamped his tiny foot. "Cos that's cheating." He scowled.

Lily sniggered behind Luna, clamping up when the imp glared up at her.

"Hellooo, Miss Luna."

A blast of icy wind and snow hit the three friends as the large oak door swung open, momentarily turning the inner hallway into a snow globe.

"Nimbie!" Luna skipped past Murdoch towards the mammoth hobgoblin, enveloping him in an enormous bear hug.

"What about me?"

Luna looked over Nimbie's shoulder and spotted the familiar white, coiffed hair of her grandmother. "Nana Violet!" She let go of the hobgoblin and bent down to hug her tiny grandmother.

When they finally let go of each other, Violet held her granddaughter at arm's length. "Oh my, I still can't get used to seeing you in your new transitional state, even after all this time."

Luna blushed. She was still trying to get used to it herself. She secretly missed her darker locks, but she couldn't deny she absolutely loved the aquamarine eyes. They made her look so surreal, like one of the light creatures of Illuminos.

Thinking of Illuminos, she asked, "Have you heard from Dahlia?"

Luna had become good friends with the bodyguard of the princess of the fairies, after she had taken them through the fae tunnels to find the first missing crystal.

Violet shook her head. "Sorry dear, she has not popped in to see me at the cottage for a while. In fact, I was going to ask you how she's been."

"I have only seen her a handful of times since the shadow walkers attacked the manor," said Luna.

"Ah, Violet. So nice to see you." Agnes Guthrie emerged from one of the side rooms. "Did you drive all the way here?"

Violet shook snowflakes from the top of her hair. "Oh Agnes, really? Have you seen the weather? You know I would never drive in that." She pointed a thumb towards the door.

Agnes chuckled. "You never change, old friend." The two women hugged. "Come, I've made us a pot of tea with some honey and scones."

"Mm, my favourite. It seems you will never change either!"

The two women chatted as they headed across the foyer, disappearing back into the room where Agnes had appeared from.

"See? Wit is the point in me slaving awae to rid the snow when folks are using the flipping fae tunnels!"

Luna, Nimbie and Lily watched as the imp stormed off in the direction of the kitchens. Once he was out of sight, the three of them burst into a fit of giggles.

"Come on, Nimbie, fancy joining us for hot chocolate and some fudge cake?" asked Luna.

Nimbie grinned widely, showing off his huge square teeth. "I won't say no to that."

Luna went after Murdoch towards the kitchens, and quickly found Jeannie the hoglin, who agreed to make their feast and bring it to them whenever it was ready. Thanking her, Luna returned to the others, and suggested they go and sit in the TV room.

Black, faux leather corner sofas took up most of the small square room, and a large, flat screen television hung on the wall opposite them. The room had only recently been refurnished, mostly as a reward for the children's bravery after the shadow walker incident, and though they could not watch live television, they had countless DVDs to choose from.

Nimbie took up an entire sofa with his large frame, his awkward size making Luna giggle, and soon after they had settled, Jeannie Gibbs bustled in holding a tray of goodies.

"Hot chocolate with lashings of oat cream, sprinkled with plenty of marshmallows," announced the cook. She placed the tray down in the middle of the floor. "Oh, and not to forget the slabs of hot chocolate fudge cake and vegan vanilla ice cream!"

As Jeannie stood back up, she caught the look of dismay on Lily's face. "Aww, sweetheart. I'm sure you can remember the taste."

"Oh, it's okay, don't worry. I can just conjure up a slice. It's not as good as the real thing, but it's close enough." A delicious looking slab of chocolate cake, almost identical to the slices in front of them, appeared in Lily's hand. Between mouthfuls of the scrumptious sponge, Lily mumbled, "It's useful being a ghost. I can conjure up anything I desire in the spirit world, well, almost anything." She let out a chuckle, spraying pieces of cake everywhere, the crumbs disappearing into thin air after landing on the furniture.

A short while later, once the plates had been licked clean – by Nimbie, of course – Violet joined them.

"Agnes was telling me about your trip into the Dead Forest this morning," she said.

Luna and Lily both nodded their heads.

"Oh, that must have bin scary," murmured Nimbie.

"It was terrible, especially when Salvador and Monsieur Chavron sensed the coven of evil witches," shuddered Lily.

Violet seemed to think about this for a moment. "Yes, I'm wondering what they are up to. I mean, it's obvious they are here to manipulate the portal."

"That's what I don't understand," said Luna. "If they gave Belinda a powerful spell to open the portal, why don't they use it themselves?"

"Because they weren't in possession of the spell."

Everyone in the room jumped as Belinda entered the room.

"Hi Violet, hi Nimbie," she greeted the visitors. "Mind if I join you?"

Violet gestured for her to sit down and Nimbie leaned over and gave her a hug as she plonked herself down beside him.

"You're sure they definitely don't have a spell to open it?" asked Luna. "If that's the case, how are the vetalas escaping?"

Belinda shrugged. "I know they don't have the spell. They knew I had a powerful spell from my ancestors; it wasn't strong enough to open the portal, just enough to crack it further. That's why they used me, because they knew I was the only one who could open it. The shadow walkers must have broken through when the barrier was at its weakest."

"But that still doesn't explain why they are here now," pondered Lily. "And how the vetalas are escaping."

"They haven't escaped." Violet suddenly slapped a hand over her mouth. "Oh dear…"

The others stared at her intensely, their eyes questioning.

She held both hands up. "Okay, but don't tell your headmistress I told you."

They all nodded their heads eagerly, except for Nimbie.

Violet shot him a look, before continuing. "Right, well, Monsieur Chavron could smell the vetalas, but once out of earshot, he informed the teachers it was only the one on the loose."

"Isn't that bad enough?" said Luna.

Violet pondered this for a moment. "Well, yes. But one is not as urgent as a group of them."

"Okay, so what are they going to do about it?" asked Lily.

"They need to track it down obviously, but it will not be that easy."

"Why?" asked Belinda.

Violet shrugged. "They need to travel to Transylvania to find out more about the whereabouts of the next crystal, the ruby."

"That's a bit cliché, isn't it?" remarked Belinda. "Evil vampires… Transylvania…"

Luna nodded her head.

"There are vampires all over the world, but they originate from the ancient ruins of Transylvania. You know the history of Vlad the Impaler?" When she saw the children's blank faces, Violet shook her head. "Oh dear, are you not learning anything about history at this school?"

"That's what I've been saying," groaned Belinda. "They don't even know the history of the grimoire."

Violet's eyes shot up. "You mean the missing grimoire?"

Belinda nodded. "I had to give those two a history lesson myself."

Violet sat silently for a few moments. Luna could almost hear her brain ticking away.

Suddenly, Violet stood up. "That could be the answer to everything!"

The older woman's remark surprised the others.

"What are you suggesting?" asked Luna. "That this grimoire holds the secret to helping us find the missing vetala?"

Violet looked down at her granddaughter, but her vision was somewhere else entirely. "Even better—"

Just then, a commotion erupted from outside the room.

"What in the blazes are you doing?"

The group all jumped to their feet, rushing out of the room just in time to see Evan Corsan running out of the kitchens with Jeannie Gibbs hot on his trail. Nimbie grabbed hold of the boy as he sprinted past him and the two of them jostled around for a few seconds until Jeannie caught up. Gripping Evan's shoulders, Nimbie swivelled him around to face the others.

"Whatever's the matter?" asked Violet.

But as Evan slowly turned his head towards them, Violet and the rest of the group recoiled. Smudged across the boy's mouth was a dark, red stain.

"Is that… blood?" spluttered Luna.

Evan Corsan grinned back at her, licking his blood-stained lips.

Chapter 10

Jeannie panted for breath, holding something out towards them between her stubby fingers. "I caught him eating this raw piece of meat!"

Violet took a few cautious steps closer. "But why?" she asked, turning to look at Evan.

Evan shrugged. "Dunno, I just had a taste for it. I was starving."

"What is going on here?"

The group turned to see Salvador briskly walking towards them. Frances Chavron appeared from the room behind him. Evan wiped furiously at the offending blood stains around his mouth, but it was too late. The two additional sets of eyes had already witnessed the horror. Salvador's olive skin turned a pallid grey, and Luna noticed that the symbols tattooed on his shaved head seemed to pulsate against his skull. He staggered backwards, stepping into Frances Chavron.

"I think we need to talk." Monsieur Chavron walked around the Spaniard, towards the boy. Taking Evan from Nimbie's clutches, he led the boy away from the group. "Come, we need to speak to your head teacher."

The two disappeared down the hallway.

"What the heck!" exclaimed Belinda, as Salvador marched after the pair.

Violet shrugged. "It doesn't look good, I know, but Mrs Guthrie will figure it out."

"Figure what out?" asked Luna. "Why would he suddenly start craving a bloodied piece of raw meat?"

"If I weren't already dead, I think I'd have fainted by now," gasped Lily.

"Has anyone seen Evan?"

The group turned as Ava Corsan and Sebastian Chavron came out of the games room. Luna was about to tell Evan's little sister that he had just been dragged off to the head teacher's room by a vampire, but suddenly felt lost for words.

"Come with me, dear, I'll take you to him." Violet gestured to Sebastian, and the two of them led the girl in the direction her brother had been escorted only moments before.

The remaining five watched in silence as they disappeared down the corridor.

"Okay, I'm kinda creeped out now," said Luna, once Violet and Ava were out of earshot.

Jeannie Gibbs shrugged her broad shoulders. "Beats me. I had best get started on dinner, can't let you all go hungry just because of this strange incident."

Luna looked to Nimbie for answers, but he simply shrugged his wide, broad shoulders.

"I have an idea," said Lily. "Why don't I listen outside Mrs Guthrie's door?"

"What if you get caught? You'll get kicked out of Blackhill for sure," mumbled Belinda.

Lily rolled her eyes. "I'll be quiet. I am a ghost after all."

"No, none of you can risk it. Miss Violet will tell us," said Nimbie.

Luna thought about this for a moment. "Will she though? I mean, it is a confidential meeting; we can't rely on her telling us. Lily is our only option."

"Well, I won't take any part in this." Belinda stormed towards the stairs. "I'm already on their blacklist," she said over her shoulder, as she took the stairs two at a time.

"I promise I won't get caught," said Lily, floating between Luna and Nimbie.

"Oh Miss Lily, I really don't think this is a good idea," said Nimbie.

"Look, if Lily gets caught, I will take full responsibility," said Luna. She turned to Lily, but her ghost friend was already drifting towards Agnes Guthrie's office.

As Lily Jackson floated along the dimly lit corridor, she held one of her hands in front of her face and concentrated. Her hand turned translucent, so much so that she could actually see the painting on the wall through it. Turning invisible always made Lily think of her hometown of East Kilbride in Scotland. One day, after once again witnessing Emma Whyte bully her best friend as they walked home from school, Lily had snapped, turning invisible and tripping the bully up to fall flat on her face. It was one of her favourite memories of being a ghost; she had felt so powerful.

Stopping outside the dark mahogany door of Agnes Guthrie's office, Lily placed an ear against the door and listened, worried that if she tried to enter the room the people inside might sense her presence. She could hear voices filtering through.

"So, what you are saying Monsieur Chavron—"

"Frances, please. Let us dispense with the formalities."

A pause.

"So, Mons… Frances. Are you saying that Evan is becoming a bloodsucker?"

Lily almost jumped with fright when she heard those words. They were coming from Agnes.

"I'm afraid so. His thoughts are already turning to his mother's side. Thankfully we have caught it just in time… before he spills blood from his first victim."

A moment's silence, then—

"We knew this was going to happen," Agnes sighed. "We thought that perhaps the Corsan siblings might take after their father, but we brought them here just to be safe. I'm thankful we did."

"Mrs Guthrie?"

The voice belonged to Ava Corsan.

"Do you mean to say that Evan and I are both half vampires?"

Someone coughed.

"Yes, dear. We have been waiting to explain this to you, as per your parents' wishes. Your mother, Patricia, is indeed a vampire, just like Frances and Sebastian here. Edward Blackhill rescued your mother when he was still a young man. In fact, it was he who introduced your parents. Your father, who is one hundred percent human, subsequently attended one of our Solstice Balls with Patricia, once we knew we could trust him with the manor's secrets"

"B-but… how did our mum become a vampire?" Evan asked.

"Your mother was born a vampire. Both of her parents, your grandparents, were full-blooded vampires, if you'll excuse the pun."

"Now I know why they scared me so much," murmured Ava.

"Perhaps the presence of my son and I has triggered the surfacing of their abilities," suggested Frances.

"Or else you and your son have caused this to happen." Salvador's tone was harsh.

"You think Sebastian and I have forced them to become vampires?"

There was a lengthily silence, then—

"Perhaps. Don't you use your eyes to hypnotise your victims?"

A deep laugh broke through the air. Lily could hear the older vampire walking around the office with his cane.

"Do you truly believe everything you see in horror films?"

"His point is not so far from the truth, father. After all, we can use our eyes to manipulate a person's way of thinking," said Sebastian.

A nervous clearing of the throat ensued.

"Well, er, yes. But my point is that people believe everything they watch on that glass box of deception."

"I only felt hungry," mumbled Evan. "I wasn't out to hurt anybody."

"Of course not, dear, we know you weren't," said Agnes.

"I've been feeling a thirst too," Ava admitted. "I wasn't sure what I was craving. It doesn't feel like you're thirsty exactly, but eating doesn't fill you up either. It's weird."

"At least we know what we are dealing with now," Agnes reassured them. "We can stop the hunger and concentrate on your new abilities."

"Will we have to drink blood from now on then?" asked Evan nervously.

"No. You will be given the same synthetic blood that

the Chavrons drink. Once we have your thirst under control, you can focus on developing your talents. While the Chavrons are here, I am sure they will help you both to enhance your new abilities."

Footsteps drew closer to the door, prompting Lily to zoom off back down the hallway into the brightly lit foyer where the others were still waiting.

"They're coming," she warned, as she swooped down beside Luna and Nimbie.

Luna nodded. "Any news?"

"Loads. I'll meet you in our room." With that, Lily floated up the staircase.

Luna headed after her but stopped when she realised the hobgoblin wasn't following. "Aren't you coming, Nimbie?"

He shook his large head back at her. "Nah, I don't want to get in trouble, Miss Luna. I'm only a visitor after all."

Luna smiled at him kindly and waved, before turning and heading upstairs to join Lily.

Belinda was in her usual spot, lying on her back on top of her bed with her earbuds plugged in. She jumped up when she sensed Lily and Luna spring into the room.

"What happened?" she asked, taking out one of her earbuds.

They could hear muffled heavy metal music thrashing through the speakers.

"Lily has got some info on the Corsans," explained

Luna, as she made herself comfortable on top of her own bed.

Belinda pulled the other earbud out and shifted into a sitting position. Two scruffy Doc Martins dangled over the side of her bed as she sat against the wall, facing the two girls.

Luna shook her head and smirked. "I thought you didn't want to get involved? We don't want to get you in trouble…"

Belinda rolled her eyes. "Just spill it."

Lily chuckled. "We knew it wouldn't last."

Belinda snorted. "I'm already involved if I make a death spell for Luna."

Grinning, Luna looked over at Lily, gesturing for her to start. Reluctantly at first, then more confidently, Lily began to recount everything that she had overheard. By the end, the other two looked taken aback.

"Wow, I didn't expect that," exclaimed Belinda.

"Hmm, I don't know," pondered Luna. "I think their animal guides are a bit of a clue. I mean, Evan has a python and Ava has a bat."

Belinda snorted. "Really? Don't you think that's a bit vampirist—"

"Hey, what's going down?"

The three girls turned to the door as a mop of blonde hair poked through the open gap.

"Hey Magnus, did no one tell you not to skulk around the girls' corridors?" snorted Belinda.

The tall boy pushed the door open wider but stayed standing in the doorway.

"Eh, as long as I don't set foot inside the room then I'm safe," he shrugged. "I was heading to the games room when I heard you talking."

"Ah, so you're nosey, and a rule breaker," added Belinda.

Luna laughed. "Ignore her. Come in, we've got news to tell."

Magnus shook his head. "Nah, I'm not getting in trouble."

"Jeez, not another goody two shoes," said Lily, rolling her eyes.

Magnus leaned back out into the hallway, his head moving left to right. When he saw the coast was clear, he stepped inside the girls' room and closed the door behind him.

Once they had finished telling him what had happened, Magnus smiled.

"Well, I think it's cool."

"Me too," said Luna.

Just then, the sound of the doorknob turning made them all jump. Magnus panicked and hid behind a curtain. The other three sat rigid, staring as the handle twisted slowly, rotating anticlockwise until it finally clicked, and the door opened inwards.

"Hugo!" they all shouted.

A blur of bright orange flew into the room and

bounded towards Luna's bed. The creature's huge, long, hairy arms instantly assaulted Luna as they flung around her neck in a tight embrace.

Magnus peeked around the curtain, letting out an exasperated sigh when he noticed it was only his orangutan animal guide.

"Don't you ever do that again!" he scolded.

Hugo, who was now sitting on top of Luna's lap, hung his colossal head, looking up at his master with woeful eyes. Magnus could never stay annoyed with the orangutan for long, and held his arms out towards him. Hugo smiled, showing off his massive yellow incisors before jumping into his master's arms.

A peck at the window revealed that Poe was watching from the other side of the glass. He did not look happy that an ape was intruding on his master's space.

Belinda stood up to open the window when she suddenly stumbled backwards.

"No!" she gasped.

Luna jumped to her feet. "What's wrong?"

Belinda slowly backed away from the window. "T-there's someone out there…"

Magnus came to stand by Luna's side. "It'll only be another student or teacher," he said.

Luna looked down into the gardens. "There's no one there."

Belinda was still backing away. "That's because

they're not in the gardens."

Magnus, who was still clutching onto Hugo, tried desperately to look over his enormous bulk.

"Okay, so maybe it's a teacher or the Edgar twins in the forest?"

Belinda shook her head. Her gaze was still focused on whatever was beyond the window.

"It's them."

"Who?" asked the other three.

"The Pendle Hill witches."

Luna pushed Belinda out of the way, pressing her face against the cold glass.

"I don't see anything, apart from trees and, well, more trees."

Belinda sank down onto her bed. "I must be imagining it. I was so sure I saw her."

Luna turned away from the window. "Her?"

Belinda wiped her nose with the back of her hand. "The leader of the coven. Or at least she was the last time I saw them."

"We should tell Mrs Guthrie," stated Magnus.

Belinda swiped her hand away from her face. "Nah, I might just be seeing things. I don't want to bother her in case I'm wrong."

"But what if you're not? Frances Chavron and Salvador both smelt their presence in the Dead Forest," said Luna.

Belinda looked towards the window and shivered. "I

don't want to rile it up again, especially after the hate I got when the shadow walkers escaped. I'll keep a close eye out though."

Luna studied the witch for a few moments. She could sense the girl's fear as she sat hugging herself on her bed. Something was wrong. They just needed to find out what.

Chapter 11

Nimbie poked his bulbous head through the open door of the games room.

"Bye Miss Luna. Me an' Mistress Violet are headin' home now."

Luna was sitting on the floor on one of the large beanbags. She had left the others to clear her head, and was happy to see the games room unusually empty. She fought with the idea of telling her nana about Belinda's sighting, but decided against it. She trusted the young witch, even after everything that had happened.

Luna struggled to pull herself upright as the wriggly beans sucked her into the beanbag's centre. Once she had finally wrestled free, she rushed over to the hobgoblin.

"Are you not staying for dinner?" she asked, slightly out of breath.

"I'd love to, but Miss Violet has prepared my favourite meal, cream mashed potatoes an' kidney an' pickle pie!"

Luna giggled. "Well, you can't miss out on that!" She leaned down and hugged the chunky hobgoblin.

"Mind you keep safe," whispered Nimbie into her ear. "Don't you be doin' anythin' dangerous."

Luna straightened up as she let go of him, tapping the side of her nose. "You know me, Nimbie, I'm always dangerous."

Nimbie's eyes widened, and Luna could not help but laugh. His worried expression was truly comical.

"I'm pulling your leg," she joked.

Nimbie looked down at his thick stumpy legs before looking back up at her with a puzzled expression. Luna shook her head and laughed.

"Bye dear!" Violet called out from the foyer.

Luna squeezed past Nimbie to hug her nana.

"I'll see you next week." Violet hugged her granddaughter back.

Luna hugged her tightly, once more deliberating whether to tell her about Belinda's recent revelation. Deciding against it, she finally let go of her nana.

"Why, that was a big hug,' remarked Violet. "Is everything okay dear?" She seemed to search her granddaughter's eyes for clues.

Luna looked away from her intense stare. "I'm just going to miss you, that's all," she shrugged. But once again, Luna was tempted to tell her about the evil witches and her dangerous plans to find out if Jonas Schmidt was lingering in the spirit realm. Watching them.

But her attention soon drifted past her nana's shoulder, noticing her car wasn't parked outside, which meant they must have travelled through the fae tunnels. They would need to leave the premises of the manor to use them; even the fae couldn't turn up unexpectedly without an invitation. Luna began to feel at ease. The tunnels were a safer means of travel than her nana's car, and would keep them safe from any unwanted visitors who might be hanging around outside the safety of the manor's barriers.

☾

After their evening meal, Agnes asked the children to meet her outside the invisible wall leading to the gardens, but when they asked her why, she would not say. Confused, the children readied themselves for the bitter cold, wrapping up in warm coats, hats and scarves.

As they huddled together beside the enchanted barrier, Augustus, not Agnes, marched out in front of them. He chanted the disabling spell under his breath, waiting until the invisible wall had opened before beckoning the children through. Silently, they followed him, trudging through the fresh layer of snow that now covered the gardens. The nights were drawing in early now, and as the skies darkened, the children became increasingly nervous. Why had they been asked to come outdoors at this hour?

Not wanting to face the wrath of Augustus, they trudged behind the fairy until he halted. Luna could just make out a few figures standing in front of him, before Augustus stepped aside to reveal Princess Xania and her bodyguard.

"Dahlia!" cried Luna. Her heart soared when she spotted the fairy. She had not seen her since the shadow walkers had escaped.

The petite fairy waved frantically over to her. Today, her cropped hair was sapphire blue, and she was dressed in her usual casual wear of black leggings and a hooded black top. Her trainers matched the colour of her hair.

Augustus cleared his throat. "Children, this evening we are training with my kind. The reason we are here on a freezing, dark, wintry night is to test your abilities in these conditions."

The eleven children all exchanged confused glances. Magnus held a hand up. Augustus nodded to him.

"Sir, are we learning fae magick?"

Augustus shook his silver mane of hair. "Thankfully you are not fairies, but I can teach you some of our basic skills, such as how to see in the dark."

Luna scrunched up her face. "But that's not possible. We don't have your eyes."

A low snigger came from Dahlia's direction.

Augustus rolled his luminous eyes. "Thank you for your input, Luna Green." He walked in circles with his hands behind his back. "I have been instructed to teach you combat in the dark, so that you are prepared to fight our enemies regardless of the time of day. Night combat is simply about adjusting your eyes to fight in the darkness."

"Can we not just use our magick to see?" piped up Tamara.

Augustus froze on the spot, before slowly turning to face the young witch. Tamara shrank backwards when she caught the look of hatred emanating from his features. He took a few steps towards the young girl.

"This is not all about magick, witch!" He spat the last word out. "Or about seeing in the dark. This is about your ability to fight without special modifications."

Tamara's head sunk into the collar of her thick woolly coat.

"What I think my brother is trying to tell you all is that it is of great importance that we prepare you for the night creatures." Princess Xania stepped forward, holding her long wooden staff. The amethyst crystal on its tip was hardly noticeable in the gloomy atmosphere, and nor was her long, deep purple gown. The princess' mahogany hair was loose, and her curls cascaded over her shoulders all the way down the length of her back. She turned to Dahlia and nodded her head.

Dahlia bowed, before taking centre stage. "Okay kids, get into pairs."

The children scattered, finding themselves a partner.

As Lily was absent, assumedly because she could already see in the dark, Luna, Belinda and Ava were left without partners, as Ava's brother, Evan, had partnered with Lucas Kane.

Dahlia guided Ava over to Luna and Belinda. "Okay, let's bend the rules and put you three together."

Belinda took a few steps away from Ava, a flicker of fear in her eyes. Admittedly, they had only just discovered that Ava was half vampire, so Luna could understand her anxiety. But Ava was a sweet girl and Luna knew she would never harm anyone intentionally.

Once the fairy was happy that they were all partnered up, she motioned for the children to form a circle around her. Once they had, Dahlia placed one foot in front of the other; holding her right hand out, she flicked out her crystal wand. A bright white light shot straight from its tip, lighting up the circle. Holding the lit wand at arm's length, the fairy circled on the spot, leaving a trace of the radiant white light emanating around the group. Suddenly, a circle of fire shot up from the ground, and the children quickly leapt out of the way.

"Stay inside the circle!" shouted Dahlia.

"I thought we were learning to fight in the dark?" muttered Magnus.

"We are. But first, we need to establish boundaries," answered Dahlia.

The petite fairy once again held out her crystal wand and directed it towards the centre of the blazing circle.

The children shuffled awkwardly inside their fiery enclosure as Dahlia murmured in Gaelic. Out of nowhere, a dark shadow sprang from the ground. Luna's eyes widened as the shadow rose, elongating into the figure of a dark humanoid.

"What the heck?" cried Angelica Lawson. "What is it?"

"It is a shadow of an unknown. We shall pretend it is a vetala," answered Dahlia calmly. She took her stance once more, one leg in front of the other, as she held her wand out towards the humanoid figure. White light shot out from the tip of the wand to fly straight at the figure. A loud zapping sound erupted through the stillness of the air as the light hit its target. The shadow bent in two, falling to the ground, as Dahlia shot out another beam of light. This time, the shadow faded away.

"Okay, who wants to go first?"

The children all looked at one another.

"But we don't have a crystal wand," piped up Evan Corsan.

"We have wands," said Tamara, waving her wooden wand aloft. She looked over to Belinda, who just shook her head. "You mean to say you don't carry yours?"

Belinda shrugged. "Didn't know I had to. Also, didn't Augustus just tell us it wasn't about special modifications?"

Tamara rolled her eyes at the goth witch, clucking her tongue.

Dahlia held a hand up. "I realise that you are not all witches or warlocks, but you must know your abilities by now?"

A loud cough erupted from behind the fairy. Dahlia turned as Augustus walked over to her side.

"The children still have a lot to learn about their family traditions."

A confused Dahlia turned to face Princess Xania. "How are we supposed to fight the enemy with a group of clueless children? Were they not hand-picked by Edward Blackhill for a reason?"

Princess Xania stepped forward, turning to face Augustus. "Brother, what is going on?"

Augustus looked up towards one of the windows in the manor. Luna followed his gaze, to see the outline of Agnes Guthrie looking down on them.

Augustus looked back to his sister. "Mrs Guthrie asked me to bring the children to you, for more personal training."

"And why is she not accompanying us?" asked the princess.

Augustus shrugged his broad shoulders. "She feels it would be good for the children to learn from a different source."

Princess Xania sighed. "Very well… though surely the children should be learning from their own kin?"

"I am in charge of their combat lessons, sister. It was my suggestion to bring them to the gardens at this hour."

"Princess Xania," corrected Dahlia by his side.

Augustus mumbled an apology, dropping his gaze onto his black, shiny brogues.

An awkward silence fell.

"I just found out today that I have vampire blood."

The cold air around them dropped a few degrees as all eyes focused on Evan Corsan.

"Stand forward, boy," demanded Augustus.

Evan shook slightly as he took a step towards the teacher. Ava stepped forward too. Xania frowned at the girl.

"I'm his younger sister," Ava explained.

Xania nodded her head in understanding. "What are you?" she asked, pointing at Isaac.

"I-I'm part warlock, but my father is a flamethrower."

"Now he tells us," remarked Xania. She pointed her staff towards Magnus Scully.

"I have telekinetic powers. I can focus my intent on harming someone or moving objects. And I recently found out that I can hold my breath for a really long time underwater."

A snigger came from one of the children as Luna recalled their visit to a local swimming pool in the nearest town. The boys had decided to compete against each other, on who could hold their breath the longest. Luna was assigned to time each of them. Lucas was the first to resurface, followed closely by Isaac and Evan.

Only Magnus remained under the pool's surface. Ten minutes had gone by, and still Magnus remained under the surface. The boys began to panic, ready to pull him up, but Luna popped her head under the water, only to see Magnus smiling, giving her the thumbs up that all was okay. Another ten minutes had gone by. Even the lifeguard was beginning to notice there was someone at the bottom of the pool. Luna would keep checking on him, and still he would smile, reassuring her that he was fine. Finally, they'd had enough, and Isaac had pulled him up to the surface.

"Hmm, as I recall, vetalas are not so fond of water," mused Xania, dragging Luna's thoughts back to the present.

"And you?" Xania pointed towards Lucas Kane.

"I am from a powerful Haitian family, a lineage of voodoo practitioners. I can do hexes."

Xania nodded her head in approval. "I have known the Edgar twins since they were six years old. I understand they demonstrated their full potential as werewolves during the fight against the shadow walkers." She pointed to the rest of the girls.

Tamara stepped forward with her head held high. "I am—"

"Witches!" hissed Augustus.

Dahlia shot him a glare. "Don't," she muttered under her breath.

Belinda held a feeble hand up. "I'm from a powerful

generation of witches too."

Angelica Lawson stepped forward. "I come from a family of shapeshifters."

The others turned to face her.

Angelica shrugged her narrow shoulders. "I can only change into a black cat."

Tamara looked more shocked than the others. "So how come we haven't seen you change?"

Angelica shrugged again. "I guess I'm just embarrassed that I don't know how to turn into anything more threatening…"

"Yet," finished Princess Xania. "You will learn to change into anything you want, and that includes your enemy." She motioned for Dahlia to continue.

"Okay, we need to rethink this whole situation. From tomorrow, we will work continuously on our new skills. This means eight or twelve hours a day, lessons need to be based solely on skills and learning more about yourselves."

Everyone groaned.

"What about Luna Green, you still haven't asked her what her abilities are," piped up Tamara. "I mean, we all know that she is a Celestian, but what exactly does a Celestian do?"

Luna bowed her head. She hated this kind of attention.

Xania laughed. "Child, where do I begin? What can Celestians not do?"

The princess looked up towards the dark sky. Thick black and grey clouds slowly sailed across the vast expanse, revealing, in that moment, the white glow of the moon. When the full moon emerged, its glow became brighter, almost blinding. Or was the light coming from another source?

The group turned their attention away from the sky, towards Luna Green.

Confused, Luna looked down at herself. Her entire body was glowing. She held a hand up before her face, studying it. A bright white glow emanated from her skin, making her feel like a human-shaped lightbulb.

She dropped her hand as her entire body vibrated. "What's happening to me?" she cried out, as her feet slowly departed from the ground.

Chapter 12

Luna's legs dangled in mid-air, her arms taking on a life of their own as they stretched up towards the sky. Her fear soon subsided as a rush of adrenaline came over her. She had never felt so alive.

All eyes were on her, but she wasn't interested in their mindless thoughts. Her power and strength were increasing by the second. With her feet still hovering above the ground, Luna lowered her arms to study her hands once again. A brilliant white light still emanated from them. She waved them around, giggling as the light shifted with her movements.

Dahlia made a move towards her, but Princess Xania grabbed hold of her arm.

"Don't touch her," she warned.

"What's happening to her?" asked Magnus.

Princess Xania smiled, her eyes fixed on the wonderful sight before her. "She is connecting with the moon."

"Should we let Agnes know?" asked Augustus. The

fairy nervously glanced up towards the window, but the headmistress was no longer there.

"We will. But for the moment, let us enjoy this wonderful and rare scene. It has been a very long time since I have witnessed the Celestian union."

"But what does it all mean?" asked Magnus. "Is she in any pain?"

Dahlia snorted. "Nah. Think of it more like plugging in one of your electric gadgets."

Magnus looked confused.

"Say you need to charge your phone, right?"

The boy nodded.

"You would plug it into a power source, wouldn't you? That's essentially what's going on with Luna right now. She is being charged by the moon."

The group fell silent and continued to watch as the light within Luna dimmed slightly. The heavy clouds had shifted once again, masking the moon's glow. Luna could feel herself lowering to the ground. When her feet touched the frozen grass, she felt an energy that she had never felt before.

"Wow, what just happened!" she cried out.

Augustus and Dahlia approached on either side of her.

"You're powered by the moon," explained Augustus.

He nodded to Dahlia, who placed a hand on Luna's shoulder. But as soon as she touched her, the fairy flew backwards, exactly as she had done when she had touched the Celestian crystal, all those months previously.

Luna rushed over to Dahlia, who now lay on her back. "Are you okay?"

Dahlia scrambled back to her feet before the girl could reach her. "Wow, that was amazing!" she exclaimed, dusting herself down.

Luna looked at the fairy, before studying her own hand. Her pale skin still had a glow to it. Turning slowly around to face the others, she witnessed the children take a step backwards.

"What does this all mean?" she asked aloud.

Dahlia appeared by her side. "It means your powers are even cooler than before!"

"My bodyguard is correct. Bringing you all out here tonight was important not only for your training but also because of the full moon. Luna, and the rest of you, needed to be made aware of what a Celestian is capable of," said Princess Xania.

"Yeah, and with our own personal human-sized torch, we'll have no trouble fighting the vetalas in the dark," sniggered Dahlia.

"Now Luna, let's show everyone what you can do," said the princess.

Dahlia and Augustus led Luna into the circle, after the petite fairy had extinguished the ring of fire around them. Luna noticed that whenever she got too close to Tamara, she backed away. Luna smirked to herself. She guessed she would not be getting anymore grief from that witch.

"Children, please stand behind Luna, or else you may end up losing a head or an arm," instructed the princess.

Without hesitation, the rest of the children quickly scurried behind Xania and as far away from Luna as they could.

Augustus and Dahlia both stayed on either side of her.

"Now, close your eyes and concentrate," said Augustus.

"On what?" asked Luna.

"What's in front of you."

Luna squinted her eyes to adjust to the darkness. She could just make out a small tree stump. "Okay, what now?" she asked.

"Focus your mind on that object and imagine it exploding." Dahlia lifted Luna's arm. "Use your hand to direct energy towards your goal."

Luna felt silly but thought it wise not to disagree. Fixing her gaze on the tree stump, she envisioned the shadow walkers that had attacked them last year. Holding her palm out towards the darkness before her, she imagined fire escaping from her fingertips, burning the monster alive. Scenes of her dad, Jack, fighting the shadow walkers flashed into her head, helping her to focus.

"You don't have to scrunch up your face," laughed

Dahlia.

Luna inhaled deeply, calming herself and focusing once more. She thought of Lazarus, the huge dragon she had met a few months back. She remembered how he had shot blasts of fire from between his razor-sharp teeth, burning down the trees in his path. The more she focused on the dragon, the more she was sure she could hear his voice inside her head, urging her to use her power. Luna felt her fingers tingle with heat, and she stared at her hands in amazement. Sparks of orange flickered from their tips. Her powers were working.

"This is it!" warned Dahlia. "Stand back!"

Luna's fingers flexed straight ahead; her aquamarine eyes focused on their target. Sparks of light flickered from her fingertips, but as quickly as they had appeared, they fizzled out.

Luna's heart sank.

"Don't give up, child." It was Augustus. "Failure is for the weak-hearted."

Luna sighed. How was that supposed to make her feel better? Taking a deep breath, she went through the motions again, focusing on the target. A tingling spread through the soles of her feet, right up towards her heart before travelling along her arms until it finally reached her hands.

A blaze of orange flames shot forth from Luna's delicate fingertips, bursting across the frozen grass, then BOOMF! The tree stump burst into a ball of flames.

"You did it!" cried Dahlia.

Loud cheering erupted from behind Luna as Princess Xania appeared by her side.

"Well done, Luna. You have taken the first step towards discovering your powers, though I'm afraid there is more for you to learn."

Luna frowned. "I can do more?"

The princess smiled. "Oh yes. Celestians are some of the most powerful beings known to exist within our realms, hence why the dark entities destroyed Celestia. Otherwise, the Celestians would have destroyed the dark realms before their inhabitants had time to threaten us here on Earth."

An anger Luna had never felt before suddenly coursed through her body. "They killed my family, and my people." Luna tightened her fists.

Dahlia stepped towards her and placed a hand on the girl's shoulder. "Save your anger. One day, you will need it."

Luna looked down at her fingers. She could still feel the heat radiating from them. Something else occurred to her and she turned to look at Dahlia.

"If I am such a powerful being, then why can't I stop the cursed blood of Amadan coursing through my veins?"

Dahlia let go of her shoulder and looked to Princess Xania for answers.

"Child, this I will never understand," said Xania

solemnly. "Although Celestians are indeed powerful beings, I'm afraid there may be some things even they cannot do. But do not lose hope. Perhaps you do have the power to solve your own predicament. After all, even us fae are constantly learning about the hidden talents of our ancestors."

"What about this missing grimoire?" asked Luna. "Could that cure me? I've heard many stories about its secrets, and the powerful spells hidden inside it."

Xania looked past Luna's shoulder towards the two young witches, Belinda and Tamara. The latter hung her head.

"I see," said Xania. It was clear that she was disappointed in Tamara and Belinda for speaking of the grimoire. "I cannot guarantee how many of the stories you have heard are true. But I can tell you that there is an ancient grimoire, and it is indeed missing, though it is yet to be established whether the grimoire belonged to an evil being, who then passed it on to a powerful witch—"

"It's true!"

The princess turned to Tamara. "That is a legend of your heritage, passed down generations of witches."

Tamara took a few steps towards them. "It belonged to the maker of evil, and he gave it to Elizabeth Drake."

"And it got stolen in the early 1900s by a traitor named Winnie!" yelled Belinda.

Luna shook her head in confusion. "Wait… hang

on… didn't we once have a school nurse named Winnie? I remember Bel… Miss Tilly telling me about her… she vanished without a trace, didn't she? It's not… it's not the same Winnie, is it?"

"I'm afraid so," said Augustus. "Winnie disappeared years ago, presumably with the grimoire."

"I'm confused, who is this evil being that keeps being mentioned?" asked Magnus.

"Satan," stated Augustus matter-of-factly.

"He's real? Satan? Seriously?" stammered Luna.

The three fairies nod their heads.

"Demons are as real as us," explained Xania. "They are the ones who control the darker realms. It was a young warlock named Bastian Hans who conjured up the beast, only to discover the hidden truths of other realms that co-exist inside our world."

"So how does Winnie fit into all of this?" asked Luna.

"She was working for Jonas Schmidt," spat Augustus.

"At least we think she was," added Dahlia.

"Was? You mean she's no longer alive?"

"Well, if she is alive, she would be well over one hundred years old by now, which seems very unlikely given her human status," scoffed Augustus.

Luna thought for a moment. "But what if this grimoire has a spell inside it that can make a person younger? Or make then live longer?"

The others pondered this for a moment.

"She has a point." Dahlia shrugged.

"And if there is such a spell, then what's not to say that there is one for curing deadly curses," added Luna.

"I like your way of thinking." Dahlia grinned. "I mean, the grimoire once belonged to Satan himself. There must be some powerful spells inside it…"

"Spells that could be used to close the portals to the darker realms," pondered Xania. "Or break them open."

The group all turned to each other.

"Perhaps we should rekindle our search?" offered Dahlia. "And while we're at it, prepare the new guardians to search for the whereabouts of the missing ruby."

"We spent many long years searching for the grimoire, what makes you think we will find it now?" asked Augustus.

"Dahlia's right," declared Princess Xania. "Evil is creeping into our realm again. We need to find the grimoire and the next missing crystal, before either falls into the wrong hands."

Chapter 13

The following morning, after breakfast, Agnes Guthrie instructed the children to meet in the library, instead of attending their first class with Hattie Bordeaux. As Luna and Lily made their way out of the dining room together, they caught sight of a flash of green, vanishing behind the doorway leading to the medical room.

"Was that Belinda?" asked Luna.

"I think so, but why would she be sneaking into the medical room?" replied Lily.

The two girls looked at each other.

"No… she wouldn't… would she?"

"Only one way to find out," replied Lily.

They waited until the foyer was clear of all the children before sliding up to the closed door of the medical room. Lily placed an ear against the wood.

"Can you hear anything?" whispered Luna.

Lily shook her head, and was about to drift through the doorway when the door slowly creaked open. A tuft of green hair poked through. Lily jumped back. Human habits were hard to break.

Belinda almost dropped what she was holding behind her back. "Poisoned rats! What are you two doing sneaking about?"

"I think we should be asking you that question," said Luna pointedly.

Belinda slid past them, gently closing the door behind her. "Not here. Let's just say I've borrowed one of Miss Tilly's special ingredients to use for our little plan."

"Well, if you don't want to get caught, I suggest you hide it before we go to the library," said Lily.

"The library? What about our history of voodoo and hexes class with Mrs Bordeaux?"

Luna shook her head. "Mrs Guthrie changed the timetable at the last minute. We have a meeting in the library tower instead."

Belinda shoved the glass vial inside the pocket of her black hooded top. "Right, let's do this!"

The three girls made their way through a door directly behind the right staircase, to reveal a hidden corridor. At the end of the corridor was a doorway, which opened to reveal a spiral staircase. Belinda, being the tallest of the three, had to duck her head as they passed through. Their feet echoed against the stone steps as they walked in circles inside the narrow tower, towards the sound of children chattering.

"Ugh, I hate it when we have to go to the library," huffed Belinda.

"Just think of the exercise," chuckled Lily, as she floated ahead.

"Hmph, easy for you to say, Casper," grumbled the goth.

The library was in the eastern tower, in a spacious circular room filled with books, the shelves stretching from wall to wall. In the centre of the room, the other nine children and all the teachers, including the Chavrons, sat in rows.

"Ah, so you have finally decided to join us," announced Agnes. "Take a seat, please."

Three chairs that had been stacked against the far wall suddenly lifted into the air, floating over the heads of the other children before landing at the very front row.

"Great," murmured Belinda. "No hiding in the back for us."

"That goes for you too, Lily," said Agnes, gesturing to the three empty chairs before her.

Lily snorted as she floated onto her chair. "Pointless," she muttered, as her bottom kept disappearing through its middle.

Once the three newcomers were all sitting sulking at the front, Agnes Guthrie began her speech.

"I am sure you must all be wondering why I have gathered you here this morning." Looking out across the room full of bleary-eyed teenagers, she smiled. "Given recent events, we have decided that you are all underprepared for what may lie ahead. As such, in addition to your usual lessons, the Chavrons and I will be teaching you the history of the vetalas, and how to fight them, so that you may understand the enemy we are facing."

Evan Corsan shot his hand into the air. Agnes nodded to him.

"Miss, is Monsieur Chavron going to be our new teacher?"

Agnes looked at the vampire. "I'm afraid Monsieur Chavron cannot dedicate himself to every lesson, for he has other commitments."

"Splendid," whispered Salvador to Augustus, who was sitting by his side.

The tall fairy nodded, a rare display of pleasure playing on his lips. Bell Tilly, who was seated on the other side of Augustus, tutted, and the fairy's smile quickly disappeared. Luna noticed this brief altercation. It was always such an oddity to see the fairy smile.

Frances Chavron quickly stood up. "But rest assured, I will be here often enough to help answer questions regarding our subject."

Augustus let out a low groan.

☾

Half an hour later, after giving the children a brief introduction to the history of vampires, Agnes snapped the textbook closed. "We will meet in the library every week. Sebastian will hand out textbooks to you as you leave. I expect you all to have familiarised yourselves with these before our next lesson."

Chairs scraped across the floor as the children began to make their way out of the library.

Agnes held a hand in the air. "Before you all go, I would like to congratulate Luna Green on her successful reunion with the lunar phase last night. We are all so proud of you."

Luna blushed. "Er, thank you, Miss, but it really wasn't anything."

Agnes Guthrie chuckled. "My dear, you really do not understand how strong your powers are. Augustus tells me you blasted a tree stump into oblivion like a fire-breathing dragon."

Luna shrugged. "I guess it was just beginner's luck."

Agnes smiled. "It is that kind of beginner's luck that we need on our side, especially if we are to face the highest degree of evil."

"What about Luna's dad, Jack? Can he not help?" piped up Tamara.

Agnes let out a long sigh. "Jack Green is insistent that he has no choice but to stay off the radar for now. He continues with his normal life, working for a wage so that, one day, he can build a better home for himself and Luna."

"But the world is in danger! He must help!" exclaimed Tamara.

Luna swivelled around in her chair to glare at the young witch.

"Jack is fully aware of the situation, and he will be here in a heartbeat should we need him. For the time being, we are only looking for answers," explained Agnes. "Which is why we are grateful we have his daughter."

The room fell silent.

"You may all leave."

The children made their way down the spiral staircase, carrying their new books on the history of vampires. Once everyone had made their way through the hidden doorway into the main hallway, teachers included, Belinda tugged at Luna, holding her back.

"Wait, we need to talk through the plan." Belinda pulled the glass vial she had stolen earlier from her pocket. "This is only one component of the potion, there are still things I need to get my hands on."

"What's inside?" asked Luna.

"Worm guts." Belinda swirled the vial, but the dark brown liquid didn't move.

"What?" gasped Luna. "No way in hell am I drinking that stuff!"

Belinda laughed. "Ironically, that's exactly where you'll be heading if I don't get this spell right." She lifted the vial to study its contents at eye level. "This isn't just any old worm's guts; they belong to a rare worm called *Mortelis vermis*. It feeds off one of the rare plants in Miss Tilly's greenhouse, at least, I think she has one in there… I still haven't found it yet."

"But if the worm feeds off that plant, surely there will be some of that plant in the worm's guts?" queried Lily.

"Yes, but I need fresh leaves from the plant. Partially digested leaves are no good. I need both the guts of *Mortelis vermis* and fresh leaves from its main food source to stop Luna's heart beating for a short while, and to help her journey into the spirit realm."

"Why can't I just go?" asked Lily. "I mean, hellooo, I'm already dead."

"We've already discussed this, Lily," sighed Luna. "You haven't been to the Ethers or the Rainbow Gate. If this is where your fate is to be decided, then I think it would be too risky for you to go."

"Yeah, you could end up in the fiery pits of Hell, toasting yer butt off for eternity," chortled Belinda.

Lily glared at the witch.

"Besides," continued Luna. "You decided your own fate by choosing to stay here after you died. The guardians of the Rainbow Gate might not let you back in."

Lily shrugged. "Suit yourself. I still think it's too risky. I mean, what if you never wake up?"

"I think I have more important things to worry

about." Luna glanced down at her ankle.

"If you two are just going to argue about this again, I'm leaving. I have an ancient spell to work out," Belinda said in a clipped tone, swiftly pushing against the hidden door and making her way along the corridor towards the main stairs.

Lily raised her eyebrows at Luna, but her friend simply shrugged, turning away and walking off in the opposite direction. Luna knew Lily was right, it was risky. But she wanted to speak to her mother. She didn't care what it cost.

☾

Agnes Guthrie was careful to ensure that no one was following her as she made her way to her office on the ground floor, constantly looking over her shoulder as she walked briskly along the dimly lit corridor. Satisfied that she was alone, she stopped in front of a painting. It was an oil painting, featuring the forest that surrounded the manor. She stared into it, studying the grooves where the paintbrush had left its indentations, somehow recreating the swift movement of trees in a motionless scene.

"Show yourself. I know you are there." She waited a few moments, staring at the trees. "I said show yourself!"

Barely visible, a small, shadowy figure emerged

from behind one of the trees.

Agnes leaned in closer, peering over her half-moon spectacles. "I demand to know who you are!"

At first, the figure seemed to move closer to the painting's edge, ready to reveal themselves. But as they drew nearer, a flash of light sprung from the painting, targeting Agnes in the chest. It left her stunned, causing her to stumble backwards into the wall.

"Agnes, are you all right?"

The sound of Agnes falling had alerted Bell Tilly that something was wrong, and she rushed to the older witch's side. Taking her arm, she guided the woman into her office, gently easing her into a chair.

Agnes, temporarily blinded by the bright light from the painting, slowly regained her sight.

"What happened?" asked Bell.

Agnes looked up at her. Bell noticed red veins throbbing across the whites of her eyes, contrasting starkly against the lilac of her irises.

"I'm afraid we are being watched… from inside the manor," said Agnes shakily.

"W-what do you mean?"

"For months I thought I kept seeing a figure, lurking behind the trees in the oil painting hanging in the hallway. I tried using a revealing spell, but it wouldn't work. I thought maybe I was just seeing things, but I could sense it every time I walked past. So, I thought I would challenge them to show themselves, but they momentarily blinded me."

Bell thought for a moment as she took in this information.

"Who do you think it could be? And how did they get into the painting?"

"I really don't know. The enchantments around the manor should stop anyone from coming inside… they should not even be able to use the painting as a portal to spy on us. Unless…"

"Unless?"

"Unless the painting was already here at the manor before we cast the enchantments."

Bell straightened. "You mean…"

The two women stared at each other.

"Jonas Schmidt…" Agnes whispered. "That would explain the mystery of his disappearance all those years ago. He's been hiding all this time… inside the painting."

Chapter 14

Luna struggled to get any sleep that night, and during the rare moments when she did, fanged creatures and shadow walkers assaulted her dreams. Belinda tossed and turned too, in the bed across from her. Her usual snoring was unusually quiet.

"Are you awake?"

Luna rolled over to face the other girl. "Yeah, I've been awake most of the night," she replied groggily.

Belinda moved onto her back to stare up at the ceiling. "Thought so. I couldn't sleep for you tossing and turning. I couldn't sleep after that night in the gardens either, when you tuned into the moon. You didn't stop glowing; it was like sharing a room with a giant, juiced-up nightlight."

"Sorry," mumbled Luna.

"Nah, you're alright. It's not your fault. Besides, I've had this death potion on my mind... I had a nightmare that it did actually kill you."

Luna snorted. "I'm more likely to be killed by the

rogue vetala."

"Same with us all. Not to mention the band of evil witches who are just waiting to kill me."

Luna sat up. Swinging her legs over the side of her bed, she looked towards the window. The sky was still dark. She checked her watch. 6.09 a.m. The sun wouldn't show at least for another hour.

A gurgling followed by a dull bang sounded. Luna froze, until she realised it was just the radiators coming to life.

"Is it still snowing?" Belinda asked.

"Nope."

Lily Jackson popped her head out from under Luna's bed, startling the two girls.

"Could you please stop doing that!" snapped Belinda. She threw her duvet off and sat up.

Lily giggled. "Sorry, I can't help myself."

"When did you get here?" asked Luna stifling a yawn.

Lily shrugged. "Just after midnight."

"You've been lurking around since midnight? You must have known we were both awake, why didn't you say anything?"

Lily shrugged again. "You weren't talking so I assumed you were trying to sleep; I didn't want to disturb you. Anyway, if you're done interrogating me, I have some new information, if you're interested." Lily sat, or pretended to sit, at the end of Luna's bed.

The other two girls looked at each other. "Go on."

"Okay. As you both know, I can't sleep because—"

"Ghosts can't sleep," chorused the girls.

Lily rolled her eyes. "At least I know both of you have been listening to me. Anyway, as I floated around the manor while you all slept, I heard voices coming from Mrs Guthrie's room. And it wasn't just her talking to herself. There was a man's voice."

"Ooh, Mrs Guthrie's a sly one, sneaking men into her room," snorted Belinda.

"I don't think that's what was going on. It was her office, not her bedroom. Anyway, I struggled to distinguish whose voice it was."

Luna thought about this for a moment. "Did he have an accent? Like Salvador or the Chavrons?"

Lily shook her head.

"Could it have been Archie Brutt?"

"Nope, I would recognise his dulcet tones anywhere. It's strange, I feel like I have heard his voice before, I just can't pinpoint who it belongs to…"

"Is that all you've got to tell us?"

Lily gave Belinda a look. "No, of course not. I overheard them talking. They were saying that they should go into the forests to look for this band of rogue witches."

Belinda perked up. "Really? So they think the witches are a more urgent threat than the vetala?"

Lily shrugged. "Seems so. It kind of makes sense

though I guess. There is only one vetala out there, compared to an entire coven of witches."

Belinda shuddered. "I knew I was right to be afraid when I sensed them the other day."

Luna pulled herself up. "I think we should speak to Mrs Guthrie. We need to tell her about your vision."

Belinda grimaced. "You think?"

Luna nodded. "The teachers have clearly been hiding something from us, and I reckon that means the situation is more serious than they are letting on. The more information they have, the better."

☾

After their lesson on botanical plants was over, Luna, Lily and Belinda waited for all the other children to leave the greenhouse, so they could speak to Bell Tilly on their own. Luna noticed Magnus hovering around too, and instantly felt guilty not asking him to stay. She nodded for him to join them, and was happy to see his face light up as he jogged over to be with them.

Luna went on to explain to Bell about Belinda's outburst a few days previously and insisted that they needed to speak to Mrs Guthrie about it, telling Bell that Belinda had been too scared to say anything until now.

Bell looked at the young witch sympathetically. "That must have been a terrible thing for you to have to deal with all by yourself. I'm glad your friends convinced you to come forward. Mrs Guthrie will be interested to hear what you have to say."

As Bell led them towards Mrs Guthrie's office, Luna could not help but notice that Bell appeared to suddenly distance herself from the wall. Looking across, Luna realised that Bell seemed to be avoiding an old oil painting, featuring the forest that surrounded the manor. Luna remembered the painting well. In fact, she had avoided looking at it since her first day at Blackhill Manor. The painting had disturbed her, the strange figure lurking behind the trees – that had appeared and disappeared as quickly as it had come – being enough to convince her to stay away.

Forcing herself to look at it now, she noticed, almost out the corner of her eye, that the same figure was back. Staring at the painting, she followed the figure as it flitted from tree to tree, drawing ever closer, only to vanish just before Luna could identify who the figure might be. Frustrated and unsettled, Luna followed the others into Agnes Guthrie's office. Bell's behaviour had convinced her; she was determined to finally ask Mrs Guthrie about the painting.

Agnes was surprised to see the four teenagers, but welcomed them into her office, exchanging a brief look with Bell. Immediately, Luna informed the headmistress about Belinda's vision, and a concerned Agnes gently coaxed the story out of the young witch, asking her what she had sensed and seen and how close she thought the witches might be. Satisfied that Belinda had told her everything she could remember, Agnes thanked them and ushered them off to their next lesson.

Following her friends to the door, Luna suddenly remembered about the painting. "You go. I just want to ask Mrs Guthrie something. I'll join you in a sec."

Belinda, Lily and Magnus gave Luna a confused look, but decided not to argue, and headed on to their next lesson, leaving Luna with Bell Tilly and Mrs Guthrie.

Agnes raised her eyebrows. "What did you want to ask me, Luna?"

Shyly, Luna explained her concerns about the painting, telling them that she had seen something, or someone, watching her from inside it, both when she had first arrived at the manor and just now.

When she had finished talking, Agnes let out a deep sigh.

"I was afraid that this might happen. You have always been so perceptive, Luna. I too have been seeing this shadowy figure for a while now. But despite using every enchantment I can think of, I cannot seem to reveal the identity of the figure. This person, whoever they are, is undeniably powerful; they must be incredibly experienced for them to have hidden for this long without us knowing who they are."

"Could it be one of the Pendle witches spying on us?" ventured Luna.

"I doubt it. Whoever this figure is they must have been spying on us since before the spells of protection were cast on the manor. I have my suspicions but…"

"What about Winnie?"

Agnes raised her eyebrows in surprise. "What makes you say that? Who told you about her?"

Bell's cheeks flushed slightly. "That would be me, I'm afraid. After Amadan attacked Luna, she kept asking why we did not have a nurse."

Agnes nodded, then turned back to Luna. "What makes you think the figure could be Winnie? None of us know why she disappeared."

"She stole the grimoire," said Luna.

Agnes frowned at Luna. "Where did you hear this?"

Bell sighed and looked apologetically at Agnes. "Salvador mentioned this to me yesterday; I should have said something to you sooner. Apparently, Augustus told him that Belinda and Tamara blurted it out during their training session in the gardens the other evening. According to them, the story of the missing grimoire was passed down to the young witches by their ancestors," explained Bell. "Naturally, Augustus and the other fairies elaborated on this story, insisting that Winnie was working for Jonas."

"Dahlia and the others thought that the grimoire could be the solution to stopping the vetala; they said that we had to find it, and so did Nana Violet. Do you think the grimoire could be the reason why the Pendle witches were in the forest? Are they still there now?" asked Luna.

Agnes stared at Luna in shock, overwhelmed by how much the girl seemed to know. She looked over at Bell. "It appears our secrecy has been in vain, Miss Tilly. The children seem to know more than we do about this situation." She sighed heavily. "I am surprised at Violet; I would not have thought she would be so loose-tongued regarding this matter. But it doesn't matter. You know now; we might as well be open with you about what is going on." Agnes fixed her gaze on Luna. "I have been trying to figure out the reasons for the Pendle witches' presence myself," she explained. "I have been in contact with a warlock in Australia, Benjamin Faulkner. He is an expert on the history of witchcraft and is currently researching the origins of the most powerful grimoire. He wants to write a book on it."

"Is that who you were speaking to last night?"

Agnes shot Luna a stern look.

Realising her error, Luna clasped a hand over her mouth. "Sorry… I couldn't sleep last night… I was walking about when I heard a man's voice coming from your office," she lied.

Agnes studied her for a moment, making Luna worry that she had been sussed out, though she knew she would lie again if it meant protecting Lily.

"Yes… I was speaking to Benjamin late last night." Agnes reached across her desk and lifted a purple satin cloth, to reveal a large crystal ball. "Please sit."

Luna and Bell sat down on the chairs opposite the desk.

Agnes lifted the crystal ball by its wooden stand, the legs of which were shaped like an eagle's claws. "I use this to communicate with other witches and warlocks across the world. Think of it as a mobile phone but without the costly bills."

Bell chortled at this.

Luna frowned. "There are others out there?"

The two witches nodded.

"How many? Why are they not here to help?"

"Warlocks and witches are very common, unlike Celestians." Agnes waved a hand across the air. "Same as vampires. But not all of them are powerful enough to help."

"Do they go to schools like Blackhill Manor as well?"

Agnes shook her head. "No, most of them attend Wiccan schools, where those with magickal heritage are taught alongside the 'norms'. Edward Blackhill built this school in order to train the best of the best, to protect our damaged portal. If we welcomed all the other witches and such, we would have a serious overpopulation problem."

"But I thought Mr Blackhill searched the world for new talent to bring back here," stated Luna.

"Yes, but you must remember, he only took children

who had been carefully chosen by their ancestors to be the new guardians. He was very selective in his choosing." Agnes studied Luna for a moment and smiled sympathetically. "I promise I will explain this in more detail to you and the other children when I get the chance."

Luna rubbed at her eyes. Her sleepless night was not helping. "Okay. So, how do you use the crystal ball?"

"I thought you would never ask!" Agnes placed both hands over the surface of the ball. Her lilac eyes gazed deep into its reflection.

Luna watched on in awe as Agnes Guthrie moved her hands back and forth, letting them hover above the glass surface. A mist seemed to fill the crystal ball, like a potion being brewed within a glass cauldron, and when the mist cleared, Luna heard a familiar ring tone.

"Hello my dear friend."

Luna leaned in closer, astonished to hear her nana's voice coming from the crystal sphere.

"Is everything okay over there at the manor?"

"Yes, I was just showing your granddaughter my old mobile phone."

Luna heard Nana Violet chuckle.

"Let me see her."

Agnes beckoned for Luna to come closer. Confused, Luna walked around to the other side of the desk, and was surprised to see her nana smiling up at her from inside the crystal ball.

"Wow! This is amazing," Luna exclaimed.

"More reliable than those modern techie things," laughed Bell.

"And with no costly bills," added Violet through the crystal ball.

"But aren't you speaking through your mobile phone, nana?" asked Luna. "I heard your ringtone…"

"Yes, but that's only because the magick has to connect to something. If I was sitting beside my crystal ball whenever Agnes called, it would come through on that," explained Violet. "But as I'm always out and about, it usually connects to my phone. How are y—"

A bleeping sound came from the ball, making the image of Violet fuzz out slightly.

"What's happening?" asked Luna.

"Nothing to worry about, just someone else on the line," said Agnes.

She quickly said her goodbyes to Violet as another face, this one unfamiliar to Luna, popped up on the crystal ball's surface.

"Agnes, thank goodness you're there."

"Benjamin, I was just talking about you," replied Agnes.

"Only good things I hope," said the man in a mild Australian accent.

"Any updates since I spoke to you last night?"

"Yes. After we spoke about the painting…" The man paused, his expression suddenly cautious. "Are we alone?"

"No, I have Bell Tilly and one of my students, Luna Green, here with me."

The man's eyes moved closer to the glass, the curvature of the crystal ball absurdly magnifying his face. Luna struggled not to laugh.

"Luna Green! Why it's such a pleasure to finally meet you."

"Er, you too, sir," she replied nervously. She felt a little silly talking to a crystal ball.

"I have informed Luna of the painting. In fact, she came to me to tell me that she too has been seeing a shadowy figure lurking inside it."

"I see. May I ask what your thoughts are on this, Luna?" asked Benjamin.

Listening to the warlock's accent, Luna understood why Lily had struggled to differentiate it from an English one, especially muffled behind a closed door. "I-I was thinking that the person in the painting might be the nurse who used to work here... Winnie," she replied nervously. She could see the man's forehead crinkle in response.

"Winnie?"

"I am sure I have told you about her before," prompted Agnes.

"Ah, of course, yes. Yes, I have been doing some research on her. Her sudden disappearance from Blackhill Manor certainly raised a few eyebrows.

Especially when Edward mentioned an incident with one of the staff."

"What incident?" asked Bell.

"It was actually with an imp. Worked in the kitchens as I recall…"

"Murdoch," whispered Luna, more to herself than to the rest of the room.

"You know him? I thought she had killed him," said Benjamin.

Luna's eyebrows shot up. "She tried to kill Murdoch?"

"Never mind that," said Agnes in a brusque tone. "What news do you have?"

Benjamin cleared his throat. "As you know, I am researching the whereabouts of the missing grimoire, and during my research, I came across an old piece of parchment containing some new and interesting leads."

"Where did you find this parchment?" asked Agnes.

Benjamin scratched his greying beard. "That is another mystery. I was leafing through yet another old textbook on the history of magick, and when I reached the chapter on the grimoire, there it was. The parchment insists that the paper used to create the grimoire was derived from ancient trees, of Celtic origin."

"How could that be? Surely the oldest grimoire would be made from parchment, derived from animal skin?" offered a confused Bell.

"One would assume so, but apparently not. If this

parchment speaks the truth, the grimoire must have been crafted from some of the oldest trees in your part of the world."

Luna suddenly remembered the story Belinda had told them a few days ago. "Didn't Elizabeth Drake witness a tall stranger pull the book out from an old oak tree?"

"The girl speaks sense," said Benjamin. "Satan himself approached Elizabeth; perhaps he conjured the book right before her eyes?"

"No, that is impossible," Agnes insisted. "The story of Elizabeth Drake harks back to the 1600s. Satan is from when time began. The grimoire is as old as the Earth. It was no doubt hidden in the tree."

The room fell silent for a few moments.

"Miss Tilly? Remember you once taught us - I think it was last summer, that plants can hear us, even retain information."

Bell nodded.

"Well, what if the trees in that same forest where Elizabeth Drake was given the grimoire could tell us their secrets?" suggested Luna.

Three sets of eyes, including Benjamin's from inside the crystal ball, looked straight at her.

"That's it!"

All eyes moved back to the image inside the crystal ball.

"Have you heard of the Tree Man?" asked Benjamin.

The two witches nodded. Luna shrugged.

"Assuming the ancients created the grimoire, the Tree Man is, well, the man to ask."

"Where does he live?" asked Bell.

Agnes rubbed her chin. "I'm sure the fae will know."

"I can head into Araig and ask?" offered Bell.

"Or we could just ask Augustus?" suggested Luna.

Bell and Agnes looked at one another, then shrugged in agreement.

After saying their farewells to Benjamin, the three of them left the office to go in search of Augustus. But as they reached the stairs, Luna found herself being accosted by a floating ghost and a green-haired goth.

"There you are!" They both stopped abruptly when they saw the teachers.

Agnes eyed the girls suspiciously. "Is class finished already?"

The two friends nodded.

"Very well. I will leave you three to catch up."

Belinda and Lily waited until the two teachers were out of sight before excitedly turning to Luna.

"What's all the excitement for?" asked Luna.

"We've got it!" squealed Lily.

"Keep it down," hissed Belinda.

"Would you two just get on with it?" snapped Luna.

Belinda produced a miniature jam jar full of leaves and a large glass vial from the front pocket of her hoodie. "I finally got all the ingredients."

Luna stared at the dark murky liquid inside the glass. "But how?"

"Let's just say that we didn't make it to our maths class today. Well, apart from Magnus, who insists that he actually enjoys listening to Mr Brutt droning on about squares and circles." Belinda rolled her eyes.

Luna looked at Lily who just shrugged in response.

"Anyhoo," Belinda continued. "Not only did I manage to slip into Bell Tilly's greenhouse again, I also managed to sneak into Salvador's office."

"Are you insane?" Luna exclaimed.

"Shh!" This time it was Lily. "I mean, surely you can tell she's insane just by looking at her?"

Belinda scowled at Lily, before giving Luna her attention again. "The *Mortelis vermis* worm, and it's host plant, which I have here, were only some of the necessary ingredients. I found the most important one amongst Salvador's collection of potion bottles. It contains tetrodotoxin from a pufferfish." After noting Luna's blank expression, she elaborated. "This stuff is deadly. Just one dose can kill thirty people."

Luna staggered backwards. "And you're going to make me drink it?"

Belinda shrugged. "You want to die right?"

"Err, yeah… but I also want to come back again."

Belinda rummaged inside her pocket again.

"Just as well we have this then." She produced another vial, this time containing an inky black flower.

Luna's eyes widened. "Is that what I think it is?"

"Yip. Rosa Diaboli. Otherwise known as the Devil's Rose. The same one that Elizabeth Drake was searching for over four hundred years ago."

Chapter 15

After Belinda's great reveal of all the deadly ingredients they had discovered, Luna suddenly lost her appetite. Deciding to skip lunch, she instead disappeared out of the arched front door. She needed some fresh air, even though the cold instantly bit at her face. Zipping her parka up to her chin, she walked around to the side of the manor, pausing when she reached the enchanted invisible wall.

Sighing, she placed her palms out before her until they came into contact with the solid invisible wall, willing it to vanish. The wall's magick vibrated through her flesh. She closed her eyes and imagined the invisible bricks crumbling away. Moments later, she reopened them, dismayed to feel the wall still intact. What was the point of being this powerful, magickal being when she couldn't even open a wall? Mrs Guthrie had said she would allow the children to know the magick words, but only when she felt she could trust them. Luna was deemed a celebrity in the magickal world, wasn't that enough to allow her access?

She dropped her hands and turned around. What was there here for a thirteen-year-old to do? Back in her hometown of East Kilbride, she had spent hours sitting in her secret place in the Calderglen woods, reading a good mystery novel. Yes, she could go to the tower library and read there, but that meant being cooped up inside. The books at the manor were interesting, but they were all so old or rare that the children were forbidden from taking them outside the manor.

"Psst."

Luna cocked her head to the side.

"Psst. Doon here."

Luna looked down to find someone tugging at the hem of her jacket. "Murdoch!"

The green-tinted imp looked up at her. "How come's yer oot ere? Ye'll freeze tae death!"

Luna was about to remark that it might be more humane than what Belinda had planned for her, but decided it was best to keep her mouth shut about their little plan for now.

"I needed the fresh air," she answered.

"Aye ye'll git that aw'right."

"If you're so worried, why are you out here in the cold with just a shirt and an apron on?"

Murdoch looked down at himself. "Cos that's wit a wear."

Luna shook her head and laughed. Crazy Scottish

imp, she thought. But then she remembered the crystal ball conversation earlier that morning in Mrs Guthrie's office.

"Murdoch, is it true Winnie almost murdered you?"

The imp stumbled backwards, but quickly righted himself, blaming the ice on the path. "Where'd ye hear that fr'm?"

She recalled the morning's conversation to him, missing out the parts about the grimoire, just in case Agnes wanted to keep their search for it a secret.

The imp scratched the tuft of white hair on top of his head. "Aye tha's right. She wis' one horrible witch."

"Do you remember what happened?"

"Aye, like it wis' yesterday."

"Do you want to talk about it?" asked Luna sympathetically, trying to hide her curiosity.

The imp shrugged his narrow shoulders. "A wouldnae mind but a'm not sure a'm allowed tae."

Luna looked all around them. No one else was about. "I won't tell," she said.

Murdoch scrutinised the young Celestian. "If yer sure, I'll tell ye. But a'think we should head indoors first. Ye'll die a frost bite before a can finish ma story."

Luna nodded and followed Murdoch back inside the manor. He motioned for her to come into the kitchens. Sensing her hesitation, he reassured her that no one would be in there, as Jeannie Gibbs, Aengus and Gobbins always had a nap before preparing dinner.

Satisfied that they were alone, Luna hopped up onto a high stool next to the island worktop in the centre of the room. The imp climbed onto another on the opposite side.

"Would ye like a hot drink?" he asked.

"I'm fine, don't trouble yourself," she answered.

"It's nae trouble at all. How's aboot a make ye a hot chocolate?"

Luna nodded her head eagerly and a smiling Murdoch pointed a long green finger towards the large fridge behind her. Luna could hear its door opening, and was about to turn around and look, when a carton of almond milk flew over her shoulder. Quickly, she ducked out of the way, watching with wide eyes as it landed on the worktop between them. Next, a small saucepan appeared over the imp's shoulder and landed on top of the gas hob. The milk carton levitated and tipped its contents into the saucepan, just as the gas came on of its own accord. Luna jolted, making her wobble unsteadily on the high stool, as the flames roared under the saucepan. Next, two mugs appeared between them.

"Is this how you cook all of our meals?" she asked. "By magick?"

Murdoch shook his head as he watched the milk simmering on the stove. Then, using his finger, he instructed the saucepan to soar through the air once more until it was levitating just above the two mugs.

Luna watched on as it poured hot milk into each one whilst a glass jar containing chocolate powder tipped its contents into each mug and a levitating spoon stirred the two ingredients together.

A steaming mug slid over towards Luna. "Thank you." She smiled, lifting the mug towards her lips, when suddenly, two large vegan marshmallows plopped into the frothy liquid.

"Sorry," apologised the imp. "But ye cannae have it withoot the finishing touches."

Luna nodded, taking a long sip of her drink; it was just cool enough for her to avoid burning her tongue. When she placed the mug down, she was left with a frothy, chocolatey moustache.

"Tae answer yer question, no. We don't use magick to cook all yer meals. That would be cheatin'. We'll only dae it if we're in a rush. Which we usually are." Murdoch tapped the side of his tiny button nose.

Luna chuckled. "Can you show me how to do it?"

"But ye already know how tae. It's all in here." Murdoch tapped the side of his head and wriggled his long fingers. Looking at Luna's confused expression, he added, "But aye, a'll help ye."

Luna smiled, taking another sip of her hot chocolate.

"So, tae answer yer first question, aboot Winnie tryin' tae kill me… it happened jist after the manor wis built."

Luna's eyebrows shot up. "Just how old are you?"

Murdoch snorted. "How old dae a look?"

"Eh, I'm not good at guessing ages."

Murdoch shrugged. "Tae be fair, a'm actually no sure. Ye lose count after a few centuries."

"Wow," exclaimed Luna. "I didn't know imps lived that long!"

"An how many imps have ye met, Miss Luna?"

Luna's face turned crimson.

"Exactly." stated Murdoch triumphantly. "All magickal creatures can live hundreds of years. A mean, look at Augustus. Even though he's a pompous git, he still looks like he's in his mid-twenties, when actually he's hitting treble figures."

Luna's eyes widened. "So how old was Winnie before she disappeared?"

"Don't ye mean, how old is she the noo?"

"You think she's still alive?"

"Aye! She has the missing grimoire. Them spells are the most powerful in the entire universe."

"How do you know? What makes you think she has it? And where did she find it?"

Murdoch shrugged. "Tales ave been circulating fer centuries… the grimoire is an evil text, Miss Green. It wis' created fae the very fire's o' Hell, and the man who confronted young Elizabeth Drake telt her as much. He made her an offer, in exchange fer being the most powerful witch in the world."

"I never heard the end of her story. Did she help the

village, and cure the little girl of the pox like she promised?" asked Luna.

Murdoch shook his head. "After that fateful meeting, she accepted the book an' headed back tae her village. But no before studying the grimoire. As legends go, she cursed the father o' the child, an' the rest of the villagers, wi' something far worse than the pox." Murdoch took a sip from his mug. "The villagers died a horrible death, a disease that spread from village tae village, eating every villager from the inside oot."

Luna scrunched her face up in confusion. "But why? I know the villagers had always been unkind to her, but from what I was told, she wanted to help the child, and she even made herbal cures for the villagers."

"Aye, but that grimoire changes people, Miss Green. It did the same tae Winnie. That was the reason she tried tae kill me. Back when she worked here, soon after Mr Blackhill had finished the manor, she came back one day fr'm the Dead Forest. She had it in her possession, the grimoire. She said the elm tree had spat it oot. Mr Blackhill got all excited; he reckoned it might have the answers tae close the portal fer good. But when he asked her for it, she turned nasty. Said 'they' gave it tae her. She would'nae listen tae reason. Mr Blackhill threw a disarming spell at her tae drop the book, but she screamed at him, and started tae cast a death spell. It was then that a' entered Mr Blackhill's office, and as she turned tae see who it wis', she cast the spell, aiming it at me. Thinking fast, a quickly jumped oot o' the way, and the spell crashed into the wall in his office, blasting a giant hole. Mr Blackhill quickly cast another hex at her, but she jist vanished."

"Vanished, how?"

"Poof, in tae thin air. Her and the grimoire."

"And to this day you have never seen her again?" asked Luna.

Murdoch shook his head. "Never bin seen again; nor has the grimoire."

Luna thought about this for a moment. "But if she still has the grimoire, why hasn't she used it to open more portals?"

The imp shrugged. "Dunno… maybe that's why the portal opened in the first place, or why it refuses tae close entirely?"

"None of this makes sense," Luna continued, ignoring Murdoch's suggestion. "Jonas Schmidt used a spell to open the Damnatorum portal, causing it to weaken and allowing the shadow walkers to come through. How can we be sure that his spell hasn't weakened the openings to the other connected dark portals, not just the Nocte Viventem? And surely such a powerful spell must have come from the grimoire, so where did he get it from?" Luna exhaled when she saw the imp staring blankly up at her.

"Finished?"

Luna blushed as she nodded.

"To answer everything you jist said: it's possible that the missing grimoire is'nae the source of these spells. Perhaps it dis'nae hold the key to closing the portals, but still holds other powerful incantations, maybe those that cause death or can bring people back from the dead?"

Luna instinctively glanced down at her blackening ankle. "Or perhaps a spell that can cure curses?"

"Aye, perhaps."

Chapter 16

Luna left Murdoch in the kitchens to prepare their dinner, passing Jeannie Gibbs on her way out. The hoglin had looked surprised to see her leaving the kitchens, but instead of stopping to engage in conversation, Luna swiftly disappeared down the dimly lit corridor. She thought of finding Lily, Belinda and Magnus, to tell them what she had just learnt. Instead, she turned and headed in the opposite direction, stopping when she reached the forest oil painting. She studied it for a few moments, concentrating on the row of trees at the front where she had previously witnessed the dark shadow. Nothing.

"Okay," she murmured to herself. Standing before the painting, she felt for the silver cord around her neck. Clasping both hands over her crystal, she closed her eyes and concentrated.

Her eyes darted about inside their sockets, the darkness behind her eyelids seeming to move like a black liquid. Finally, the darkness dissipated, and faint patches of colour seeped through. As Luna opened her eyes, familiar shapes and objects came into view. The forest lay spread out before her. Somehow, her idea had worked; she was inside the painting.

Luna carefully took a few tentative steps towards the trees. It was so surreal… everything was formed from brush strokes… it was like she was inside an animation of her own surroundings.

"Hello?"

Her voice echoed through the eerie stillness. She could hear nothing but her footsteps. There was no birdsong; no sound of the leaves and long grasses gently rustling in the breeze. Luna walked a few steps further, then stopped. The faint sound of feet, pounding against solid ground, resonated through the silence. Luna turned to look behind her, half expecting to see yet more forest, or even a blank canvas, but all she could see was the hallway opposite the painting. Turning back to face the forest, she was met with another sound.

"I'm not here to cause you any harm," she called out, as she moved closer to the trees.

Peering into the gloom, she could just make out an outline of a figure, running into the thickest part of the forest. Desperate not to lose them, Luna ran after them, keeping the figure in her sights, but just when she thought she was catching up, the mysterious person would appear further away again.

"Please stop!" she called after them. But it was no

use, they kept running further away.

Eventually, Luna stopped moving and leaned against a tree, her mind racing as she tried to figure out what her next move should be. A branch snapped above her head. Panicked, she glanced upwards, squinting into the murky canopy, until she spotted a shadowy figure lurking between two trees. The figure was obscured by the greenery, making it hard to tell if it was male or female.

"Hello?" she called out again.

This time, the figure didn't turn to run, instead moving closer towards her. She braced herself as the figure edged nearer, almost out of the shadows, as though they wanted to be seen.

"Luna, what are you doing?"

Luna's eyes snapped open. She found herself back in the hallway, in front of the painting.

Archie Brutt had grasped her arm and was shaking it gently. "What's going on? Are you okay?"

"I was, er…" Luna pulled away from the teacher, fixing her eyes back on the painting. She peered closer into it, but there was nothing there.

"Is everything all right out here?" Agnes Guthrie asked, emerging from her office.

"I was just coming to see you Mrs Guthrie when I found Luna Green standing here. She seemed to be in some sort of trance," explained Archie.

Agnes looked at the teacher, then at Luna.

"Come in, both of you," she demanded.

Luna sheepishly followed the headmistress into her office. Archie Brutt walked behind, closing the door after him.

"What's going on, Luna? Did you have another vision?" asked Agnes as she gestured for them to have a seat.

Luna slowly shook her head as she settled into a chair.

"She was holding onto her crystal," said Archie.

"I thought I could use my powers to try and enter the painting. I wanted to see who was inside," explained Luna.

Agnes studied her for a moment. "Did it work?"

Luna slowly nodded her head, her eyes cast down to the floor.

"Remarkable," whispered Agnes.

Luna's eyes shot up. She had not been expecting that kind of reaction from the head.

"I had never thought of that. I had considered using a spell to get inside the painting, but using your crystal to teleport inside is just outstanding." Agnes thought for a moment before adding, "But it was also a very dangerous and foolish thing to do on your own."

Luna hung her head.

"Did you see who it was?"

Luna shook her head. "I was chasing after them for a while, but just as they were about to show themselves,

Mr Brutt broke my concentration."

Agnes looked at the teacher, then back at Luna. "We are dealing with someone who doesn't want to be found. Whoever it was you saw, they were no doubt ready to attack you. It sounds like Mr Brutt just saved your life."

Luna shuddered.

"From now on, you mustn't undertake anything like this again, is that clear?"

Luna nodded.

"Good. You may go back to your room before dinner."

Luna hurried out of the office and past the painting. She had no urge to look at it. Not after this experience. Agnes was right, it had been a terribly dangerous thing to do. What had she been thinking?

"Hey, I've been looking everywhere for you."

Luna looked up. It was Magnus.

Seeing her distressed expression, Magnus gently pulled her to the side. "Are you okay?"

Luna shrugged. "I have a lot to tell you. Meet me outside my room in ten minutes; I'll tell you everything."

Magnus nodded.

Luna hurried up the stairs and didn't stop until she reached her bedroom.

"Luna, there you are." Belinda jumped up from her bed, causing Poe to squawk in fright.

Luna sighed as she flung herself down on top of her

bed. She wished everyone would leave her alone for five minutes. She needed to think.

Belinda tilted her head quizzically. "Okay, I can tell something's up. But before you get into that, I just want you to know that I've finished preparing your potion."

Luna stared at her. Really? This wasn't the time for her to be breaking more rules. "How do you know it works?" she asked nervously.

Belinda shrugged. "Dunno. That's just a risk we have to take."

Luna thought for a moment. "Couldn't I just use my crystal?"

Belinda shook her mane of green hair. "I don't think so. I'm not familiar with that method anyway."

There was a light knock at the door and Belinda quickly hid the glass vial under her duvet cover.

"Come in."

Magnus peeked his head around the gap and the girls sighed with relief, motioning for him to come inside. Magnus entered cautiously, not overly pleased to see Belinda's raven perched on the headboard of the young witch's bed. The two of them stared each other down for a moment, as Magnus made his way towards Luna's bed. Satisfied that the boy was not about to disturb his peace, Poe closed his eyes and nestled his head into his feathers. Magnus sighed with relief, and promptly made himself comfortable at the end of Luna's bed.

Once he was settled, Luna told her friends the entire

story, from her magickal hot chocolate with the imp to her entering the painting. When she had finished talking, the other two looked at one another.

"Wow, you did all that using only your crystal… you're sure you didn't mutter some spell under your breath or something?" asked Magnus.

Luna nodded.

"Maybe you *could* use the crystal to travel into the Ethers," pondered Belinda, completely in awe of Luna's abilities.

"I don't know… I'm not sure I can go that far. I mean, I need to go into a coma to enter the Ethers and I'm not sure I can teleport without being conscious," explained Luna.

Magnus shook his head. "This is too risky. Mrs Guthrie has already warned you once. What if we can't revive you, Luna? What if you die?"

The two girls looked at one another.

Just then, Lily burst into the room. "I have an update," she gasped. "After dinner, a few of the teachers are heading into the forest to look for the band of black witches." She looked at each of them.

The three friends shrugged.

"Don't you see? This is the perfect opportunity for us to do the necromancy spell."

Luna got up from the bed. "I don't know. I'm already in a lot of trouble."

"But I thought this was what you wanted? To find

your mum and ask about Jonas Schmidt."

"I think he's in hiding, just like Winnie," said Luna. She told Lily what she had just told the other two.

"Wow, so there really is someone lurking in that painting. But… if you don't visit the Ethers, we will never be able to find out whether Jonas and Winnie are still lurking around on Earth. I've tried to ask around, but no one will tell me anything. You're a Celestian. They might actually give you the answers we need," said Lily.

"She's right," added Magnus. "I don't want you to die, even for a second, but at least if you find your mum then maybe she can answer some of our questions."

Belinda pulled the vial from under her duvet. "Are you ready to risk it?"

Looking at the desperate eyes of her friends, Luna steadied herself, then nodded. They needed her. Everyone did. She couldn't give up now.

Chapter 17

Black clouds swirled overhead, bunching together like an angry army of starlings, swarming towards the waning crescent moon to engulf the only light that dared to shine on this darkest of nights.

Magnus waited by the tall window in the upstairs hallway. His head peeked out from just above the window's ledge. His eyes scanned the dark gardens below for any movement. He could just make out the treeline beyond the manor's invisible barrier, the trees swaying in a silent dance, until the forest was completely obscured by the darkness as the clouds finally enveloped the lunar light.

As the darkness swam before his eyes, he noticed a stream of bobbing lights floating together in a single row, making their way towards the forest.

Along the hallway, in the girls' bedroom, Luna stared at the murky dark green liquid for what seemed the hundredth time that night. She tore her eyes away to glance at the small alarm clock, the one she relied on to get both her and Belinda up in the mornings. It flashed 11.51 p.m.

"Nine minutes until midnight," said Belinda, following her gaze.

"How long now do you think?" murmured Luna, her growing anxiety making her feel sick.

Suddenly, the door to their room burst open, and a red-faced Magnus stood in front of them.

"They're gone!"

"At last!" Lily exclaimed.

Luna held the round vial before her eyes. "What did you say was in this again?"

Belinda opened her mouth to list off the ingredients just as Luna held up her hand.

"Forget it, I don't want to know."

Magnus closed the door behind him and made himself comfortable at the end of Belinda's bed. He felt a pair of beady eyes watching him and turned, his gaze eventually meeting that of Poe the raven.

"Does Poe have to be here?" Magnus nervously looked away as the raven continued to stare him out.

Belinda made a snorting sound. "Yes. He's my familiar."

"Animal guide," Magnus corrected her.

"You may call them animal guides, but us witches have a more personal bond with ours. He's my familiar, end of."

Magnus held both hands up. "Okay, no need to bite my head off." He nervously glanced back at Poe, who to his horror was now sitting on the bed right next to him.

"Bloody hell!" He scrambled to the other end of the bed, trying to get as far away from the raven as possible.

The others burst out laughing.

"Yeah, all right, laugh at me why don't you. Have you seen the beak on that thing?"

Belinda looked furious. "How dare you! He's not a thing—"

"Cut it out you two, this is not the time," Lily reprimanded them.

Magnus and Belinda pulled a face at each other, before begrudgingly turning their attention to the task at hand. The three watched in silence as Luna continued to study the vial.

"Hate to say it, Luna, but we don't have all night," said Belinda. "I mean, we don't know how long the teachers are going to be away for."

Luna glowered over at her. "I thought you said it would seem like I'm only away for minutes?"

Belinda shrugged. "To us, maybe. To you, it might feel you're away a while longer."

"Do I need to drink all of it?" Luna lifted the vial closer to her face, sniffing at its contents. Her face contorted as the acrid smell of sour milk hit her nostrils.

"I added some mint leaves to help with the taste,"

offered Belinda.

Luna shot her a look. "Cheers. I really think the two mint leaves are going to do a great job at quelling the awful taste of worm guts."

Muffled laughter erupted from the end of Belinda's bed, and the three girls instantly turned to look at Magnus.

"Sorry, I just remembered that Luna's vegan. And now she has to drink worm guts."

"Thanks for reminding me, yet again. Believe me, there is no way I would be doing this if I had another choice."

"Hey, I haven't mentioned it before."

"Well the other two have!"

Lily and Belinda shifted uncomfortably.

Luna sighed, lifting the vial to her mouth. "Anyway, let's do this. And remember, if I don't make it back…" Luna paused. "Well, you'll think of something."

Magnus, Lily and Belinda looked at one another in panic, but as they drew their attention back to Luna, she was already swigging back the vial's contents. When it was empty, Luna instantly choked, both hands clutching at her throat. Her face turned increasingly red with each second. Lily reached for her, but Belinda batted her ghostly hands away.

"This is meant to happen."

Luna stared frantically at the three of them. Her aquamarine eyes glistened red, bulging out as she continued to grasp at her throat. Luna had assumed she would throw up when the thick liquid touched the back of her throat, but instead, she had felt her muscles tighten. Almost instantly, she had found herself struggling to breathe, and as she grappled at her throat, spots of red clouded her vision. She could just make out her three friends on the other side of the room, watching on helplessly as she struggled to breathe. But thankfully, it all ended as quickly as it had started, and she soon felt the last breath of air leave her lungs.

A sensation of lightness overcame her then, and she felt herself falling into a void of darkness. Was this how it felt when you died? Had her mother experienced nothingness too? Luna tried to shut these thoughts out, allowing the darkness to swallow her as she continued to fall.

Chapter 18

When she opened her eyes, Luna was surprised to see that she was no longer surrounded by darkness. Instead, a barren landscape stood before her. Red hues filled the space where the sky should be, and a haze of vapour rose from the endless dunes of black sand.

Looking down, Luna discovered that she was sitting on the ground. She ran her fingers through the sand, allowing the grains to fall through her fingers. It felt real. She pushed herself up and walked in circles. There were no landmarks in sight. She appeared to be in the middle of a desert. Every direction had the same outlook. No buildings or trees stuck out from the barren landscape. Luna shook her head. Was she really in the Ethers? Or has she accidentally died and gone straight to Hell?

Panic boiled inside her belly as dark thoughts of being stuck here for an eternity blurred her vision.

"Can I help you?"

Luna turned rapidly, causing her injured ankle to twist awkwardly. She fell to her knees as pain spiked through it. Terrified, she watched as an enormous hand came into view, its thick sausage-like fingers, outstretched towards her. Luna slowly looked up to find the hand's occupant, but almost lost her balance when she took in the tall figure looming above her.

"I don't bite," boomed a man's voice.

Cautiously, she accepted the beefy hand and allowed the stranger to pull her back up onto her feet. Fresh pain bolted through her ankle, but this time, she wasn't aware of it as much. She was too focused on the newcomer's strange appearance.

Standing at least eight feet tall, the man grinned toothlessly down at her. But it was his eyes that made Luna suck in a deep breath. There were three of them blinking down at her. Each dark green iris was missing a pupil, and looked more like a cabochon than a human iris. They would not have looked out of place hanging around someone's neck on a delicate gold chain.

"Are you a cyclops?" Luna asked.

The giant man laughed. "No, but you're almost right. I'm a tricyclops."

Luna squinted up at him. "What's the difference?"

The creature scratched at his wiry black beard. "Well, most cyclops only have one eye in the centre of their forehead. As you can see, I have a few more than that."

Luna looked puzzled. "But your eyes aren't like normal eyes. How can you see out of them?"

The tricyclops let out an enormous belly laugh. "I found you, didn't I? My eyes may look strange to you, but they work just as well as yours. I'm what they call a seer." He leant down, so that he was facing her. "And I know I'm right in saying that you don't belong here."

"I'm not sure where here is though," answered Luna sheepishly.

"Don't worry, you're not in Hell, well, not yet." The giant let out another boom of laughter.

"So, am I in the Ethers?"

The tricyclops stopped laughing and took a step backwards. "Yes... but you shouldn't be. Nor do you have time to waste talking to a tricyclops."

Luna nodded her head solemnly. "I used a potion to induce me into a death-like coma, so I could visit here to find my mother."

The creature's large forehead wrinkled, and all three eyes squinted down at her.

"That was very careless of you, but also very brave. May I ask who your mother is?"

"Jocelyn Green." Luna felt herself slowly relaxing in the tricyclops' company.

The creature scratched at his beard again as he stared into the distance. "I can't say the name is familiar, but I am sure there are others who know of her. Come, I will show you where to go."

Luna began to follow the tricylops when he suddenly turned to face her.

"Oh, I almost forgot." He held out his large beefy hand one more time. "The name is Forcas."

"Luna Green."

☾

They must have walked for at least three miles through the desert, and still the landscape had not changed. Luna felt her breathing becoming ragged as she struggled to keep up with the tricyclops' enormous gait.

"Where is this place, Forcas? Where are we right now?"

Forcas stopped in his tracks. "We are exactly where you don't want to end up after you die. Believe me, I hope for your mother's sake that she isn't here."

"Are we somewhere worse than Hell?"

Forcas made a clicking sound. "Nowhere is worse than Hell." He began walking again. "This place is neither Heaven nor Hell. More like a place between. But sometimes souls get lost here, and cannot find their way to the Rainbow Gate, thus trapping them in an endless desert of loneliness."

"Where are we going now then? Are you taking me to the Rainbow Gate? I've heard that's where I need to go." Luna felt a shift in the tricyclops' demeanour. Maybe he was trapped here against his will, she thought.

"I can show you how to get to the Rainbow Gate, but I'm afraid I cannot go with you," he told her.

Luna looked up at him, and he turned towards her, surprising her by answering her thoughts.

"I can leave here if I wish to do so, but I choose to remain, so that I can guide the lost towards their chosen path. Your fate, Luna Green, has yet to be decided. The Ethers may be your fate, or it may not, but a decision has yet to be made. Once you reach the Rainbow Gate, it is up to the guides who guard it as to where your final destination will be."

"How did you know I was here? I mean, if souls get trapped all the time, then why did you appear when I needed you?"

"I told you, I am a seer. Gifted with the foresight of things yet to come. Your energy is much stronger than that of any soul I have sensed since entering this damned place. Unfortunately, I do not always find the souls who are lost here, until it is too late. By then, they have already vanished into this vast nothingness." Forcas fixed his strange eyes on Luna, staring through her. "But you already know what foresight is. You have powerful abilities, my Celestian friend. But a word of warning. This is no place for a rare and sought-after being. Danger lies everywhere, especially in this place."

Luna shuddered. She was about to ask him what dangers he was talking about when suddenly the ground beneath them shook violently.

"What the—"

"Stand back, child!" Forcas flung out one of his enormous arms, pulling Luna back just as a train thundered past them.

The sound of brakes screeching sliced through the dusty air, followed by a vast puff of white steam as the train came to a sudden halt before them. Luna shielded her eyes from the sand that had been whipped up into a miniature sandstorm beneath the train's wheels.

After a moment, she dropped her arm, marvelling at the magnificent sight before her. An old-fashioned steam train sat on top of the sand; Luna could see no railway tracks, and wondered how the train could have possibly travelled through the endless desert. But somehow, it had, and now it was here in front of them, as though waiting for a new passenger.

"Climb on, Luna," Forcas told her. "This will take you to the Rainbow Gate."

"Will you come with me?" she pleaded. In the short time she had known him, she had grown fond of the gentle, three-eyed giant.

"I'm so sorry, but this is the furthest I can travel."

A door swung open before them, and Forcas gently nudged Luna towards it.

"It's okay, child."

Luna hesitated at first, but quickly realised that there was no point turning back now. She had come this far. She might as well keep going. And she knew she could trust Forcas, even though they had only just met. Stepping through the open door, she turned to bid farewell to the tricyclops, but the door slammed shut with a loud clap. Staring through the glass, she could only watch as Forcas became nothing more than a tiny dark spot on the red dusty horizon.

Chapter 19

The train instantaneously sped up, and Luna almost fell over, quickly grabbing onto the nearest pole to stop herself from falling flat on her face. It felt reminiscent to travelling through the fae tunnels, except the feeling of movement was very much noticeable this time, whereas in the fae tunnels it felt as though you were standing still while the world moved around you.

Luna carefully made her way over to one of the seats. The interior of the train looked not unlike the train that ran from East Kilbride to Glasgow, which she had used multiple times before. Except that train did not run on steam, nor did it glide along invisible railway tracks.

She took in the rows of empty seats, until she came across the back of a head, belonging to someone who was sitting at the very end of the carriage. Luna began to make her way down the aisle, grabbing onto the back of the seats to help with her balance. But when she got closer to the person, she hesitated. What if they were not as friendly as Forcas?

Squinting her eyes, Luna tried to identify whether the head belonged to a human or something else. The head featured a mass of matted, grey hair, obscuring any other features that might have helped her. Plucking up her courage, Luna continued along the aisle towards them.

"H-hello?"

The head remained completely still, not even twitching.

"Umm, would you be so kind as to tell me when to get off? I'm trying to get to the Rainbow Gate?"

The head remained still. Luna edged closer until she was almost facing the mystery someone. Suddenly, the head turned, and both the owner of the head and Luna screamed at the same time.

"Ya scared the bejeezus out of me, child!"

Luna was instantly relieved to hear a female voice.

The strange woman plucked earbuds out from both of her ears and turned to examine the culprit who had almost given her a heart attack. She chuckled. No such thing was possible in the Ethers. They were both already dead.

Luna gasped as she took in the woman's appearance; her sharp features were reminiscent of a wicked witch from the fairy tales she had been told as a child. Her long hooked nose almost touched her upturned chin and her eyes were like small black beads, rattling around beneath a narrow crinkly forehead. Her grey, frizzy, matted hair finished the look of a madwoman. All she was missing was a greenish tint to her skin and a broomstick.

"Can I help you?" she asked in a crackly voice.

"Er, yes. I was wondering when to get off?"

The old woman's eyes narrowed at her. "There is only one stop, and that is the Rainbow Gate."

"Ah, so there won't be any stops in between?"

The old woman clucked her tongue. "Of course not! This isn't just any old train you know."

Luna's cheeks reddened. "I-I guess not."

"Now sit yerself down child and take in the view."

Taken aback by the woman's sharpness, Luna took a seat in the row directly across from her, sneakily glancing over at the woman now and again. The woman was wearing blue jeans, a pale blue chunky knit jumper and battered white trainers. In her lap, she held a large tan handbag. Just a normal person after all.

Sensing her stares, the woman turned sharply.

"Do you even belong here?"

"Er, what do you mean?"

"Well, if you'd just popped yer clogs then you would have met the reaper, who'd have told ye about the train and where it goes."

"I er, I didn't meet any reaper," stammered Luna.

"Hmm, then something's not right."

The woman turned away to look out of her side window. Luna followed her gaze, taking in the view beyond the dark windows. It was just like being on an actual train, with the scenery zooming past. She turned her head to the right to look out of her own window.

"Oh!" Luna clasped a hand over her mouth, shocked at what she saw. Instead of black sandy desert, waves of foamy sea water splashed against the glass. The train was travelling over a stormy ocean, the waves seeming to almost submerge the train as they crashed against the doors and windows.

"Yeah, I'm pretty shocked myself," piped up the woman. "It's not something you expect to see when you're travelling by rail… even on a train like this one."

"What happened to you?" asked Luna, her curiosity overcoming her fear of the woman's temper.

The old woman turned back to face her. "I died, obviously." She said this matter-of-factly, like it was an everyday normal occurrence. Narrowing her eyes at Luna, she said, "But I sense that you are not entirely there yet."

"I… um…" Luna was about to explain when the woman continued to talk over her.

"It won't be long until I meet my maker. I should have known that old hag Mildred had poisoned my tea! If there's an ounce of justice left in this world, it will be her who goes to the fire pits, not me!" She pointed a long spindly finger down towards the floor. "I can't wait until she pops her clogs. You mark my words, I'll make sure she goes down for what she did to me." Her expression turned solemn. "Though I guess that's not my decision. If I'm allowed upstairs, I will travel back for a nightly visit, just to scorn her. But…" She shuddered. "If they decide I have to stay here in the Ethers, well, then I'm well and truly f—"

The train came to a sudden halt, its brakes screeching as Luna was sent hurtling towards the seat in front of her. The old woman got to her feet. Tucking her large bag under her arm, she made her way towards the exit. When she reached the doors, she turned back to Luna.

"Dear, I think you need to prepare yourself to meet your maker." The doors swung open and the woman promptly disappeared through them.

Luna struggled to get back to her feet after the bumpy ride. She quickly glanced out of the window, surprised and relieved to see that they were no longer on the ocean. Instead, crystal blue skies winked back at her, decorated with the most beautiful vibrant greens, reds, purples and pinks dazzling all around.

"Wow, this must be Heaven."

"Er, fraid not, miss."

Luna looked down to where the voice was coming from, almost losing her balance when she discovered a pig with two heads standing on its haunches, staring back up at her.

"I'm your conductor for today. Sorry I didn't have time to greet you on my rounds, but you were the last pickup."

Luna wasn't sure how to reply. The pig wore a blue uniform, complete with shirt and tie. Across his chest hung a ticket machine, and as he turned aside for a moment to check on the other leaving passengers, she clocked two small pink wings poking through the back of his blazer. Luna bit into her bottom lip to stop the giggles that threatened to surface.

"Ticket please." The strange creature held out a trotter.

"Er, sorry, I didn't know I needed to buy one," stammered Luna.

The two heads cocked to the side, and two sets of beady eyes stared up at her. "When you met the reaper, did you not buy one then?"

Luna stared down at the creature. "No, I never met him."

The pig scratched each head, slightly knocking off his two peaked hats. "Hmm, that doesn't sound good. Not good at all."

"Where do people get money from anyway, if they are already dead?" asked Luna.

The pig snorted. "You ask too many questions." Turning around, it pointed a trotter. "If you make your way over to that queue, you will find out where to go."

Luna didn't know which head to look at; both seemed to talk at the same time, and their snouts made a snorting sound each time the pig finished a sentence.

"Are you listening?"

"Er, yes, sorry. Which queue?"

The winged creature pointed a chubby hoof over his left shoulder. Luna looked over the pig's two heads and sighed when she spotted the mile-long queue.

"I have little time. Is there any way I can make it to the front?"

"Sorry, princess, but none of us have very much time, else we wouldn't have ended up here. You'll have to wait like everyone else."

"Right, sorry." Luna was about to leave when she thought of something. "Is it alright if I ask you a few questions?"

The creature looked at his left wrist, and Luna was surprised to see a modern digital watch.

"Not possible, I'm afraid. I need to get back onto the spirit train to collect more souls."

"It will only take a few seconds of your time."

The pig looked at his watch again, then sighed out a loud snort. "Fine, what is it then? Are you scared that you'll be dropped down to the fiery pits of the red man himself, or are you worried you're not pure enough for the big guy up there?"

Luna stared at him as he pointed his hooves up and down, and a saying flashed through her brain: 'As Above, So Below'. For a moment, she lost herself in her thoughts, contemplating the statue of a deity Belinda had near her altar. It was named Baphomet, and its meaning felt quite poignant in this moment. Good or evil? A tapping sound dragged her back to the present, and she looked down to see the impatient train conductor drumming his hoof against the ground.

"Er… neither, actually. I was wondering whether you get to know the spirits who come here? Do you remember any of their names?"

The creature turned both heads back in the direction of the queue. "Does that answer your question? Hundreds, if not thousands, pass through here on a daily basis. How could I possibly get to know any of them?"

"I don't know… perhaps some of them have stopped and talked with you before? Like we are now?"

Both the creature's faces were becoming pinker with every second. Luna thought it best to push on.

"Have you ever met Jocelyn Green?"

The creature's heads stretched out on either side to turn and look at one another. Then, for the first time, only one of them spoke.

"Can't say I've ever heard that name before."

The other head did not look so convinced, but it eventually nodded in agreement with its twin.

"Sorry we can't help. Maybe someone can at the Rainbow Gate."

Luna mumbled a brief thank you and made her way over to the mile-long queue. Something in the train conductor's demeanour had changed, and just as Forcas had pointed out, Luna was all too familiar with foresight. Right about now, that foresight was telling her that the pig creature had been hiding something from her.

Magnus paced up and down between the beds, stopping now and then to glance down at Luna's crumpled body on top of her bed. Her face was peaceful, like she was sleeping, but her usual glow was rapidly diminishing before their eyes. He was sure she was turning an unhealthy shade of blue.

"How long now?" he asked, for what must have been the tenth time since Luna had collapsed.

Belinda checked her watch. "She's only been under for half a minute. Relax, she still has plenty of time before we need to bring her back."

"How will we know when she has found some answers?" Lily asked nervously.

"We won't. All we can do is give her as much time as possible," said Belinda.

"What if we can't bring her back?" whispered Magnus.

Belinda and Lily caught each other's gaze, and Magnus knew the answer was not what he wanted to hear.

Chapter 20

It felt like a scorching summer's day, except this wasn't your usual earthly heatwave. Luna wiped her brow, amazed to feel no perspiration on the back of her hand, as she carried on walking towards the lengthy queue of what appeared to be silhouettes of 'normal' people.

But as she reached the end of the queue, it shocked her to see that it ran for miles and miles. The front was nowhere to be seen. Scanning the crowd, she recognised the grey frizzy hair of the woman from the spirit train, and decided to approach her, but was quickly bombarded with moans of complaints about skipping the queue from the people behind.

Mumbling an apology, Luna insisted that she wasn't trying to skip the queue but was instead trying to say hello to an old friend. Grumbling, the others in the queue begrudgingly allowed her to approach the old lady, who was still wearing her ear buds.

The woman jumped when Luna tapped her on the

shoulder. "Bejeezus child! If I wasn't already dead, you would have been the death of me!" She plucked her earbuds out and waited for Luna to explain herself.

"I'm sorry, er…" she paused when she realised she had not properly introduced herself to the woman earlier.

"Madge," the woman answered.

"Madge. I'm Luna Green."

Luna heard sharp intakes of breaths coming from the people behind and in front of them, and Madge's demeanour took a dramatic turn, her mouth dropping open. Confused, Luna looked around, taking in the other 'normal' looking people and their same expressions of shock.

"Have you heard of me?" Luna finally asked.

Madge looked down. "Yes, I have."

"And me," said the man behind.

This started a chain of 'and me too' responses which chorused down the line.

Luna turned her attention back to Madge. "What do you know about me?"

Madge shrugged. "You are famous in these parts, or maybe infamous is a more appropriate term."

"But why?" asked Luna.

Madge looked her up and down, her gaze settling upon her hair. "It's obvious isn't it? You are the last Celestian alive. Or at least, you were."

"I guess that makes sense. Do you know my mother

as well then? Jocelyn Green?"

Madge looked at the people behind Luna, as though seeking confirmation. She fixed her black eyes on Luna's once more. "I have heard of her, yes. She is your mother. An important part of your heritage."

Luna felt she was finally getting somewhere. "Have you heard anyone saying that they have seen her here?"

Madge looked past Luna's head again, but before Luna could say anything, the older woman replied.

"No. As far as I know, she is not here."

Relief flooded through Luna. The last thing she wanted was for her mum to be stuck in a place like this, with nowhere to go.

"That's good to know." Luna paused. It was harder to gauge what the response would be to this next question. "I was also wondering whether you have heard of Jonas Schmidt?"

If the woman wasn't already dead, Luna would have been convinced that she was witnessing this woman's death. Her face froze in an expression reminiscent of someone pressing the pause button on a horror film.

"I… er… I have heard of him," Madge finally stammered.

"Is he here?"

Madge's face returned to normal. "I wouldn't know. I mean, I have only just arrived, like yourself." She seemed to study Luna for a moment, her small beady black eyes widening in shock. "Unless… you shouldn't be here, should you? Child, what on Earth are you playing at?"

"I had to come. I need to know where my mother is, and Jonas Schmidt. People I care about are in danger…Wait, how come you knew my mum wasn't here and not Jonas?"

The woman shrugged. "You mustn't play with the dead. Go back now, before you die for good."

"But then all this will have been for nothing. I need to get to the Rainbow Gate, maybe someone there can tell me the truth."

"Do you think this is some sort of a fairy tale? This is no place for a living person, especially one whose time is not yet up!"

"Please," begged Luna.

Madge studied her for another few seconds, then sighed. "You are a stubborn one, aren't you? Fine. We will try to sneak you to the front of the queue."

"And how are we going to do that?" asked the man behind.

"I'm a witch," Madge smirked. "I have ways."

Before Luna had time to thank the old woman, she felt her body being gently pushed through the centre of the line of people, as though she was a ghost herself, whizzing through them like mist. Some people jumped out of the way to avoid her, while others simply shuddered, unaware that she had quite literally passed through them. The experience of travelling through another human body was completely disorientating, and each time she passed through, she was overwhelmed by the emotions going through that individual's mind, making the whole thing even more unsettling.

It was not until she finally came to a stop that she realised she had been holding her breath the entire time, and she let out a spluttered gasp. Gradually, she felt her body fill out again, as though it was being inflated, and as she looked up, she was stunned to discover that she was now at the very front of the queue.

"Excuse me!"

Luna turned to apologise but her words became stuck in her throat. The person standing behind her was the thinnest man she had ever seen. He towered over her, his lanky frame at least six and a half feet tall. But what was most shocking was that both of his eyeballs were hanging out of their sockets, dangling against his cheekbones.

Luna twisted her head away as bile threatened to make an appearance. Still facing away from the strange man, she heard a series of squelching noises before someone tapped her on the shoulder. Luna slowly turned towards the man, relieved to see that his eyes were now back inside their sockets where they should be.

"Ah, I can see you better now," said the stranger. Then it was his turn to look shocked. "Why, you're a Celestian! Why are you here?"

"NEXT!"

The man looked over Luna's head, then back down at her. "I think it's best if you go first. I'm sensing that you don't belong here."

Luna nodded, silently thanking him, and made her way through a white mist. With great apprehension, she continued to walk into the unknown. She struggled to see two feet in front of her. Was she walking through clouds? No, of course not. She wasn't in the sky. But then, she wasn't on Earth either. She was somewhere in between.

When at last the mist dissipated, she found herself in a large clearing. But instead of the beautiful Rainbow Gate she had imagined, she felt rather cheated and puzzled by the sight before her. Yes, there seemed to be an enormous gate up ahead, though apart from its size there was nothing particularly special about it, but what stalked the front of it was not at all what Luna had expected. Sheep, and plenty of them. Normal looking sheep, grazing the grass. Except this grass wasn't green, it was blue.

Luna shrugged and carried on walking forwards. She did not have time to stop and puzzle over the scenery. She needed to find answers, and quickly. As she approached the grazing sheep, Luna narrowed her eyes. Her pupils widened in surprise. Each sheep appeared to be encircled by a miniature rainbow.

"Wow," she exclaimed out loud, smiling joyfully at the beautiful red, purple, yellow, blue and violet colours arcing around their middles. "How cute."

She approached the sheep closest to her. It did not look up from its grazing as she bent over, reaching out her hand to stroke it. Unexpectedly, the sheep suddenly turned its full attention to her, and Luna stepped back in horror. The creature's eyes burnt a fiery red, and its mouth hung open, revealing triple rows of the most terrifying, razor-sharp teeth she had witnessed since Amadan.

Chapter 21

Luna let out an ear-piercing scream as she jumped back to avoid the creature's bite, but she ended up falling onto her backside. All she could do was watch helplessly as the flame-eyed sheep edged closer, its jagged teeth grinding menacingly.

Luna's vision clouded over. All she could see was the shapeshifter, Amadan, her mind reliving the moment when he had first attacked her back in the forests of Araig.

"Enough!"

The brusque male voice brought Luna back to the present moment as the sheep-like creature quickly spun around and scurried away from her.

"What on Earth are you doing here?"

A dark-cloaked figure loomed above Luna. Panicking, she turned and scrambled backwards across the ground.

"Child, I am not here to hurt you."

Luna squinted up at the stranger as he held his hand

out to her. She couldn't make out his features – the large hood he wore shrouded them in darkness – but as Luna stared at his proffered hand she recoiled, taking in the raised red scars crisscrossing across the surface of his skin.

Reluctantly, she accepted the stranger's offered palm, but as soon as their hands touched, he quickly let go as though he had been burnt. Luna dropped back to the ground.

"Why did you let go of me?" she asked.

The stranger waved his hand frantically, as though it was on fire. "You must leave, immediately!" he insisted.

Luna heaved herself up to face the cloaked figure. "Are you a grim reaper?" she asked.

"I am not a reaper. I am the guardian of the Rainbow Gate."

The figure took a few tentative steps towards her, and Luna tried her best not to flinch as he loomed over her. Just then, the man's giant hood fell back to reveal his face. Luna recoiled: like his hand, the man's features exhibited angry red lacerations. The man drew back as Luna struggled to her feet.

"What happened to you?" she asked, dusting herself down.

The figure turned away, staring into the distance. Luna followed his gaze, amazed to see that the rather dull-looking gates had been transformed. Tall, golden gates rose like a beacon through the mist, with a huge rainbow of colours arcing through them.

The figure turned back to face her. "I have been the guardian of the Rainbow Gate since the dawn of time." He shrugged. "These scars are part of me now. For years I have fought every creature who has tried to pass me to get to the gates." The man rolled up his sleeves to reveal more scar tissue.

Luna studied the stranger's face before taking a few steps towards him. The face behind the red angry scars was the face of a man. There were no tentacles; no fangs; no burning eyes. He was just a human being. His piercing blue eyes gazed down at her, softening as he spoke.

"Why are you here, child?"

"I'm here to find my mother."

His thin, almost grey lips frowned. "When our hands touched, I felt your energy, and I can safely say you are not ready to meet your maker. But now you talk of seeking your mother?"

Luna nodded.

"You have voluntarily come here to seek her out?"

Luna nodded again. The man rubbed the stubble on his chin, before turning away. Luna watched curiously as he reached inside his cloak, and when he turned back to her, she saw he was holding what looked like a stone tablet. He bent down and placed it on the ground between them, then with a flair of his hand, scribbles of names floated out of the stone into the air before them.

"Name?"

"Er, Jocelyn Green."

The man dropped his hand, making the floating words zoom back inside the stone.

"I know who you are, Luna Green. You are one of the few remaining Celestians. You will not find your mother here."

"Why didn't you say that before?" snapped Luna. "I have little time as it is!"

"Then you must hurry back to the living."

"Can you at least explain where she is then? Or Jonas Schmidt?"

The man glared down at her. "I know of neither. Now GO!"

"But you must know something? I can't have almost died for nothing!"

The man let out a sigh. "All I know is that Jocelyn has never been here. I would know. As for this man, Jonas… well, I think he has visited, but got sent back."

Luna frowned. "Sent back? To where?"

The man shrugged. "It was beyond my jurisdiction. If I remember rightly, he was looking for something."

"Something?"

"Or maybe it was someone. Regardless, I have answered your questions as best I can; now you must leave or else you will die for real."

Luna looked down at her ankle. "I might be here sooner than you think."

The man followed her gaze. "You're infected?"

Luna nodded. "Amadan. I'm looking for a cure."

"In Jonas Schmidt or your mother?"

Luna shrugged. "I thought Jonas would know, since he was the one who released the shapeshifter. As for my mum, I just wanted to see her once more. I want to believe she is at peace. My best friend, Lily, who's a ghost, hasn't seen her in the afterlife."

"I'm sorry I couldn't give you more answers. I hope this has at least given you some peace of mind that she is not wandering lost in the Ethers. This isn't a place where you would want to be lost."

"How do I get back?"

The man placed two fingers in his mouth and let out an ear-piercing whistle. To Luna's horror, the rainbow sheep scuttled towards them. She backed away, but the man held out his hand to stop her.

"Don't be afraid, they are harmless. Well, only if they know you are not dead." He chuckled softly to himself.

The sheep surrounded Luna, their sharp teeth snapping.

"Now, close your eyes."

Glancing down at the terrifying sheep creatures, Luna looked up at the man dubiously. He shrugged at her, and eventually, she reluctantly closed her eyes.

The rainbow sheep circled around her, and when Luna peeked through one eye, it amazed her to see the miniature rainbows that surrounded each of them combine into one magnificent rainbow.

"It's okay, you can open your eyes now," called the man.

Opening both eyes, Luna stared in awe at the giant rainbow that lay before her, starting at her feet and arching up into the mist, before disappearing from view.

"If you walk over the bridge, it should take you back."

Luna stared in disbelief. Then she remembered the sheep with the sharp teeth. At first, she couldn't see them anywhere, until she looked closer at the rainbow. They were all hiding underneath.

"Child, you must hurry!"

Luna took a step onto the rainbow. It felt solid, a though it were made of stone, yet she could see straight through it. Cautiously, she took another step, then another. After a few more steps, she turned back towards the man.

"I didn't catch your name," she called out.

"The name's Rogue. When you next hear that name, it will be nearly your time."

Luna laughed nervously, before turning back and continuing her walk over the bridge. As she reached the highest point, she began to feel dizzy and disorientated. Pausing for a moment, she took a few deep breaths, before beginning her descent. Her breathing became more laboured as she walked down the other side of the rainbow bridge, and she stopped once or twice to catch her breath. Her legs grew weaker as she continued, and she feared she would not reach the end of the rainbow. She stumbled onwards, worried that she might fall over the side at any moment, but the thought of the sheep beneath pushed her further, until at last her left foot touched the ground on the other side.

Then, everything vanished, and she began to fall.

Chapter 22

Belinda looked at her watch for what seemed the hundredth time since Luna had 'died'. She could have sworn that her friend's face was changing to a mottled purple blue-ish colour. Was this a sign of rigor mortis setting in?

"Okay, I think we need to wake her up." Belinda reached over Luna's lifeless body, checking her pulse.

"Is she still breathing?" asked Magnus desperately.

Belinda looked up at him. He hadn't stopped pacing since Luna went under.

"Her pulse is very faint, but that's normal under the circumstances," Belinda reassured him.

"Someone is coming along the hallway," Lily whispered, floating over to the closed bedroom door and placing an ear against it.

Magnus rushed over to the window. It was pitch black outside.

"No sign of the teachers," he said.

"Poe is keeping watch, he will let us know when they

return," Belinda assured them. "Whoever's outside is probably just passing."

"But we're the last room on the corridor," hissed Lily.

"Can you still hear them?" whispered Belinda.

Lily leaned against the door again. "No... maybe I imagined it."

"Wait, her eyelids are fluttering!" cried Belinda.

Lily and Magnus rushed back over to the bed as Belinda felt Luna squeeze her hand.

Unbeknownst to her friends, Luna was experiencing her own internal nightmare, screaming relentlessly as she continued to freefall into the abyss. It felt never-ending, and she could not help but fear that Rogue had lied to her and sent her to her death. Then, suddenly, she saw a familiar sight come into view. Below her, in the centre of the darkness, was her bed, with her body lying across it. Belinda, Lily and Magnus were leaning over her. How could she be looking down at her own body?

Before another thought could enter her head, she felt a whooshing sensation envelop her, and with a soft thump, she landed back inside her own body.

"What's happening?" The voice that came out of Luna's mouth was alien to her own ears.

"You're back!" cried Lily.

Luna tried to push herself up, but her entire body ached as though she had been through another battle with Amadan.

"Take your time," soothed Belinda. "Your soul needs to adjust back into the shell of your body."

Luna scrunched up her face, but even that hurt.

Belinda and Magnus pulled Luna up into a sitting position against the headboard, and Magnus gently arranged her pillows behind her head. Luna looked across at him with searching eyes. How sweet, she thought. Then, like a switch had been flicked, she felt her heart flutter back into life. She noticed Magnus' face flush red as he quickly pulled away, taking an awkward step back.

"What time is it?" asked Luna, looking at Belinda, deliberately shifting her gaze away from Magnus.

Belinda checked her watch. "It's just gone midnight. You've only been under for five minutes."

"Really? But it felt like hours!"

"What did you see?" asked Lily eagerly, sitting down beside her.

"Can I have water first, please?"

Belinda handed her a pre-filled glass while Magnus made himself comfortable on Belinda's bed. The goth sat cross-legged in the middle of the floor, watching as Luna gulped down her glass of water like she hadn't drunk anything in days. Once she had finished, she held onto the empty glass, staring ahead of her as she tried to remember what had happened.

"It was the strangest thing. I woke up in this desert of black sand, except there was no sun, but the sky was red."

"Ooh, sounds like Mars," offered Lily.

Belinda threw her a look. "Let Luna tell her story."

Luna, unperturbed, carried on. "It scared me; I thought I might be in Hell. And then this three-eyed giant approached me, but his eyes weren't like ours, they were green stones, like the cabochons you get on a bracelet or necklace."

The other three listened attentively as Luna told them more about the tricyclops, Forcas, and how he had led her to the spirit train, where she had met a witch called Madge, who had ended up helping her get to the Rainbow Gate. When she had almost finished her tale, Poe let out a loud screeching sound, flapping his impressive wings.

Luna snapped out of her storytelling trance, cowering against the wall.

"Turn off the light!" exclaimed Belinda in a harsh whisper.

Magnus jumped to his feet, clumsily tripping over Belinda's abandoned Doc Martin's in the middle of the floor. Regaining his balance, he grabbed the light switch, and the room fell into complete darkness. Belinda switched on a torch, laying it on the floor so the light wouldn't shine upwards.

When she saw Luna cowering, Belinda reached over and squeezed her hand. "It's okay, Luna," she reassured her. "Poe is only warning us of the teachers' return from their search in the forests."

Luna turned to face her friend. "What are they searching for?" she croaked.

Magnus frowned. "Don't you remember? They went out searching for the coven of dark witches."

"It's okay," said Belinda. "It's normal to feel disorientated after coming round." She turned back to face Luna. "What happened once you got to the Rainbow Gate?"

Luna shifted her gaze back to the wall. "I, er… I met some sheep." Luna shuddered as she remembered their vicious-looking teeth.

"Sheep?" Belinda looked questioningly over to Lily before turning around to look at Magnus. She shone the torch in his face so she could see his expression, but ended up blinding him instead.

Luna carried on. "They had rainbows arcing around their bodies, like sideway halos. I thought they looked cute and harmless, like most sheep, but when I went to pet one, it opened its mouth wide open and revealed these horrible rows of sharp spiky teeth."

The three others looked at one another again. This was not what they had expected at all.

"Luckily, I was saved in the nick of time by Rogue. He was very kind. At first, I thought he was a grim reaper, for he wore a long, black, hooded cloak." Luna smiled to herself. "But he explained that he was the guardian of the Rainbow Gate. I asked him about my mum, and Jonas Schmidt. He'd heard of both, but unfortunately, he hadn't come across either of them."

The room fell silent as each of them waited in case Luna had more to add. When she said nothing, Belinda piped up.

"Did this guardian explain what the sheep were?"

Luna shrugged as she continued to stare ahead. "I guess they protect the Rainbow Gate or something. But in a way, they helped me to get back here."

"Did they bite you?" gasped Lily.

"No, their miniature rainbows joined to make a giant rainbow bridge."

Lily looked over at the other two. She needed little light to see the expressions on their faces. Magnus looked well and truly confused, but Belinda looked surprisingly unfazed.

"They sound awesome!" remarked Belinda.

The room fell silent again, just as the creak of a floorboard shifting sounded from outside their room.

"I knew it!" hissed Lily. "Someone's been listening in."

Belinda carefully got to her feet and tiptoed over to the closed door. Slowly, she pulled the door handle down, opening it wide enough to peer out. Craning her neck around the edge of the door, it took her a moment to adjust to the darkness, and by the time she could see into the hallway, the sounds of muffled feet had padded out of sight. Sighing, she closed the door.

"Well?" asked Lily.

"There was definitely someone out there listening. The question is, who was it… and why?"

Chapter 23

Luna got a good night's sleep despite the events of the early hours, and as she headed down to breakfast that morning, she felt more refreshed than she had in a long time. Even though it was a Sunday, the children were expected to get up early for breakfast. Some didn't bother, skipping their first meal of the day and waiting till lunch, but on this Sunday morning, the dining room was full. It was hardly surprising: the children were desperate for answers after the teachers' visit to the forests the previous night.

As Luna sat down between Magnus and Belinda, she sensed their weariness.

"No sleep?" she asked, as she tucked into her cereal.

Belinda grunted something under her breath and turned briefly to glare at Luna. The young witch was still wearing her eyeliner from the previous day, and the smudged makeup did nothing to alleviate the dark bags under her eyes.

"How could you sleep last night after everything that

happened?" mumbled Magnus, his voice rough.

Luna shrugged as she continued to spoon her cornflakes into her mouth. She felt surprisingly well, and her appetite had miraculously reappeared after weeks of nausea. "Maybe I've been born again."

Belinda threw her a look of disgust. "Never mind that, we need to find out who was spying on us last night."

She scanned the length of the table, pausing when she reached Tamara Hobbs. The young witch, sensing that she was being watched, glanced up briefly from her plate of fruit. Belinda glowered back at her, prompting Tamara to drop her eyes.

"Guilty as ever."

"Really?" Magnus rolled his eyes. "Tamara's way too obvious."

Belinda shrugged. "She looks guilty to me. Plus, she's always suspected us since your monkey sneaked into her dorm room."

"Ape," corrected Magnus.

"Whatever," snapped Belinda. "Just look at her, she can't even look at us."

Luna pushed her empty bowl away. "I don't think it's Tamara. What about the teachers? Or Angelica Lawson? Didn't she say she could change into a black cat?"

Belinda shrugged. "Yeah, but what would she gain from listening in? And anyway, the footsteps were too heavy to be a cat. And to answer your other theory, the teachers were in the forests, remember? Or has your zombie state wiped out that part of your memory?"

"But not all the teachers went." Luna nodded her head towards the top table where all the teachers sat in a row, eating their breakfast.

Bell Tilly looked over at their table, catching Luna's eye. She gave a half-hearted smile before reaching for her mug. Luna could sense the younger teacher's weariness, which was very out of character. Bell was always bubbly, even first thing on a Sunday morning.

Half an hour later, after Jeannie Gibbs and Gobbins had cleared the dirty dishes from their tables, Agnes Guthrie rose to her feet. The room was already eerily silent, so there was no need for her to ask them to pay attention.

"From everyone's faces, I can tell that we have all suffered a restless night as a result of these uncertain times. As you are all aware, myself, Salvador, Augustus and Miss Tilly went into the forest last night to try and discover the whereabouts of the escaped vetala. Monsieur Chavron also accompanied us, and it was he who picked up the scent of the creature."

Luna could not believe she had forgotten about the Chavrons. Her eyes darted to the two empty seats at the teachers table where the Chavrons usually sat.

"After our search, Frances Chavron and his son, Sebastian, had to leave on business. But they have assured us that they will soon return. Though our search was unsuccessful, Salvador did pick up the scent of the Pendle witches. It seems they are still hiding here in our forests." She glanced over at Belinda, giving the girl an all-knowing look. Belinda looked down at her hands and began to nervously pick at her black nail polish.

Evan Corsan threw his hand into the air. Agnes motioned for him to speak.

"Why did you go so late at night? Couldn't you have waited until daylight?"

A tutting sound came from Augustus' direction. Salvador's dark eyes threw him a sideways glance.

Patient as ever, Agnes explained. "The vetalas are creatures of the dark; it would be most strange to find one rambling about in the daylight." The headmistress clapped her hands together, startling everyone, including the teachers. "Now, instead of our usual lessons, we shall do something entirely different from tomorrow. I would like all of you to wear something warm and bring rucksacks for food and supplies. We will spend the day travelling through the forests, so comfortable footwear is also a necessity."

Evan flung his hand up again. "Are we going to search for the witches?"

Agnes shook her head. "No, but it will be a bonus if we run into them or discover their hideout. Tomorrow we are going to the forests to meet with our magickal neighbours, and to ask them a few questions along the way."

She took her seat, giving the children permission to leave, and the sounds of excited chatter filled the ominous silence.

"What do you think Mrs Guthrie was talking about? Who do you think we will meet tomorrow?" asked Magnus, as they made their way to the foyer.

Luna shrugged. "More fae, perhaps?"

Magnus walked towards the games room, stopping when he sensed Luna wasn't following.

"I'm going to the library, catch you later," she called after him.

Luna made her way through the secret doorway and up the spiral steps, hoping no one else had decided to spend their Sunday in the library. Thankfully, once she reached the oval room, she was pleased to see that she was alone. Luna loved the tranquillity of the library, and the smell of the old books, and though she missed her secret haven in the Calderglen woods back home, the cosy library tower was a welcome substitute.

Heading over to the history section, she scanned the shelves for what she was looking for. She wanted to learn more about Celestia. After her time in the Ethers, she had come to realise that her life might not be as long as she had anticipated. Anything could happen, at any time. She needed to find out more, not just about herself, but about her ancestors and her homeland.

Luna scanned from the floor to the middle of the

bookcase, until she could no longer read the words on the spines of the books. She glanced over at the ladder on the other side of the room. It was attached to a rail, and was designed to slide across the bookshelves, allowing easy access to the books higher up. But instead of retrieving it, Luna held onto the crystal around her neck and imagined her feet lifting off the ground. Her crystal pulsated like a heartbeat, beating faster, until she could feel her body becoming lighter as her feet gently parted with the stone floor. But just as her body began to hover above the ground, she felt the pulsing of the crystal slowing back down, until she could feel her toes touching the floor again.

Not one to give up, Luna kept trying, and after a few failed attempts, Luna tried a different tactic, imagining a halo of bright light engulfing her entire body. This seemed to power up her crystal, and it began to pulsate at a higher frequency. Heat radiated outwards from its raw edges, until her entire body rose into the air. Luna could feel empty space beneath the soles of her feet, even through her trainers. She opened one eye, amazed to see that she was staring directly at the books on the top shelf.

"Wow!"

Luna whipped her head around, looking for the owner of the voice, but the sharp movement made her power falter, causing her body to drop.

"Miss Luna!"

Luna descended towards the floor, stumbling forwards until she crashed into a bookcase.

Luna turned to see Nimbie grinning at her.

"Nimbie! It's so good to see you!"

The large rotund hobgoblin threw his thick short arms around her waist, squeezing with everything he had. Struggling to breathe, Luna deftly wriggled out of his embrace.

"Is Nana Violet here too?" she asked.

"Just me." The hobgoblin took a few steps back, his large broad teeth smiling up at her. "I told Miss Violet that I wanted to see you, an' she told me to visit."

"Fae tunnels?" guessed Luna.

Nimbie nodded his enormous head.

Luna smiled. "How long are you here for?"

She made her way towards the chairs by the fireplace, Nimbie's footsteps thudding behind her as she plonked herself down in the nearest one. Nimbie, knowing he wouldn't fit in any of the others, dropped his huge posterior onto the floor, reminding Luna of the first time they had met back at Nana Violet's cottage.

"Miss Agnes said I can stay fer tea."

Luna beamed. She had missed Nimbie so much, and the fact that he had taken the time to come and visit her made her heart feel full of love for the hobgoblin.

"What were you doin levitating in the library?" Nimbie asked.

"I was trying to find a book."

Nimbie's big doleful eyes looked up at her quizzically. "I didn't know you could fly."

Luna giggled. "Neither did I, but the thought popped into my head, so I thought I would try using my crystal." She glanced over at the bookshelf. "I'm trying to find something on Celestia. I really want to learn about my heritage. Princess Xania took me and the other children out into the gardens the other night to practise our magick, so we could learn how to see the vetalas in the dark—"

Nimbie's bushy eyebrows knitted together in the middle. "You mean you learnt to use torches?"

"Haha, no, Nimbie. We were supposed to be learning spells to manifest light, so we can fight the vetalas when the time comes, but when the moon appeared from behind the clouds, my entire body lit up. I could feel the moon's energy pulsing through my veins. Princess Xania says the moon is like a battery charger for me." She giggled as she envisioned herself plugged into a wall socket.

"Ah, lunar energy is most important fer Celestians."

"You mean you already knew? Do you know anything else about my kind?"

Nimbie scratched the small patch of ginger fur on his chin. "I know a little, but I can help in finding more out fer you."

Luna jumped off her chair and dived onto the hobgoblin, hugging him ferociously. The two of them giggled and laughed as they wrestled.

When they had finished laughing, Nimbie's expression turned serious.

"What's the matter?" asked Luna.

Nimbie shook his head, his pointy ears swaying with the motion.

"I don't like this danger you're being put in. The vetalas are nasty creatures. It ain't fair fer them to be putting you in danger."

Luna sat back in her chair. "What brought this on?"

Nimbie shrugged. "I don't trust those vamps."

Luna frowned. "You mean the Chavrons?"

Nimbie nodded. "There's sumthin not right about them." He shivered, even though he was sitting directly next to the fire.

"You think they have something to do with the vetala escaping?"

"Nah, we all know that's cos of the damaged portal. But sumthin doesn't add up."

Luna thought about this for a moment. "Yeah, I know what you mean. Why are they here? I know Mrs Guthrie invited them, but what I don't get is why? I mean, we fought off the shadow walkers by ourselves with help from the fae and my dad… but then, why would a vampire come all the way here from France just to tell us what a vetala is, when we can easily find out for ourselves?"

Tap, tap.

Luna and Nimbie turned their heads towards the doorway.

Frances Chavron shadowed their only exit, his cane tapping against the stone floor. Luna's eyes shifted to his mouth. A devious grin prominently displayed his two very sharp incisors.

Chapter 24

"**M**onsieur Chavron, I thought you were away on business?" Luna's voice was unusually high-pitched.

Much to Luna's horror, the older vampire ventured past the threshold of the doorway. His well-polished shoes clicked against the stone floor as he sauntered towards them, swinging his cane. The cane's ruby handle glinted each time it caught Luna's eye. He stopped short a few feet away from them.

Nimbie scrambled to his feet. "Would you like a chair, sir?"

Frances Chavron took off his top hat, placing it under his left armpit. "No, thank you. I shall not outstay my welcome." He looked over at Luna, who remained seated. "Yes, I was away on business, but I am needed more here."

Luna felt her cheeks redden. "We meant nothing by—"

Frances Chavron clicked his tongue, cutting her off.

"My dear, you do not need to explain your concerns away. I completely understand that sharing your exquisite home with two blood-sucking vampires is extremely alarming. But I can assure you both that my son, Sebastian, and I are here at Mrs Guthrie's request. We are assisting her in finding the vetalas. I can sniff them out just like Salvador can smell black witchcraft emanating from the heinous coven who are also stalking your forests."

Luna smiled nervously. "I understand. We were told all of this. But if you don't mind me asking, what business did you have to attend to away from the manor?"

"Miss Luna! You can't ask someone of authority such a question!" exclaimed Nimbie.

Frances Chavron let out a sharp laugh. "Very brazen, Miss Green. Not to worry, I don't mind at all."

Nimbie shuffled over to Luna's side as the vampire paced before them, his cane clicking rhythmically against the floor.

"We are planning a trip to Romania, and it was my duty to seek the approval of the elders for yourself and Agnes Guthrie to visit."

Luna's eyes widened. "M-me?"

Nimbie placed a supportive hand on her shoulder.

Frances stopped pacing and turned to face her. "Why yes. You are a very special being, Miss Green."

"But what can I offer the elders? I'm only a child."

Frances edged closer to her, making Luna lean back in her chair.

"You may be a child, but like my son, Sebastian, you are wise beyond your years. Besides, once I informed them of your existence, they were most eager to meet you."

"But why?"

Frances Chavron threw his hands up in the air. "Child, I do not know of their intentions. But if I were you, I would not refuse their invitation." Giving her an intense look, he clicked his heels and turned, before swiftly departing from the library.

Once they had recovered from the shock of the vampire's appearance, Luna and Nimbie left the library in silence. The hobgoblin hurried after Luna as he tried to keep up with her long strides. Instead of heading to where all the other children were, she made her way to her dorm room.

☾

"So, Poe, what's been going down?"

Belinda lay across her bed on her belly, while her raven perched on her headboard. The large black bird cocked its head to the side, letting out a loud squawk.

"Hell yeah, that's what I thought."

She rolled over onto her side when she heard Luna enter the room, chuckling with amusement as Luna, in her haste, almost closed the door in Nimbie's face.

"Hey, Nimbs, how are you?" Belinda raised her hand in greeting, and the hobgoblin gave her a high five on his way by.

"Hey, Poe." Nimbie went to high-five the raven but received a high-pitched warning not to come any closer. Nimbie scurried away over to Luna's side of the room.

"What's up?" asked Belinda, sensing Luna's distress.

Luna stood facing the window, her arms crossed over her chest.

"We just got spooked by a vampire," answered Nimbie as he struggled to climb onto the end of Luna's bed.

Belinda straightened up, swinging her legs over the side of her bed.

"Whoa, which vamp?"

"Frances." Luna turned away from the window to face them.

Belinda frowned. "I thought they were away?"

"Same, but I guess not. Apparently, the vampire elders are dying to meet me."

Belinda's face contorted as she fought to keep a straight face. "Was that pun intended?"

Luna shrugged. "Dunno, but I have a horrible feeling about this." She plonked herself down on her bed.

"I mean, you are famous. It's hardly surprising."

"It's not funny, Belinda! I'm only thirteen, what do they need me for?"

"Um, maybe because you're the last living Celestian, duh." Belinda hit her palm against the side of her head.

Luna snorted. "Why can't all twelve of us go to Romania? Why just me?"

"Don't worry, Miss Luna. Miss Agnes hasn't even asked you yet."

Luna smiled over at Nimbie. "You're right. Frances Chavron could just be saying that to make me worry. Especially after he overheard the two of us talking about him."

"Ooh, now this I want to hear. Do tell," said Belinda leaning in closer.

☾

After the meal, Nimbie asked Agnes Guthrie whether he could take Luna out to the gardens, and Agnes gladly obliged, knowing that Nimbie would not let any harm come to her. Darkness had fallen early – it was winter, after all – and Luna shivered beneath her thick, woolly coat. The heavy snowfall that had descended over the past week was now crisp with the evening frost, and patches of snow draped like a thick cape over the sculpted hedges. The only light came from the many manor windows, blinking down at them like dozens of rectangular glass eyeballs, and a sliver of moonlight, the waning moon only giving out a third of its light.

"Tell me why we are out here again?"

"To practise your magick, Miss Luna."

"But it's so dark out here. Why don't we wait till tomorrow? Unless you're going to teach me more of the fae magick we were practicing the other night?"

"I can't teach you fae magick, but there are other ways for you to see in the dark." Nimbie stopped in the centre of the gardens, in the middle of a large patch of the grass. "Right, call Theodore."

Luna closed her eyes and thought of the beautiful creature. Instantly, he came into her mind, clear as day. When she opened her eyes, the handsome unicorn was standing right before her.

"Theodore!" She rushed over to him, both arms outstretched.

The unicorn lowered his muzzle, and they hugged.

"I still don't know how you arrive by my side so quickly," she giggled, as Theodore affectionately nibbled at her neck.

"Telepathy," answered Nimbie.

Luna gave him a look. "I know that, but how does he travel here so fast?"

Nimbie shrugged his broad shoulders. "Just does."

"So, what do we do now?" asked Luna, reluctantly letting go of Theodore.

"Hold on to your crystal," instructed Nimbie.

Luna gripped it tightly like she had in the library earlier. "Okay?"

Nimbie nodded towards Theodore. The unicorn

raised his head, pointing it towards the dark sky. Luna felt her crystal heat up, then vibrate, until something akin to electricity began to crackle through her fingers. Suddenly, a bright white light beamed from the unicorn's horn, shooting upwards into the sky before falling towards Luna. As it made contact, she felt a bolt of energy pass through her body, not like an electric shock but more like an energising power surge. Luna looked down. The beam now radiated from her, flooding the air with a brilliant white light.

"Wow!" exclaimed Luna. "How is this even happening?"

"Connection," answered Nimbie solemnly. "You and Theodore together have the ability to transverse thoughts into reality. The crystal simply helps to make that connection."

The gardens were lit up like a football pitch, and when Luna let go of her crystal, the light did not fade.

"Now the both of you can magick together. You are stronger as a team."

"What should I try next?" asked Luna.

The hobgoblin shrugged. "Why not levitate, like you did in the library?"

Luna nodded. She reached for her crystal again, when Nimbie stopped her.

"You don't need that anymore, you're already connected." He threw his short arms wide apart.

Luna understood, and with that, she threw all of her

energy, directing it towards the sky. She could feel a push on the soles of her feet, but just when she thought she was being lifted, her trainers crunched against the frozen grass.

"Everything is energy: the grass, the trees, even the elements," coached Nimbie from the side lines.

Luna listened, but as his voice became distant, she felt the wind rising around her, curving about her body like a mini tornado. Her arms instinctively lifted from her sides, slowly raising themselves skywards. Later, she would understand that her powers were drawing in the multiple energies around her, just like Nimbie had predicted.

The wind continued to whirl around her, and only when she heard a cry did she open her eyes, amazed to discover she was floating in mid-air.

"You did it!" cried Nimbie from below.

Luna looked down. She was at least six feet in the air.

"Don't lose concentration," yelled the hobgoblin.

Luna suddenly felt sick as she became aware of the waves of energy shifting around her. "Okay," she murmured to herself. "I can do this."

Taking a deep breath and closing her eyes, Luna imagined herself floating back down to safety. A few seconds later, her feet landed with a soft crunch back on land.

"Amazing!" she cried, her eyes wide.

Nimbie hobbled over to her, throwing his short arms around her waist. But as he did, they both heard a loud crackling sound, as the energy in Luna's body reacted to the presence of another living thing.

"Whoa, so much energy," laughed Nimbie. "Like a telly."

Luna looked at her hands, turning them around. Small sparks of light darted across her palms, before fizzling out. Then, everything went dark.

Luna felt a muzzle nibbling at her ear. "Theodore," she giggled, as the unicorn tickled her with his white mane.

Luna wanted to practise more, but Nimbie had to leave Blackhill Manor before it got too late, or Violet would worry about him. They said their goodbyes, and Luna reluctantly headed back inside.

She found Lily floating in the hallway, staring into the forest painting.

"Are you okay?" Luna asked.

But Lily didn't budge; she continued to stare straight at it.

"Lily!"

Startled, Lily turned to her friend. "Oh, Luna, sorry. I never saw you there."

"What were you staring at?"

Lily shifted her gaze back to the painting and shrugged. "Thought I heard someone say my name."

"And it came from the painting?" asked Luna.

"I think so."

Luna stepped beside her and looked into the painting. It wasn't so long ago that she had entered the painting to try and find out who was watching them.

"Who do you think it is?" asked Lily, breaking their eerie silence.

"I have my theories. At first, I thought it might be Winnie."

Lily turned to face her. "What made you change your mind?"

"I saw someone watching me through the trees. Although I couldn't make them out, I felt a weird energy from them."

"So, you don't think it's a woman inside the painting?"

Luna shrugged.

"Who do you think it is then, if it's not Winnie?"

"Remember when Jonas Schmidt channelled himself through me?"

Lily nodded her head.

"What if the reason he could do that was because he's still here in the manor?"

Lily's pale face stared back at the painting. "You mean to say that all this time, since he damaged the portal over a century ago, he's been watching us from inside the manor?"

Luna nodded. "It makes sense. How else could he have possessed me? There are so many protection spells around the manor." Luna shuddered. "We should leave, it's not safe to talk here."

Lily stared back at the painting, but she failed to notice the dark shadow flickering between the trees.

Chapter 25

Monday dawned bright and crisp, with the sun finally making an appearance, cutting through the heavy slated clouds. But though the rays of light beaming through the forest canopy were welcome, the children wished the sun could provide warmth as well. It was bitterly cold, and as they trudged through the snow and mud, trying their best not to disturb the eerie quiet of the forest, the children wished their headmistress had picked a more inviting day to leave the comfort of the manor.

Agnes, Salvador and Augustus led the children through the shadows of the forest, leaving the Edgar twins to prowl at the back of the group, their senses on high alert in case of danger. The eeriness that surrounded them added to the sense of mystery, for Agnes had still not told them where they were going, or who they were meeting.

Luna walked in the centre of the group with Belinda trudging alongside her, followed by Magnus and Lucas.

Tamara and Angelica strode with their heads held high behind the teachers, and Luna became increasingly annoyed by their air of importance the further they ventured into the forest.

An hour passed, then another. The children were exhausted, and their feet hurt, not to mention that hiking through uncharted forests without the knowledge of their destination or purpose was taking a toll on their sanity. In fact, they had been walking for so long that when Agnes Guthrie finally halted, Tamara, not expecting the sudden change of pace, bumped into the back of the head teacher.

Ignoring her clumsiness, Agnes held a hand up to alert the others, and one by one, the group gathered in a tight circle.

"Thank you to every one of you for continuing on this journey without questioning or complaining. I wanted you all to experience this encounter without prior knowledge, so that you may rely on your instincts, not on prejudice or forethought."

Luna and Magnus exchanged worried glances.

"May I introduce the tree guardians." Agnes looked up into the nearest tall hawthorn tree.

The children followed her gaze to one of the higher branches. Luna held her breath, her eyes searching every twig and shadow, but nothing jumped out at her. She was about to complain about this to Magnus when something moved between the leaves, something green and furry, which proceeded to scuttle along the tree's rough bark. At first glance, it looked like moss, but when it began to crawl down the tree towards them, the children became alarmed.

"Don't be afraid, children. These little creatures are wickles, they won't hurt you." Agnes stretched an arm up towards the tree, her hand reaching out to touch the cluster of green fur. At first, the creature scuttled sideways, like a crab, but after a few sniffs, it somehow sensed the owner of the hand, and jumped down, landing onto Agnes' outstretched palm.

A few of the children jumped backwards as the green, furry, spider-like creature began to weave in and out of the head teacher's fingers. Unperturbed, Agnes let out a peal of giggles as the creature tickled her skin with its fluffy coat. Luna leaned in closer, enraptured by this new and exciting creature of the forests. It was not much bigger than your average house mouse, fitting comfortably inside Mrs Guthrie's palm, and its spindly legs, five on each side, were coated in the same dense moss-like fur as its body.

Sensing her interest, the creature suddenly pounced from Agnes' hand onto Luna's shoulder. Shocked by the creature's sudden appearance, Luna almost jolted in surprise, but Agnes quickly caught the wickle and held it once more, cupping it between both her hands. The little creature's small black eyes blinked through the darkness of its new occupancy.

Smiling, Luna leaned towards the head teacher, holding out a tentative hand. "It's okay, Mrs Guthrie, I'm ready."

Agnes nodded, before carefully placing her cupped hands over Luna's. As soon as the creature gently dropped into her palm, Luna let out a hysterical giggle. Its furry legs tickled her skin. She could see the wickle's eyes peering out between the gaps in her clasped hands.

"It's okay little guy," she soothed. "I won't hurt you."

Slowly, she opened her hands, until she was sure the creature wouldn't jump from them. Its little eyes stared up at her quizzically, and then its small mouth opened, to reveal rows of tiny sharp teeth. Luna's hand wobbled at the sight of them, not sure if it was going to bite. She glanced over at Mrs Guthrie, who smiled in return, nodding reassuringly.

"Hello, Luna. So nice to finally meet you."

Luna's eyes darted back to the creature. "Did you just speak?"

The wickle nodded its little green head.

Luna's eyes widened. "Are we communicating telepathically?" she asked. She was aware that she was speaking out loud, but the same scenario had occurred between herself and Lazarus not so long ago, when the dragon had told her to speak through thought.

"I can hear him too," piped up Tamara.

A chorus of 'me too' from the other children told her

much the same.

"Wow, a talking spider."

"Not exactly, Miss Green, I am a wickle, remember. One of many who guard the trees."

"Sorry," she mumbled.

The wickle suddenly leapt from her hand, leaping rapidly onto the next person, then the next, until it landed back on the bark of the hawthorn tree. The group of children jumped about, patting themselves down, unsure whether or not the wickle was still on them.

Luna laughed, then turned back to the hawthorn tree, just in time to see the wickle blend back in with the green moss on the tree's bark. A few seconds later, that same mound of green moss sprouted hundreds of legs, and dozens of wickles scuttled back and forth along the rough bark, some jumping high in the air to land on the next tree.

As the children gazed in awe at the spectacle, Agnes remained standing before the tree, and the wickle, who Luna assumed was the original one who had just spoken to her, turned to face the older woman.

"What brings you here, witch?" asked the creature in its high-pitched voice.

Luna could hear Tamara clicking her tongue from somewhere behind her. She obviously thought the wickle's remark was rude. If it was, Agnes Guthrie did not let on.

"We seek answers," the headmistress explained. "We

have a band of dark magick witches hiding amongst your trees, and I came to ask if you, as guardians of the forest, have come across any?"

The wickle blinked at her, before scuttling back-and-forth sideways to confer with the other wickles. A ripple of high-pitched tones collided together, making no sense, before the original wickle scurried back to face Agnes Guthrie once more.

"We have not seen these witches you speak of, but we have sensed another, even darker presence within our forest."

Agnes turned her head slightly as she felt a new presence appear by her side.

"Tree guardian, what do you know of this evil you speak of?" Augustus asked.

The wickle blinked its beadlike eyes up at him. "Your Majesty." The creature bowed its diminutive head.

"Just Augustus will do," corrected the fairy.

Luna watched him squirm at the mere mention of his royal background.

The wickle scrambled upwards before jumping onto one of the tree's branches. "Some of us followed this dark creature when it emerged from the Dead Forest. It made its way south-east, towards—"

"The edge of the forest," finished Salvador, who suddenly appeared from the back of the group.

"Was it a vetala you saw?" asked Augustus.

The wickle nodded solemnly. "A hideous monstrosity, dripping with hunger. It was sniffing the air as it made its way blindly through the forests."

Salvador walked in circles. "This isn't good, not good at all. A hungry vetala on the loose amongst the 'norms'."

"You mean, it's escaped into the 'real' world?" Luna's voice squeaked with panic.

"Unfortunately, yes," stated Agnes gravely. "And there can be no doubt that it is searching for its next victim."

Chapter 26

The group hurried back to the manor after their brief encounter with the tree guardians, and Agnes Guthrie immediately ordered an emergency meeting with all the teachers, including the Chavrons. The children, meanwhile, were told to go to their rooms and stay there until further notice.

As usual, Luna and Belinda had the pleasure of Lily's company in their dorm room. The ghost was drifting around the centre of the room, much to the other two's annoyance.

"Why aren't we being included in the meeting? It's like we're not part of this," pondered Lily.

Belinda lay on her side, hugging her pillow, while Luna stared out of the window, looking beyond the dark tree line of the forest.

"Obviously we're not to be trusted," sniffed Belinda.

Lily continued to float back and forth. "I think it's you they don't trust."

Belinda's pillow suddenly flew towards Lily, only to

pass through her, hitting Luna instead.

"Would you two quit it!" Luna marched towards the door, hesitating as she reached for the door handle.

"What are you planning on doing?" asked Belinda.

Luna swung around to face them. Her usually pale cheeks had a strange pink tinge to them. "I don't know, but I'm sick of being tossed aside whenever real danger is present."

"That's not true," stated Lily. "You're the one who accompanies the teachers on tasks."

"If you're talking about my meeting with King Engogabal and Lazarus, that was because Amadan bit me. Mrs Guthrie was seeking the help of the king, to find a cure."

"You helped them find the first crystal after the shadow walkers escaped," piped up Belinda.

"Because I was already outside of the manor, and they needed a guardian of the athame to discover it. There was no time to waste once the shadow walkers escaped. Look, this isn't about me, it's about all of us."

Lily perched on the end of Luna's bed. "Luna's right. This isn't the time to be fighting amongst ourselves."

"Think about it, Belinda. You were the one who fought Amadan on your own. You didn't just save Hugo's life but the lives of all the children."

Belinda blushed in response to Luna's praise, displaying a side to her that neither of the other two had witnessed before.

"Well, I needed to win back everyone's trust… after I betrayed you all," the young witch mumbled.

Luna thought for a moment. "Why do you think the wickles hadn't seen the Pendle witches?"

Belinda shrugged. "Maybe because they're not in the forests?"

"Nah, they are definitely out there." Luna went back to stare through the window. "Unless they have something to do with the vetala leaving the forest."

"You think they lured it out?" gasped Lily.

Belinda shot to her feet, startling the other two. "That's exactly it! They wanted to draw attention away from themselves, so they let the vetala loose, because they know the teachers at the manor will follow it. This way they can sneak around unnoticed while the teachers are far away from the manor."

☾

Luna hurried down the flight of stairs, jumping over the last three steps into the foyer. Ignoring the fresh pain in her right ankle, she spun around towards the corridor on her right, and without hesitating, sprinted along the dimly lit hallway until she reached the familiar bronze plaque. Taking a deep breath, she pulled the handle before barging through the open doorway.

"It's a trick!"

Eight heads spun around to stare directly at her.

"What is the meaning of this!" snapped Augustus.

All six of the teachers, and the two Chavrons, sat or stood across from one another at an extendable mahogany table. Agnes Guthrie was standing at the head of it. On the wall above her, a lifelike oil painting of Edward Blackhill stared down at them all, as though he too was part of the discussion.

"Speak girl!" spat Augustus.

As usual, Bell Tilly urged him to calm down.

"Sit," demanded Agnes. She pulled an empty chair out from the table.

Luna bowed her head, suddenly feeling foolish. She could feel their eyes boring into her as she made her way over to the table.

"I er, I was just thinking—"

"Ha! So this sudden intrusion is just based on a whim, is it?" snorted Augustus.

"Will you please be quiet for once and let the girl explain," hissed Bell by his side.

Bell's defence gave her courage, and Luna looked up at the teachers, speaking in a firm voice. "The reason the wickles never saw the Pendle witches is because the witches are the ones who lured the vetala out of the forest. They did it so they can sneak back inside while all of your attention is focused on the vetala."

The room went quiet as everyone took in this additional information, but just as Augustus looked as though he was about to cry out again in protest, Agnes

Guthrie spoke.

"That seems like a reasonable explanation as to why the tree guardians never saw the witches inside the forest. They were already outside, luring the vetala out."

"But how?" asked Salvador. "It would need to be starving to want to eat a witch."

"Unless…"

Everyone at the table turned to look at Frances Chavron.

"Unless they have a child with them."

The other teachers stared at the vampire in horror, waiting for him to confirm their worst fears.

"The only way to lure a vetala is by the promise of a proper meal." Frances Chavron scraped his chair back as he rose to his feet. "A child's blood."

Chapter 27

The room was eerily quiet as everyone tried to process what Frances had just told them. Augustus and Salvador looked shocked at first, then determined; Archie Brutt looked horrified, as did Luna; Hattie looked furious at the thought of a child being used as bait, and Bell was crying silently, her gentle disposition not suited to such traumatic news. Ever the leader in these situations, Agnes took charge.

"We must investigate this, and quickly. It might just be that the witches aren't in the forests anymore, and the vetala has simply wandered out into the human world of its own accord."

"We can't take that chance," whispered Bell. "We would never forgive ourselves."

Luna stood silently, deep in thought. What if Agnes Guthrie was right, and they had just left the forests? Given up on the whole idea of trying to open the portal? The witches would need the athame and one of the five crystals to open it, and the only way they were going to get those was to break into Blackhill Manor and steal the athame. And even then, they would need to find the right crystal before they tried to open the portal. Perhaps they had just given up.

As the teachers began to discuss tactics, Luna was ushered out of the room by Bell, who had noticed Luna's withdrawn demeanour and had instantly assumed that the girl had gone into shock. Concerned for Luna's wellbeing, but conscious that she was needed in the room next-door – mostly to ensure that Augustus didn't suggest anything too rash – Bell stood outside the door and talked to Luna for a few minutes, just to make sure she wasn't going to pass out. Once she was satisfied that Luna was going to be okay, she advised her to go back to her room, and promptly disappeared back into Agnes Guthrie's office.

"You did the right thing."

Belinda appeared silently by Luna's side, as if by magick, though Luna knew that Belinda was just very good at sneaking up on people.

"I don't know," Luna murmured. "I could be wasting everyone's time on some wild goose chase."

Belinda shrugged. "First of all, it was my idea, not yours, and second, at least it will finally get us doing something, rather than just sitting doing nothing. It's like we're just waiting for something to happen, rather than going out there and doing something about it."

Luna turned to face her. "Wasn't that what we were

doing yesterday? Searching for answers from the tree guardians?"

"Not really. It was just another excuse to waste time, when really we need to get out there and fight."

"Do you feel ready for that?" asked Luna.

Belinda rolled her eyes. "Jeez, I've been ready since I arrived at this dump."

☾

Everyone had been asked to meet in the manor's foyer, and Agnes swiftly explained to the children that there was a possibility that a child had been abducted by the Pendle witches, to use as bait. No one was to be left behind in the manor in case the witches were now lurking in the forests, waiting for the teachers to leave so they could steal the athame from the 'defenceless' children, or the rest of the vetalas had somehow escaped and intended to feast on the children while the teachers were absent.

Luna's head was swimming with ifs and buts, so much so that she didn't process that the rest of her classmates were preparing themselves to leave the manor. All of them, teachers included, were standing in the hallway, kitted out in their warm winter clothes, before Luna had even made her way up the stairs to her dorm room.

Seeing Luna staring blankly at the scene in front of

her, Agnes Guthrie clapped her hands together. "Hurry Luna Green! We have to get going before it gets dark!"

Snapping out of her trance, Luna jogged up the stairs two at a time, grabbing her thick padded coat that still lay in a heap at the end of her bed from the morning's outdoor excursion. She stopped momentarily to gaze out of the window. Most of the snow had melted away, but the sun was already low. All too soon, it would disappear behind the treetops.

Luna bolted out of the room to join the others, her anxiety clogging her senses, making everything seem muffled. Mrs Guthrie had just informed them that they could not bring their animal guides, and the fear emanating from the children was almost palpable.

"I still don't see why we can't wait until the morning?" whispered Magnus to Luna as she joined him in the crowd.

Luna shrugged. "I was thinking the same... unless they know something that we don't."

"Like what?"

Agnes ushered the group out of the front doors, where Urus greeted them at the bottom of the steps. The large oxman turned and led them down the driveway towards the entryway, where the enormous gates loomed into view.

"If we had found the missing grimoire, then we wouldn't need to leave the manor in search of these rats," hissed Tamara to her friend Angelica.

Bell Tilly turned to the girl. "If you have any idea where this grimoire is, Miss Hobbs, then we would be more than happy to stay behind and conjure up miracles."

Belinda chuckled from behind the girls. Tamara swung around to glare at her.

"This is all your fault! If you hadn't brought your little goth fan club here none of this would have happened."

Belinda snorted. "Give it up already—"

"Girls!" barked Salvador. "This is not the time for childish insults."

Urus stopped when they reached the tall gates, and a golden padlock appeared from thin air, snaking around the centre of the adjoining gates. Luna heard the clicking sound of an invisible key being turned, and the golden padlock dropped to the ground as the tall ornate gates creaked slowly inwards.

The children filtered through, stopping when Agnes held up her hand. Using her wand, Agnes waved a series of invisible symbols into the air. It reminded Luna of when she had first arrived at the manor, and Nana Violet had drawn the same symbols on the bark of an ancient oak tree.

Sure enough, the same thing happened, and a mini tornado appeared in the air before them. It swirled around them, opening wider until it formed a tunnel. Agnes guided the group to enter, just as Luna's Nana

Violet had urged her car through the tunnel all those months ago.

Luna instantly felt dizzy as the tunnel span up and around them, like a huge kaleidoscopic hula hoop encircling them. As they reached the end of the tunnel, white lights instantly blinded them.

Agnes hurried forward, waving both arms above her head. "Violet, dim the headlights!"

"Oops."

The lights dimmed, and after a minute or two, once their eyes adjusted to their new surroundings, Luna was surprised to see her nana hanging out the driver's window of a minivan.

"Nana, what are you doing here?"

Violet jumped out of the driver's side to greet her granddaughter. "Hello darling." She grabbed Luna in an enormous bear hug. "I think you'll find I'm the transport, my dear."

Luna left her nana's embrace to take a look at the blue and white VW camper van. "Where on Earth did you find this?"

"Ach, I borrowed it from the local bric-a-brac man in Ballycastle. He won't notice it missing."

"You mean you stole it?" gasped Luna.

Violet giggled. "They were closed. I'll zap it back into their yard later on once we're finished here."

"Right everyone, pile in," ordered Agnes.

"Eh, how on Earth are we all going to fit inside of

this?" remarked Isaac Newman, as he struggled to carry his rather rotund boar up the steps of the camper van.

"Isaac! I specifically instructed you not to bring your animal guides," exclaimed Agnes furiously.

Isaac slumped his shoulders. "Sorry, Miss."

Agnes shook her head. "Oh well, he is here now. Carry on."

Isaac smiled as he continued to push the boar through the doorway. Salvador tutted at the boy, and with a flick of his hand, the boar floated upwards into the van. An impressed Isaac sprinted up the steps after him, followed by the rest of the group.

"Whoa," exclaimed the children, as they entered the van. The space inside stretched out to the size of a single decker bus.

Once everyone had settled in their seats, Agnes seated herself next to Violet.

"Where should we look?" Violet turned the key in the ignition.

Agnes shrugged. "Maybe start at the perimeter of the forest?"

"That's a significant area to cover. Might take us hours just to get around it," said Violet.

"It's a start," said Salvador, who was sitting next to Augustus in the row behind them.

"Where do you think we should look first, Monsieur Chavron?" Agnes half turned in her seat to look back at the vampire and his son.

"I think the perimeter is a good start, although I feel they will have moved further into the nearest town."

Violet shrugged. Putting the van into first gear, she did a three-point turn, and the camper van and its passengers began their bumpy ride towards the main road.

Chapter 28

Darkness enveloped them as the camper van stalked the outskirts of the forest's edge. Two hours had passed, with no sightings, and the children's eyes had grown tired of peering into the gloom.

"This is pointless, we are obviously searching in the wrong place," said Agnes, sitting on the very edge of her seat, her face almost touching the windscreen. The darkness made it impossible to see anything along the outskirts of the forest, let alone further in.

"Maybe we should go on foot," suggested Violet. "That way we will be able to hear them approaching, and those of us with more attuned senses can try to sniff them out."

"I think that's a better idea," said Salvador from behind, his tone sharp.

"Of course it's a better idea." Augustus rolled his luminous eyes. "I mean, did anyone really think this contraption would help us find anything? Going on foot was always the only valid option."

"Oh really?" Bell raised her eyebrows at the fairy. "Forgive me if I am wrong, but has it not taken us two hours to drive around the edge of the forest? Walking the entire perimeter would have taken at least four," snapped Bell.

Augustus clucked his tongue. "Well, maybe you should have given us all a ride on your broomstick instead."

Luna listened on as the two continued to debate against one another. She could never fully understand why they always had to disagree with each other's plans. She knew that Augustus was a generally disagreeable person, but his attitude towards Bell was completely uncalled for. It made Luna wonder whether there was more to his hatred of witches than he let on, and whether what had happened to his brother, Cassieus, had just been the tip of the iceberg. One day, she would find out the truth.

"STOP!"

The van screeched to a halt as Violet performed an emergency stop. The passengers in the back flew forward in their seats, and Violet cursed silently to herself, ashamed that she had forgotten to magickally insert seatbelts when she had cast the bigger van spell. Thankfully, no one got hurt.

"Whatever is the matter?" Violet asked Agnes.

"Look!"

Violet peered out into the darkness, to where her friend was pointing. She was about to say she couldn't see anything, when a flash of white ran across the road right in front of them. Then, just as suddenly, it stopped, turning to look straight at them.

"It's a child," gasped Agnes.

The figure ran towards them so frantically that, blinded by the van's headlights, they thumped against the front of the bonnet.

Violet placed her hand on the door handle.

"Wait, we don't know if this is a trick," warned Agnes.

The rest of the group were now out of their seats, standing behind the two women and peering over their shoulders into the darkness beyond. Those at the front could make out what looked like a little girl, laying in a heap on the floor by the car bonnet. She looked pale and thin, and her whole body was shaking.

"She needs help!" exclaimed Bell. "Hurry, we need to get her inside."

Violet and Agnes sprang into action, climbing out of the van and rushing towards the slumped figure. The other teachers climbed out after them, wands and other magickal objects at the ready, in case of any unwarranted attacks.

"Poor child, she's so young," said Agnes, as she lifted the girl's head. The girl's eyes rolled back behind her eyelids. "Quick, we must take her back to the manor for treatment."

Salvador lifted the girl into his arms and began to carry her towards the van. But just as he placed a foot on the first step, a low hissing sound came from the surrounding forest. The teachers stopped dead. The children had remained inside the camper van, but even they could sense the atmosphere changing all around them.

Salvador was the first to move, as he quickly heaved the girl up into the van. "Hurry children, take the girl and stay inside!"

Salvador let go of her as the Edgar twins rushed over to him and took the girl from his grasp, before promptly jumping back out to join the other teachers, slamming the door behind him. The children rushed to one of the windows to get a good look outside. Agnes, Violet, Salvador, Augustus, Bell, Hattie, Archie and the Chavrons stood back-to-back in a circle, their eyes and ears fixed on their surroundings, their weapons at the ready. Bell's casting stones jangled softly in her hand, while Salvador held his right hand out towards the space before them, his signet ring poised for attack.

"Show yourself," demanded Agnes.

Silence followed.

Moments later, the hissing sound continued.

"It's coming from over there," said Augustus.

He pointed his crystal wand towards a tree with low-hanging branches, the base of which was covered by thick undergrowth. A rustling sound came from nearby. Agnes shifted her stance, nodding to the others in a secret code. Understanding their leader, the group drifted towards the clearing. A few kept their backs turned, in case of an unprovoked attack from behind. Agnes and Violet held their wands before them, pointing them directly at the brambles next to the line of trees. A slight movement alerted the group to move closer.

"Who's there?" called Agnes.

With extreme caution, she moved closer still, her wand consistently aimed at the spot where there was movement. The rest of the teachers closed the space between them, eyes searching all around.

"I can smell it," announced Frances Chavron.

"The vetala?" whispered Salvador.

The vampire nodded.

Salvador was about to alert Agnes when something horrific emerged from behind a tree.

"Burning broomsticks!" shrieked Bell.

The hunched figure sniffed at the air and the group froze in response, not daring to move in case of an attack. As though sensing their whereabouts, the creature crouched, slinking out of the shadows of the trees. The group held their breath as they took in the nightmarish monstrosity before them.

The creature possessed a humanoid skull, and its body was not unlike that of a tall, lanky human being.

Except that its back was permanently bent, its spine curved into a half moon shape, forcing its long arms to act as a secondary pair of legs to help it propel itself along the ground. Its skin was thin, almost translucent, and it bore no clothing. As it crawled towards them, they could see the creature's blue and red veins pumping through its body like a distorted roadmap. It stopped and sniffed at the air again. Its nostrils bore only two slits that flared open as it breathed in and out. Its bony arms were long, hanging down by its clawed feet, and long, knife-like fingernails protruded from each digit.

Someone in the group moved, making the creature snap its head towards them. Its milky white eyes stared in their direction, whilst its lipless mouth snapped open, revealing a set of long fangs. It made a chattering sound deep in its throat. Was it calling to others?

"What are we waiting for? Attack!" Frances Chavron ran forward, his own fangs extending to their full length.

The others ran after him, yelling at the vetala. The creature hissed angrily, not expecting its prey to put up a fight, before disappearing back into the shadows of the forest.

"What's happening, can you see?" Magnus stretched over Lucas and Isaac to see what was going on outside the van's windscreen.

"They've run after it!" cried Lucas.

Magnus squeezed past the boys, pressing his forehead up against the glass. "How can you see anything, it's so dark?"

"Did you see the vetala?" asked Luna. She had remained beside the little girl, watching over her with a concerned expression.

The child lay across two seats, her eyes still closed; she hadn't responded since they had brought her in. A cut on her forehead was drawing the attention of the Corsan siblings, and Luna watched as they licked their lips, not once taking their eyes off the girl. Luna drew closer to the child, determined to protect her.

"I think I did," said Lucas. "But everything happened so quickly, and then the teachers and the twins ran off into the forest."

"I can't believe they have just left us," moaned Tamara. "Are the doors locked?"

Magnus reached over to the driver's side and clicked the button down. "They are now."

Belinda leaned over the unfamiliar girl and began to gently move the girl's head from side to side, studiously inspecting her face.

"What are you doing?" asked Luna.

"Checking for bites," replied Belinda.

"You think she's infected?" Tamara backed away. If she was pretending not to be scared, her face wasn't particularly convincing.

The Corsan siblings edged closer.

"Keep back you two!" warned Luna.

"It's too tempting," cried Ava. "You don't know how

hard it is to control the urge once you smell fresh blood."

"I'm sure you'll get used to it. Now back off." Belinda's tone was final as she glared at the two siblings. Then, satisfied that they were not going to attack the unconscious child, Belinda resumed her inspection. "She's clean. Fortunately for her, it looks like the vetala hasn't eaten yet."

"Well, that's good news," sighed Luna with relief.

"But if it hasn't eaten, there's still time for one of us to be its dinner," squirmed Tamara.

"I think the teachers will have caught him by now," said Lucas, turning away from the window. But just as he did, he spotted movement by the edge of the forest. "I don't want to scare you guys, but I think there's someone out there watching us."

"Are you sure it's not the teachers coming back?" asked Magnus.

Lucas backed away from the front of the van. "Not unless they've all changed into black capes…"

Belinda barged past the boys to the front of the van and peered out of the windscreen. Almost instantly, she began to back away, the look of fear on her face telling the others everything they needed to know.

"I-it's them," she whimpered, scrambling towards the back of the van, knocking over the other children in her haste. "They've finally found me."

Chapter 29

The children ran to the back of the van, their scrambling making the vehicle rock back and forth. They pushed Luna to the front in their panic, knowing that she was more powerful than the rest of them, though whether she was powerful enough was a question that echoed through everyone's minds. Petty as ever, Tamara Hobbs pushed Belinda out from the huddle, making her collide into the back of Luna.

"I deserved that," Belinda grumbled to Luna.

Luna turned to her. "Stop thinking that all of this is your fault. We are all here to protect one another; we need to start acting like guardians instead of cowards." She raised her voice for Tamara's benefit.

"And what do you expect us to do?" snapped Tamara.

Luna could hear a hint of fear in the witch's voice. "Defend ourselves," she replied.

All the children turned and looked at one another. But before they could act upon their response, the camper van shook from side to side, slowly at first, then gaining speed as the children were jolted back and forth. They could hear cheers and laughter coming from outside the van as the band of witches continued their onslaught. Then, just quickly as it had started, the rocking stopped. The children held onto each other, their eyes darting between the windows on either side of the van.

A metallic screeching sound made them all shriek in terror, and Belinda's eyes popped with fear as a hand bearing long, razor sharp nails scraped along the metal that separated them from the evil outside.

"Come out, come out, my little traitor."

Belinda's eyes widened with horror. Luna held onto her arm, giving it a squeeze to let her know that she was there.

"We know you're in there…"

Cackles of laughter erupted from either side of the camper van.

Tamara gave Belinda an almighty shove. "She's here, come and take her!" she called out.

The other children turned to glare at her, and Luna's aquamarine eyes grew dark as they bored into Tamara's.

Tamara looked down, disconcerted by Luna's fierce gaze. "I only said what everyone here is thinking. Come on, it's only her they're interested in."

"No, we are all in this together," declared Luna, curling up her fists, ready to do some serious damage to

Tamara if she didn't shut up.

Belinda pushed forward. "She's right, Luna. I started all this. It's up to me to finish it."

But just as she began to walk towards the front of the van, the door screeched open, and a hooded figure peered through the doorway. Belinda backed away as the head slowly turned to look at her.

"Ah, there you are traitor."

The rest of the witch's body climbed inside the van. She was cloaked from head to toe in a long black robe, and her eyes, like Belinda's, were accented with heavy black eyeliner. As she flung her hood back, her long, poker-straight black hair was revealed, along with a face as white as chalk, which made her black lipstick stand out from her face like a bruise.

"The teachers are on their way back," warned Belinda, her voice trembling.

The witch let out a hearty laugh as she walked towards the group. "No, they're not. We just saw them heading deeper into the forest."

Luna noted that the witch was not much taller than herself, and not much older, though with her heavy makeup it was hard to tell. She wore black from head to toe, from her slashed, fitted top to her thick, chunky rubber heeled boots, laced up to her mid-calf.

The witch held out her hand, exposing her long black talons. "Come with us, Belinda, you don't belong here with them."

"No!" shouted Belinda. "Leave me alone, Talia, I won't go with you!"

The other witch drew closer, her face scrunching up with rising anger. "How dare you speak my name!"

"Did you think I wouldn't tell them who you are?" snarled Belinda.

The witch laughed, dropping her hand. "They know us as the Sisters of Jonas."

"How original," scoffed Luna.

The witch flicked her dark eyes towards Luna. She seemed to study her for a few minutes, taking in the girl's appearance. "So, this is what a Celestian looks like in the flesh?" She edged closer to Luna, sniffing the air between them. "Ah, that explains the sweetness I could smell in the forests." She turned her head to look over her shoulder. "Sisters, come in and have a look at this. We seem to have found ourselves an even greater prize."

Two more cloaked figures entered the van, both of them taller than Talia. One of them sported a short bob of dark purple hair, and the other wore her vibrant pillar-box red locks in an intricate braid. Like Talia, both of them had deathly pale features, and their lips were adorned with thick, black lipstick.

"Is that really what I think it is?" said the red-haired witch, staring hungrily at Luna.

"Tell the other sisters to look out for the teachers," ordered Talia.

"Don't worry, they're keeping watch," said the purple-haired witch.

The next few moments passed in silence, as the groups stared each other out, until Magnus finally succeeded in pushing his way through to stand in front of the girls.

"It's time you left," he ordered.

Talia looked him up and down, before bursting into a cacophony of laughter. The other two joined in.

"Huh, you sound just like a cackling bunch of witches," Magnus scoffed, undeterred.

Talia abruptly stopped, followed by the other two. "And who might you be?" she sneered.

"My name is irrelevant."

"Magnus Scully," called out Tamara from behind him.

Magnus snapped his head around to scowl at her, making her flinch.

"Well, well, we have ourselves a wannabe hero," sniggered Talia.

Someone coughed in the background. Talia and the other two peered over the children's shoulders.

"Ah, I see you have our bait."

"She's staying here with us," Magnus insisted.

"Now, now. Your boyish features don't suit being angry. You are far too cute to scrunch them up like that." Talia looked down at the little girl, who remained unconscious. "You can keep her. The vetala probably had a bite already. We're not here for her." Talia's eyes darted back to Belinda.

"I'm not going anywhere with you," said Belinda, her voice stronger now that she had both Luna and Magnus by her side.

Talia sized her up, seemingly unbothered by Belinda's significant height advantage, before turning to Luna. "If I'd known a Celestian would be here, I would have prepared more for this meeting—"

"Sisters! The others are heading back!"

It was the first time since the witches had arrived that Luna witnessed a look of fear pass over Talia's face. The other two witches turned and ran for the door, but Talia wasn't giving up so easily, grabbing onto Belinda's hand and dragging her towards the exit.

"NO!" screamed Belinda, trying frantically to pull away from the other witch.

Instinctively, Talia took out her wand and pointed it at Belinda, preparing to utter an incantation, while Magnus leapt towards them and grabbed Belinda's other hand, trying to pull her further inside. In that moment, the van began to vibrate, and within seconds, it slowly began to lift off the ground entirely. Everyone screamed and Talia dropped her wand, instantly releasing Belinda to try and retrieve it. The other two witches were hanging out of the doorway of the van, their legs dangling frantically.

Belinda snatched her arm away from Talia and

turned to find Luna. Her instincts were right; Luna stood rigid, her hands clasped around her crystal necklace. Her aquamarine eyes centred on the trio of witches. It was she who was making the van levitate.

Talia quickly picked up her wand, before turning to use it against her foes. She paused when she saw Luna's stance. Once again, a look of fear crossed her face, and she turned towards the exit, grabbed her two comrades, and leapt out of the van.

Belinda tried to follow them, clinging to the chairs as she tried to make her way along the aisle of the shaking van. But she was too late. By the time she reached the door, the witches were nowhere to be seen. Suddenly, the van dropped to the ground, almost making Belinda fall out of the open door.

Once they had all righted themselves, the rest of the children all gaped at the Celestian. Then, a cheer erupted.

"Well done, Luna!" they all yelled, except Tamara, who was sulking at the back of the van.

"What happened here?" Agnes Guthrie stuck her head through the open door of the van.

The teacher's had finally returned.

Chapter 30

Luna knocked lightly on the door of the medical room, and moments later, a tired and dishevelled Bell Tilly answered.

"Is it okay to come in?" asked Luna, peering over the young teacher's shoulder. She could just make out a slight form lying on the bed in the centre of the room.

Bell nodded, opening the door wider to allow Luna to enter.

"How is she?" asked Luna, as she made her way over to the bed.

Bell shook her weary head. "I've been up all night monitoring the girl. She seems fine, and thankfully, no bite marks from the vetala."

"Has she woken yet?"

"Yes, I have spoken with her briefly. But her experience has left her incredibly shaken, so I think it's best if we leave her to sleep for as long as we can. It will help her mind adjust to her ordeal."

Luna studied the sleeping girl. Her pale face was

blotchy with tear stains, and dark circles hung beneath both eyes.

"It must have been terrifying coming face to face with such a monstrosity," continued Bell.

Luna was about to voice her agreement when she sensed movement. The girl was stirring from her sleep. Edging closer, Luna watched as the girl's eyelids fluttered open. It took a few moments for her eyes to adjust, but once her gaze settled on Luna, the girl recoiled, pushing herself up against the bed's headboard.

"It's okay, she's a friend," soothed Bell, sitting herself gently on the edge of the bed.

Luna stepped back as Bell fussed over the girl. She felt terrible that she had scared her; she knew her appearance wasn't exactly your average look.

"I-it's okay," croaked the girl. She sat forward, allowing Bell to puff up her pillows, before looking at Luna. "I'm Clarissa, nice to meet you."

"Luna," replied the young Celestian, smiling warmly.

Bell checked the small bandage on the girl's forehead. "Cut's clearing up quicker than expected."

Clarissa muttered her thanks to the young teacher as Bell placed the bandage back over the wound. Luna thought back to when the Corsan siblings had smelt her blood, and opened her mouth to tell Bell about the incident, before quickly deciding against it. The last thing the girl needed right now was to discover that she was living under the same roof as a pair of bloodthirsty vampires.

"Do you feel like talking?" asked Bell.

The girl shrugged. "I guess so."

"Shall I fetch Mrs Guthrie?" asked Luna.

"No, it's fine. The fewer people the better," said Bell. Turning to the girl, she asked, "How old are you?"

"Nine," she replied.

Luna detected a soft northern accent that matched the accents of the witches they had encountered in the forest.

"Do you remember how you got here?" continued Bell.

"I-I don't know… I remember being approached by a group of strange-looking women. They lured me into a forest, and then…" The girl shook.

"It's okay," soothed Bell. "Take your time."

Luna frowned. "Where did they find you exactly?"

Clarissa wrinkled her forehead. "Here, I guess."

"Where is here exactly?" Bell gave her a stern look, but Luna, deciding to ignore her, carried on. "It's just that your accent is from the north of England, the same as Belinda's, which doesn't make sense if you're from around here."

"I-I don't know… I don't remember… maybe they kidnapped me back in England…"

"But wouldn't you remember? Surely you have a

home and a family somewhere?"

Bell took Luna's arm and dragged her out of the room, waiting until they were out of earshot before turning on her.

"What is your problem? The poor girl has been through enough without you interrogating her."

Luna shrugged. "Don't you think it all seems suspicious? I mean, how did she end up here? She's clearly not a local, so what happened? Did the witches bring her with them?

"She could be visiting with her family. We do get tourists you know."

"But her accent is exactly the same as Belinda's, don't you think that's a bit too much of a coincidence? And why doesn't she remember anything?"

"Luna, please! The poor girl has been through a terrible time; she's probably suffering from temporary amnesia as a result of the trauma. Where she is from is irrelevant. Once she has regained her strength, we will try to restore her memory and return her to her family. In the meantime, I think it is best that you leave her alone." Before Luna could comment, Bell stepped back inside the room, closing the door in her face.

Sighing, Luna trudged down the hallway to the games room to find Belinda and the others.

"Well, that was clever," said Belinda, after Luna filled her in.

"Why? Don't you agree? Clarissa has the same

accent as you and the Sisters of Jonas. Don't you think that's strange?"

"I haven't heard her speak yet," shrugged Belinda. "Why does it matter anyway? Maybe they just brought her with them."

Luna looked over at the boys playing on the Xbox. "It makes little sense, that's all. Why go to the trouble of kidnapping a girl from their area and travelling with her all the way here? It makes it sound so pre-planned, which means they must have known about the escaped vetala before they came over."

Belinda seemed to think about this. "Who knows… maybe it's just a coincidence?"

Voices from the hallway drifted in through the open doorway of the games room, drawing Luna's attention. She could just make out the Corsan siblings talking to Sebastian Chavron. The siblings seemed to be hanging onto his every word. Luna caught a few words, including fresh blood and meat, and she wondered whether Sebastian was trying to teach them how to manage their thirst after the previous night's incident. She sincerely hoped that was the case. The last thing they needed was a threat from within their own ranks.

Luna sighed again. Why were they all sitting around doing nothing when there were bloodthirsty killers out in their forests? They should be planning their next move, not just waiting around for the vetala or the witches to find them again. Luna's mind drifted back to the grimoire. What if the witches found it before they did? What would happen then? Unless the grimoire was nothing more than a fairy tale.

Luna got to her feet, leaving the games room and heading down the hallway towards Mrs Guthrie's office. She was tired of all this confusion. She needed answers. But as she reached the door and prepared to knock, a familiar voice drifted through from the other side. Luna listened for a moment, scratching at her memories. Not that long ago, she was certain she had spoken to this person. But who were they?

Like a lightbulb switching on, she finally remembered. But it couldn't be… she had only spoken to this person when Nana Violet had conjured him up. Shaking her head, Luna turned the handle, pushing her way into the office. Agnes Guthrie was standing before a long, ornate, bronze mirror. But it wasn't her own reflection staring back.

"Mr Blackhill!"

Chapter 31

Agnes Guthrie rushed over, pulling Luna into the office and quietly closing the door behind them.

"Come closer, my dear. Let me see you in your true form," said the familiar voice from the mirror.

Luna's legs felt like lead as Agnes guided her towards the mirror.

"I-I don't understand," stuttered Luna. "How is this even possible?"

"There isn't much to understand, my dear. Remember when your Nana Violet contacted Mr Blackhill's spirit through an incantation spell last summer?" said Agnes.

Luna nodded.

"Well, that's exactly what I have done, except I've used this mirror to manifest Mr Blackhill. After I discovered how easy it was to contact Mr Blackhill's spirit, I came up with this idea."

"Please, Agnes, call me Edward, we're amongst

friends."

Luna shuffled closer to the mirror. The old head teacher was the same age as when she had last seen him in her nana's kitchen, though his attire was slightly different; today, he was dressed in light brown trousers and a tweed blazer. His tall stature took up the full mirror's reflection, giving the illusion that the young Edward Blackhill really was standing before them.

"How are you?" asked Luna.

"As well as one can be when dead," chuckled the young Edward. He gave her a warm smile. "I hear that your powers are becoming stronger?"

Luna nodded. "Yes, sir. I have recently learnt how to use the moon as a power source."

Edward scratched his chin. "Ah yes, that makes sense. Has your father been back to the manor?"

Luna shook her head.

"Hmm, I can understand why he wants to lead a normal existence, but I'd have thought he would have stayed a little longer to help you settle in to your new abilities."

"He started a new job, sir, and didn't want to risk losing it."

"Please, call me Edward."

Luna and Agnes looked on as Edward walked in circles. Now and then, he would disappear from view, confusing them. Realising his mistake, he quickly popped back.

"Ah sorry, I keep forgetting I'm not in the same room," he chuckled.

"Edward, the reason I summoned you was to ask if there is any truth to the rumour that the grimoire was stolen."

Mrs Guthrie's voice was calm, but Luna could detect a hint of desperation in her tone. Luna looked at her, then back to Edward. She wanted to know the answer just as much as her headmistress did.

"Yes, I believe so. The last time it was seen was when the manor was first built."

"And who was the last person to see it?" asked Agnes.

"Good question." Edward paced again, remaining in view this time. "I would like to say it was myself, but unfortunately, I have never held the book. The fae guarded it with their lives. Originally, I believe it was passed from realm to realm, but the constant fear of it ending up in the wrong hands took its toll, and the fae took it upon themselves to guard it."

"So how do you know it actually exists?" asked Luna.

"I first learnt of the grimoire when I was apprenticed to Jonas Schmidt. He spoke about it in one of his alchemy tutorials. As students, we considered it to be the holy grail of magick." Edward stopped pacing. "The grimoire has been around since the Earth's creation, and the athame was its partner in crime."

Agnes and Luna's eyes popped wider.

"The athame is millions of years old?" gasped Luna.

"Why of course! It controls the darker elements of this world. The evil entities of the realms we are fighting against were here long before humans walked the Earth."

"How come you never taught us any of this while you were still alive?" asked Agnes.

"Unfortunately, I am still learning. The spirit realm is a rich source of knowledge, and I am constantly coming across new information."

"So, there is no point in seeking the Tree Man," said Agnes, more to herself than to the room as a whole.

"You want to speak to the Oak King?" said Edward, startled.

Agnes went on to explain about her conversation with Benjamin Faulkner, and how he had suggested they seek the advice of the Tree Man.

"I can understand where Benjamin is coming from, but the grimoire, as I have just explained, originates from the Earth's creation. It was made from the first saplings that grew on Earth. The Oak King will not be able to assist you in finding the origins of the grimoire, though he may be able to help you in other ways."

"Where would we find the Oak King, if we do wish to find him?" asked Agnes.

Edward scratched his chin, raising his eyebrows. "Well, that is easy. He can be found in one of the oldest forests in Scotland."

"Scotland," repeated Agnes, more to herself.

"Okay, what else do you know?" asked Luna. "Where did the athame come from?"

"I have an inkling, but I do not wish to elaborate until I find out more from my spiritual teachers. When I do learn more, I will inform you of my findings. In fact, it would be useful to speak to all the children about this matter. Perhaps I could take over one of Archie's history classes."

"Like a virtual lecture?"

Edward laughed. "Yes, something like that, but I would be here in this mirror, at the front of the classroom."

"That is a superb idea," said Agnes. "It would be great for the children to meet you in person." Realising her mistake, Agnes laughed. "Well, almost in person."

The three of them laughed in unison.

"I look forward to that." Edward's tone became grave. "On a more serious note, I need you to be very careful about entering the forests."

"Because of the vetala?" asked Agnes.

Scratching his chin, Edward stared back out at them with a haunted expression. "Unfortunately, I sense this creature isn't the only thing roaming the forests."

Agnes shook her head, making her neat chignon sway back and forth. "We have already had the pleasure of meeting Jonas Schmidt's fan club."

"Yes, so I heard... but I sense there is someone else lurking in the shadows." Edward paused. "I fear Winnie is still here."

Agnes walked over to the mirror, stopping inches from the late Edward Blackhill's reflection. "But that is impossible..."

"Wouldn't she be at least over a hundred years old?" asked Luna.

Edward shook his head. "Does that really mean anything? I mean, look around you." Edward splayed his arms out. "Everything is possible in this magickal existence."

"Fair point," muttered Luna.

"What does she want?" asked Agnes. "The missing grimoire?"

Edward moved closer to the glass. "If the secrets of the grimoire are true, and a spell to destroy the darker portals exists within those pages, then we need to find it as soon as possible."

"But if such a spell existed, wouldn't the fae have given it to you to cast years ago?" asked Luna.

"The grimoire will not reveal its secrets to the fae, nor any creature of the light. The fae were protecting it against the darkness. Until it went missing."

"So, the grimoire is evil?" asked Luna.

Edward shrugged. "Not all of it. They say its creator was the ruler of the dark realms, but again, this is something I am learning more of as we speak."

"But wasn't it the devil himself who gave it to the witch, Elizabeth Drake, in the seventeenth century?"

"That is the story witches are told as children. But its creator could not use the book for his own selfish needs. He could only access the magick within via another powerful being. Elizabeth Drake is the ancestor of Winnie O'Toole."

"The nurse Winnie?" gasped Luna.

Edward nodded his young head. "Again, I have only just learnt of this knowledge. I discovered that Winnie's surname was actually Drake, making her a relative of the late Elizabeth."

"But could it just be a coincidence that they have the same surname?" asked Agnes.

"No, they are most definitely related. And my instincts are telling me she was the one who took the grimoire."

"If she did, then isn't she the rightful owner, since they gave it to her ancestor?" added Agnes.

"Not entirely. It belongs somewhere safe, away from the darker realms. If Winnie is a supporter of Jonas Schmidt, then her intentions for the grimoire are not good."

"We have spoken to the wickles, and they tell us they have not seen or heard of the missing grimoire in these forests," said Luna.

"You did well to seek out the guardians of the trees, but their knowledge on the grimoire is less applicable than that of the Oak King." Edward turned his head to look behind him. "I must go, I fear it won't be long until more vetalas escape."

Agnes rushed forward. "Wait! Should I seek out the Oak King?"

But already Edward's reflection had misted over, leaving Luna and Agnes to stand in silence, staring back at their own reflections.

Chapter 32

Agnes sent Luna back to her room with more questions than answers, after asking her to keep their conversation with Edward Blackhill a secret until further notice. She was glad Belinda wasn't in their room when she arrived, for she knew she wouldn't have been able to keep her mouth shut about what she had just witnessed in Mrs Guthrie's office.

Luna stood before the window between their two beds, staring out into the gardens. Her eyes scanned over the familiar sculptures. The snow had thoroughly melted away, restoring the gardens to their normal appearance. She longed for the spring when the flowers would break through the soil with their amazing displays of colours. Although she loved the snow and how magical it looked, she wasn't one for the cold.

Her eyes moved further up to the perimeter, where the gardens met the forest. If you squinted your eyes a certain way, you could almost make out the radar of magick that protected them from the dangers beyond. It looked like a heat wave; a distortion of invisible curves dancing above hot tarmac.

It had always astounded Luna that the invisible barrier acted like a one-way mirror, whereby they could see the forests beyond the manor, but from within the forests, the manor was hidden from view, with the invisible barrier making it look as though there was nothing but trees there. Anyone looking at the manor from the other side of the barrier would not know it was a deception.

Luna's thoughts drifted back to last summer, when she had thought she had seen a dark figure standing at the forest's edge, looking up at the manor, watching. How could this be if they could only see the forest's reflection? How did they know the manor was right there?

"Winnie," she whispered. "Only she would know the secrets of the manor and its barrier. But then, if Winnie is hiding in the forests, who is in the painting?"

"Who are you talking to?"

Luna spun around to see Belinda strolling through the door.

"Eh, nobody. Just thinking out loud."

Belinda scrunched up her features. "Okay, I still stand by my first impression of you, weirdo."

Luna gestured to herself, then to Belinda. "Pot. Kettle." She laughed, eyeing up the witch's hair. The goth had recently learnt a spell to enhance the colour, saving her a fortune on bleach and hair dye.

Belinda waved a hand in the air, dismissing her roommate's mockery.

Still laughing to herself after leaving their room, Luna went to look for Magnus, assuming he would still be in the games room. But as she reached the foyer, she thought she saw the new arrival, Clarissa, making her way along the corridor towards the dining room. No one was around, though she could hear the familiar sound of the boys shouting and cheering from the games room. Instead of going to join them, Luna turned and followed the girl, wondering why she was out of bed. She knew Mrs Guthrie had gathered the rest of the teachers for a meeting, but why was this girl making her way towards their meet up? Unless they had asked her to join?

Not convinced with this last thought, Luna sneaked towards the corridor that led to the dining room and listened out. She could just about make out Mrs Guthrie's voice drifting down the hallway, but when Luna peeked around the corner, she couldn't see the girl outside the dining room doors. That's strange, she thought. She hadn't heard the girl knock, and if she had entered unannounced, Luna would surely have heard the doors creaking open. Thankful for the carpeted floors, Luna sidled along the wall, stopping outside the giant doors and placing her ear against the wood. The sound of a heated debate ensuing greeted her. Clearly the teachers were struggling to come to an agreement.

Perhaps Clarissa had turned the corner, and was eavesdropping through the walls of one of the teacher's offices in the next corridor?

Slowly edging her way past the dining room doors, Luna crept along the corridor until she reached the corner. There, she stopped. She could just make out an unfamiliar voice, and then Clarissa answering. Perhaps one of the teacher's had left the meeting to talk to her? Except that Luna didn't recognise the voice. Peering around the corner, she could just make out a lone figure, facing the wall, aiming their animated gestures at the painting on the wall outside Mrs Guthrie's office. Luna's stomach dropped. Clarissa was talking to the person in the forest painting.

Luna was about to step out and confront the girl, when suddenly, someone from behind grabbed her, and an icy hand clasped across her mouth, preventing her from screaming.

"Shh."

Luna swung around to face her assailant. "Lily!" she hissed.

Lily Jackson quickly grabbed her by the arm, leading her away from prying ears. Once they reached the foyer, Lily turned to her.

"You're going to ruin things!"

"What do you mean?" hissed Luna.

"Come on, we can't talk here."

Lily dragged Luna back to their room, startling

Belinda as they burst in through the door.

"Are you going to explain to me why you stopped me!" shouted Luna.

"What's going on?" asked Belinda.

Luna stood in the middle of the room with her arms crossed, her face furious. "That girl, Clarissa, was talking to someone in the forest painting, but this one here stopped me from saying something."

"What?" Belinda looked shocked.

"The only reason I stopped you was so you didn't ruin my spying," explained Lily.

"Ruin your spying? If we had approached her, we could have stopped her there and then!" snapped Luna.

"Guys, please." Belinda held both hands up as she stood between the squabbling pair.

Luna and Lily turned their backs on each other.

Looking between the two of them, Belinda tried to process what was going on. "Wait… so you're saying Clarissa was talking to the person hiding in the painting?"

The two girls turned around, nodding slowly.

"And neither of you thought to approach her?"

"I was trying to," said Luna. "But this one stopped me."

"Like I said, I was trying to spy on her, to see who she was talking to. I was worried that if we approached her she would just deny all knowledge, and we would never find out who is in that painting."

"Did you recognise the other person's voice?" asked Belinda.

"No, I had only been there a few minutes when Luna appeared."

"You're a ghost, surely you could have just made yourself invisible," Luna huffed.

Lily shook her head. "I was worried she would sense me. Some powerful witches and other magickal beings can do that."

"But she's a little girl! She can't be that powerful. You're just a chicken."

"No I'm not! Just because she's younger than us, doesn't mean she isn't powerful."

"Guys!"

Lily and Luna jumped at the sound of the young witch's holler.

"Pack it in, will you? We'll never get anywhere if you two don't stop bickering."

The two girls looked down with guilty expressions, until Luna plucked up the courage to speak.

"I'm sorry. Belinda's right. We won't get anywhere if all we do is fight amongst ourselves." Sitting down at the top of her bed, she patted the covers, offering Lily a seat.

After a second of consideration, Lily joined her.

Belinda sat across from them. "Okay, if we are going to find out who this traitor is, we need to teach Lily to conceal herself from powerful magickal beings."

Lily slumped her head forward. "Believe me, I've tried."

Luna absentmindedly fiddled with her crystal around her neck as she tried to think of what to do.

"That's it!"

Both Luna and Lily jumped.

"Why don't you use your crystal to make yourself invisible," said Belinda. "I mean, you used it to become part fish to find the onyx crystal in the vanishing lake."

"Good idea!" Lily jumped to her feet. "Luna's way more powerful than I am. I bet if you make yourself invisible, she won't be able to sense you."

Luna held her crystal protectively with both hands. "I don't know… that was a while ago now. I don't know if I can do it." Closing her eyes, she cupped the clear crystal between the palms of her hands. After a few moments, a white mist appeared around her body, creating a halo effect.

"Wow," exclaimed Belinda. "It's like an aura."

Only seconds after the mist had appeared, it slowly faded away.

Luna opened her eyes. "It never lasts long. No matter how much I try, I can't seem to raise the same vibrations as I did when I became part fish."

"You need to remember how you felt when you did," explained Belinda. "Most powerful magick requires a strong emotion to make it work."

Luna thought for a moment. "Okay, hang on. Let me

try again." Luna closed her eyes again, and as before, a halo of light appeared around her body. Then, quite suddenly, Luna disappeared.

"What just happened?" cried Belinda.

The two girls rushed to their feet, waving their arms in front of them, expecting to come into contact with their friend.

"Luna, are you there?" called Belinda frantically.

They listened out, but no reply came back.

"This was a stupid idea!" cried Lily.

Just then, they heard a low swooshing sound, and Luna suddenly reappeared.

"What the—" began Belinda.

"Whoa, I'm never doing that again!" exclaimed Luna.

"Where did you go?" asked Lily.

"Nowhere."

"How can you just go nowhere?" asked Belinda.

"Like I said, I popped into oblivion, or at least, that's where I think it was."

"I thought you were supposed to be turning yourself invisible?"

Luna shook her head. "I tried, but I just ended up in this pitch-dark nothingness."

"Hmm, well, I guess that won't work. Unless Luna wants to practise some more, I can try and find us an invisibility spell."

"Do you think you can do one?" asked Lily.

Belinda sniggered. "If I can make a necromancy spell, then I'm sure an invisibility spell will be a walk in the park."

The other two shrugged. "Good point."

"Tomorrow we have Miss Tilly's class, so that gives me an opportunity to smuggle some herbs for the spell."

"Great, while you work out a spell, we'll do a bit of investigating ourselves," said Lily.

"Doing what?" asked Luna. "I thought we weren't going to follow Clarissa until we suss out the invisibility spell?"

"Yes… but there are other things we can investigate."

"Like what?" said Belinda looking up from her book of shadows.

"Like where Aengus and Murdoch hide the chocolate biscuits in the kitchen!"

Belinda and Luna both rolled their eyes, until they remembered Lily couldn't eat anything.

Lily laughed and shrugged. "What? I just like driving Murdoch crazy."

☽

The raven plucked at the last tendril of flesh from his chosen fresh meal. Satisfied that it had depleted his hunger for the day, Poe thought of his warm bed back at the manor. The winter sun was already fading behind the treetops. It was time to head home to roost.

Hopping up to the highest branch, Poe stretched out his wings and propelled himself into the air, his beady eyes searching ahead. Soaring high above the trees, he eventually spotted a familiar sight, one that he understood was the doorway to his master and safety. He let out his call, a guttural squawk, as he prepared for the strange impact of being sucked through an invisible barrier.

He flapped his impressive wingspan faster as he prepared to take the plunge, when suddenly, something shot up from below, hitting him directly in the centre of his chest. The raven immediately descended to the ground, spiralling headfirst like a gunned down fighter plane. Then, just as Poe was about to hit the forest floor, he suddenly vanished, and where his body should have collided, a large black feather appeared, floating slowly to the ground.

Chapter 33

"The coast is clear."

Luna poked her head around the corner that led into the kitchens. To her horror, Lily was already making her way over to the large industrial fridge.

"Psst, what are you doing?"

Lily opened the fridge door. "Looking for snacks, duh."

Luna ducked down and scurried into the kitchen, hiding underneath the high worktops.

"I thought you were only joking when you said we should sneak into the kitchens," she hissed when she reached her ghostly friend.

Lily chuckled. "I thought you knew me by now."

"Yeah, so did I."

"Ooh." Lily's eyes lit up and she reached a hand inside the fridge, fumbling about for a minute. Eventually, she pulled something out from the very back.

"What's that?"

Lily shrugged as she unwrapped the suspicious package. "Ugh, it's raw meat," she squirmed, throwing it back into the fridge.

"Can you smell that?" asked Luna.

Lily turned to her friend. "Of course I can. I may be dead, but I'm not completely senseless." She tilted her head to the side for a minute, then reached back into the fridge to retrieve the meat. "You know this might be of use after all."

"Why?" Luna asked. Then it clicked. "If you're thinking what I think you are, no. Not a good idea."

Lily chuckled. "But it would be funny just to see their reaction."

"If dangling a bit of raw meat in front of the Corsan siblings is your idea of fun then leave me out of it."

"I just want to see if they have fangs yet."

Luna shook her head at her friend.

Lily shrugged, closing the fridge door and looking around. "The pantry, of course!" Lily floated over to the other side of the kitchen towards a door. "That must be where the biscuits are." Lily grasped onto the door handle and yanked it open.

"ROAR!"

Lily screamed as something small and green jumped out at her.

It took a moment for Luna to realise what was actually going on, and when she did, she buckled over with laughter.

"How did you—"

"A knew yeh were up to nae good." Murdoch marched out of the pantry and stared menacingly up at the two girls.

"B-but I saw you leave," cried Lily.

"I'm an imp. We can disappear then reappear in a different place."

"Really? I never knew that," said Luna.

"Have yeh not learnt anythin yet in yer classes?'

Both girls shrugged.

"I was told imps can shape shift, and that they have wings, like a gargoyle," said Lily. She craned her neck to see behind the imp.

Murdoch's green tinted face became tinged with red. "Well, this imp ain't like the others!"

"How come?" asked Luna.

To their surprise, the imp lifted his shirt over his head. The two girls instinctively turned away, but when Murdoch said 'ta da' they both dared to peek. The imp had his back turned towards them, revealing two tiny stumps that sat on either side of his shoulder blades.

"Where are your wings?" gasped Lily.

Murdoch waved his tiny hands above his head and a burst of bright light exploded before them. When the girls opened their eyes, they could hear a flapping sound.

"Wow, they are, um…" began Lily.

"Spectacular," finished Luna.

The imp looked smug as he flapped his gargoyle like wings. The stone-coloured grey scales looked sparse in some parts, and the wings weren't as wide as the girls had expected.

"But why do you hide them?" asked Luna.

"Isn't it obvious," whispered Lily by her side.

Luna tried to hide her distaste, but her friend was right; they were not the prettiest of wings. In fact, they reminded her of the wings of an enormous insect. But wanting to spare Murdoch the embarrassment, she gently nudged Lily, whispering to her to keep her thoughts to herself. It was obvious the imp was proud of his natural enhancement.

"I hide them cos I ain't git a top that will fit through them. I get freezin yeh see. An' they git in the way of ma work." Another ball of light burst into the air, and Murdoch was suddenly wearing his oversized shirt again. "Anyhoo, that's not why we are here, is it Miss Jackson?" The imp tapped his tiny foot impatiently against the stone floor.

"We were looking for ingredients for baking," lied Lily.

"And have yeh asked permission tae bake?"

"Eh no, but now that you're here, is it okay if we do?"

"Enough, Lily," snapped Luna. "We were looking for biscuits to steal."

Lily glanced over at her friend. If looks could kill,

thought Luna.

"At least yer honest, Miss Green."

Murdoch turned to Lily and began to berate her, telling her she should be ashamed of herself for trying to steal and even more ashamed for lying.

While Lily was facing the wrath of the imp, Luna felt a weird sensation pass over her. It was a feeling of sheer panic, which continued to rise from the pit of her stomach. But the strange thing was, it wasn't coming from her.

Luna fled from the kitchen, ignoring Murdoch's shouts. The feeling of despair was growing stronger the further she ran, and when she reached the manor's foyer, the feeling became unbearable.

"Poe, where are you?"

Luna looked up towards the landing between the staircases. Belinda stood before the tall window, looking out into the gardens below.

"Are you okay?" called Luna, her heart beating fast.

Belinda swung around at the sound of her voice and hurried down the staircase. "Have you seen Poe anywhere?"

Luna frowned. "No, sorry. Maybe he's out hunting?"

"He's been out for hours, and I can't sense him." The tall girl clenched and unclenched her fists, her anxiety carved into her face. "This isn't like him at all."

"You can't sense him? Not even a little bit?" Luna was concerned now.

"Whatever's wrong?" Bell Tilly emerged from the door leading down to the greenhouse.

"Poe is missing, and I think he's in trouble." Belinda's voice was shrill with panic.

Bell instantly took charge. "Come with me. Let's go into the gardens and have a look."

The two girls followed Bell through the doorway between the staircases, treading carefully down the narrow steps. Luna could feel the heat immediately, radiating from the greenhouse beyond. Bell led them through rows upon rows of plants, the leaves whipping at their faces, until the young teacher stopped at a glass door, mumbling an incantation under her breath. The door whipped open, breaking the magickal barrier, and Bell rushed out into the gardens, followed by Belinda and Luna.

The three of them called Poe's name as they jogged through the gardens, following Belinda as she ran towards the invisible barrier, her voice frantic.

"Poe!"

Bell craned her neck to look up at the sky as Luna wandered towards the gate, sensing something was wrong. But as she was about to place a hand against the invisible barrier surrounding the perimeter of the gardens, it began to vibrate. A sudden feeling of déjà vu overcame her as the surrounding air changed, followed by the sound of the invisible barrier being sucked open.

Luna jumped back as two familiar figures burst

through the magickal barrier beyond the gate. Leonard and Travis Edgar pounced through at the same time, but Luna noticed there was something different about them. The twins were usually jovial after their daily run in the forest, but they both looked terrified, like something had been chasing after them.

"Whatever's the matter?" asked Bell.

Leonard Edgar was bent over, his hands clasping his knees as he panted for breath. Luna and Bell exchanged worried glances.

"Have you seen Poe?" asked Belinda desperately.

Leonard straightened up. "You mean your raven?"

The girl nodded.

Leonard shook his head. "No."

"Did you see anything unusual in the forest?" asked Bell.

The twins looked at one another. Luna noticed that the brothers were sweating profusely. Travis was the one to break the silence, his words fractured by heavy panting.

"M-Miss… I think… I think we may have killed the vetala."

Chapter 34

Bell Tilly hitched her skirts up and bolted towards the manor. Luna and Belinda stayed with the Edgar twins, giving them time to catch their breath, before following their teacher back inside.

Bell almost ran into Salvador as she crashed through the doorway into the greenhouse, scattering the bunch of dried flowers that the warlock had been holding all over the stone floor.

"What on Earth!"

"I'm so sorry, but something important has just happened."

Seconds later, the four children appeared behind Bell. Salvador took one look at the twins and instantly knew something bad had happened. Taking charge, he led them upstairs into the foyer, telling them to go into the kitchens and ask Jeannie Gibbs for water, before marching down the hallway towards Agnes Guthrie's office.

Luna, Belinda and the twins all perched on the high

stools at the countertop, while Jeannie Gibbs fetched cold water from the American style fridge. When the door to the kitchens swung open, all five of them turned their heads to see Agnes, Bell and Salvador, followed by the Chavrons.

Luna felt awkward as the adults crowded around the twins. She looked across to Belinda, who in return looked back at her. They both shrugged, wondering whether they should both leave, but as Luna rose from her stool, Agnes turned away from the twins and smiled.

"It's okay, both you girls can stay."

They moved over to the long rectangular walnut table, each taking a chair. Agnes waited until the Edgar twins had taken a long drink of water before speaking again.

"When you're ready, boys, let us know what happened in the Araig forest," she said soothingly.

Bell seemed on edge, drumming her fingers against the table's surface. Salvador looked over at her from across the table, narrowing his eyes. She took the hint and stopped.

Travis placed his empty glass down, before glancing sideways at his brother. Leonard licked his lips nervously, nodding his head. They were ready to talk.

"We—" They both laughed awkwardly as they spoke at the same time.

"It's okay," Leonard reassured his brother. "I'll tell them. It was me who killed it." Turning his attention to the others, he began to explain. "Travis and I were on our usual run in the forests, you know, in our true forms."

Luna nodded. The twins always went running in their werewolf forms.

Leonard continued. "I stopped running after I picked up an unusual scent. At first, I thought it was a dead animal. You know that sickening smell of rotting flesh?"

This time, it was Frances Chavron who nodded in agreement. Luna shuddered.

"I followed the scent until it got stronger, not realising my brother hadn't stopped along with me." Leonard took another sip of his water, before continuing. "As the smell became even stronger, I was half expecting to come across an animal's corpse, or worse, a human. Then, I saw something move in the undergrowth. It was so pale and grotesque that, at first, I thought I was seeing a naked person who had been injured by something. That's when I saw its eyes, looking up at me from the thick vegetation. The creature had no irises... no pupils. Its eyes were completely white."

Bell made a gasping sound.

"The eyes of a vetala," whispered Frances.

"But how can that be? Don't they only come out at night?" Salvador questioned.

"It is unusual, but not impossible, for them to be out

during the day, especially at dusk when the light is fading." Frances explained.

"What happened next?" asked Agnes, ignoring the two men.

"I-I moved closer, sniffing the air between it and me, and that's when the creature lunged…"

Luna noticed that the boy was trembling. She couldn't blame him. His story was bringing back horrible memories of Amadan.

"Did you get bitten?" asked Frances.

Leonard shook his head. "It never got the chance. I-I attacked, clawing at its throat."

The boy brought his hand up to his face and seemed to study it. That's when Luna and the others noticed the dark reddish-brown stains around his nails.

"Are you sure it's dead?" asked Agnes.

The boy shrugged. "It looked dead."

"We must check immediately!"

Luna jolted as Frances kicked back his chair, causing it to land on its side on the floor. The others nodded in agreement, and Agnes promptly went to alert the other teachers about the twins' ordeal. Agreeing that only a few should go out to investigate, it was decided that Augustus should replace Bell, while Belinda was told to stay behind, with Agnes promising that they would look out for Poe on their way. Luna was instructed to come with the group, much to her disappointment. She hoped the other children wouldn't hold it against her that they always chose her to attend these outings. She never wanted to, but something told her it was for her own benefit.

The group followed the Edgar twins into the forest, and Leonard sniffed the air when they reached the spot where he had last seen the creature. Sure enough, they could just make out a pale form lying amongst the shrubbery. The smell was extremely strong, and Luna knew that she would not forget this scent in a hurry.

Augustus and Frances Chavron approached the spot carefully, whilst Salvador and Agnes held back, their hands covering their noses. Using the end of his cane, Frances poked at the lifeless body.

"It's definitely dead," he announced, pulling the cane away.

Augustus leaned over to get a better look. "What an ugly creature," he snorted.

"So would you be if you had lived for thousands of years on a diet of rodents, or just about anything it can get its teeth into," said Frances.

Augustus rolled his luminous eyes at the vampire. "This must be a valuable reminder of why you choose not to kill for blood."

Frances chuckled, nodding his head. "Why, of course. That's the reason I am still so handsome."

Augustus shook his mane of silver hair.

"What made it come out in the daylight?" asked Agnes. "Hunger?"

Frances knelt down beside the creature's lifeless body. The others cringed at the thought of being so close to the thing. "It looks as though this vetala was already dying when Leonard came upon it."

"So I didn't kill it after all?"

"You may have done it justice, but no, you certainly weren't the cause of its death. No doubt hunger had made it so desperate that it was forced to come out in the daylight."

"Do you think this is the same one we encountered the night we found Clarissa?" asked Agnes.

Frances straightened up. "There's a good chance it is. But let's not rule out the possibility that others may have escaped. There is a lair here somewhere in these forests where this one has been hiding. If we can find out where it is, then we can strike during the daytime and get rid of any others."

"What should we do with the body?" asked Salvador.

"Take it with us."

The group looked at the vampire in horror.

"Whatever for?" snorted Augustus. "We need to burn the corpse and be rid of its filth at once!"

Frances stared down at the shrivelled up vetala. "No, we need to show it to the Architects."

"In Transylvania?" gasped Agnes.

Frances nodded. "Immediately."

Chapter 35

Luna's head was in a whirl, her thirteen-year-old mind overwhelmed by the events of the past few days. Only a year ago, she had been an ordinary teenager, living in Scotland, going about her dull, monotonous existence. And now? Luna stared down at her bed, trying to take in how much had changed. Nothing was the same anymore. Even when she looked in the mirror, she did not see the Luna Green she had been born as. She was part of a bigger story now; she was the only surviving Celestian, besides her father, and a guardian of the athame. But what did that really mean? She knew she was special, but why? What made her different to any of the other children at Blackhill? What was it that her teachers weren't telling her?

"This is amazing, Luna!" Lily exclaimed, floating around her best friend.

Lily's exclamation shocked Luna out of her thoughts, and she turned back to the pile of clothes that now occupied her bed, recommencing her search for her favourite sweatshirt.

"Why? I'm going to Transylvania to meet up with ancient vampires. I could end up as their next meal."

Lily chortled. "Bit extreme. These guys are ancient; as old as the hills. That's why they're called the Architects. They served the original vampire back in the fifteenth century.

"The what?"

"Vlad the Impaler."

Luna stopped what she was doing. "You mean the original Dracula?"

Lily nodded. "These vamps were his dudes. Cool, isn't it?"

"Yeah… terrific. How do you know all of this?"

"Um, I listen in class. Unlike some—"

A knock on their bedroom door stopped Luna from retaliating to her friend's comment.

"Luna, are you ready?" Bell Tilly popped her head through the door.

Luna had spied her blue sweatshirt sticking out from under her bed, and she promptly bent down to retrieve it. "Ready as I'll ever be," she muttered, as she pulled the sweatshirt over her head.

Luna followed Bell to Agnes Guthrie's office. As they entered, Agnes greeted Salvador, Augustus and Frances Chavron. But it was the long bronze mirror that drew her attention the most. Like the last time, a familiar figure smiled back at her through its reflection.

"So nice to see you again, Luna."

"And you," she mumbled to the younger version of Mr Blackhill.

"No time for that, dear," said Agnes, as Luna went to sit down on the only empty seat left. "We have arranged with King Engogabal to travel through the fae tunnels. We don't have time to travel the usual way."

"You know there are other ways to travel?" smirked Frances Chavron.

Agnes nodded. "Yes, but I am afraid we don't have the resources to manifest teleportation. The fae tunnels are quicker and will get us to our destination in half the time."

"Have you considered that the Architects might not allow us to pass through their sacred land?" Salvador enquired.

"We shall arrive a few miles from where the elders live. I have alerted a local by the name of Flavius to expect us. Once we arrive, he will guide us to them," explained Frances.

Agnes clapped her hands. "Right, are we ready?"

"I have one thing to add."

Everyone looked towards the mirror.

Edward peered out at them. "I think taking the body to the elders is a good thing, but I am worried they will not accept that a werewolf caused its death."

"I agree," added Frances. "Vetalas are resilient. They could not be struck down by claws and teeth alone."

302

"Then what killed it?" asked Agnes.

"Like I said in the forest, it was already dying from exposure. These creatures need to remain in their nest of darkness during the light hours. Hopefully the Architects will be able to determine its exact cause of death, and tell us the best way to defeat them, should a swarm of them escape before we find the next crystal," said Frances.

"There is no way I am travelling with that dead corpse. The smell is unbearable!" hissed Augustus.

"I shall bind it with clove magick. That should help with the smell, and will prevent it from decaying any further during our journey to Transylvania," Agnes informed him tartly.

As the group talked in unison, Luna took the opportunity to ask Edward Blackhill a question that had been bothering her since she had first arrived here at the manor.

"Er, Mr Blackhill, do you happen to know anything more regarding my mum?"

Edward edged closer to the mirror. His blue eyes twinkled against the reflection from his wiry spectacles. "I am so sorry Luna, but your mother's whereabouts are still unknown. Her spirit cannot be detected amongst the dead or the living."

Luna eyed him suspiciously. There had been a subtle shift in his expression; she knew he was lying. But what exactly was he hiding from her? And why was the location of her mother's spirit such a big secret? Luna opened her mouth to contest his theory of her not being found, when Agnes quickly interrupted, guiding the girl away from the mirror.

Bidding farewell to Edward, the group made their way outside. Stars twinkled in the clear midnight sky as the group huddled beside the arched door to the manor.

"What are we waiting for?" asked Luna.

Agnes nodded her head towards a looming figure approaching along the driveway. It was carrying something in its arms.

"Ah, thank you my dear friend," Agnes greeted the giant oxman, Urus, as he approached them, carrying the body of the vetala.

Luna squirmed as he placed its body down before them at the top of the steps. This was the first time she had properly looked at the grotesque creature, but now she was wishing she hadn't bothered. Its papery grey skin revealed black veins zig zagging like a road map across its entire naked form. As Urus laid it down, the creature's head lolled to the side, making Luna jump back. White milky eyes stared lifelessly out of a protruding eye socket, and its large, pointy ears flopped on either side of its small, bald head. The vetala's bony arms were long and skinny, but on further inspection, Luna noticed thin webbing underneath the creature's armpit, almost akin to the wings of a bat. The top of its back arched like that of a stretching cat, and its bony legs were twisted together, indistinguishable from one another. The creature's hands and feet were bat-like as well, and featured long, sharp claws. Luna felt sick to her stomach, as her eyes wandered back to its face. The incisors on each side of its lipless mouth curved long and sharp, almost touching its chin area. Luna shuddered as she thought of its favourite meal.

"Stand back!" informed Agnes.

Salvador led Luna down the steps as they watched Agnes wave her wand towards the vetala's body. The corpse floated up into the air and Bell promptly appeared at Agnes' side, chanting softly. With Bell chanting and Agnes waving her wand like a conductor leading an orchestra, they kept their eyes fixed on the vetala as it revolved in mid-air. A ball of twine appeared, twisting around the creature's lifeless body, which rotated like a roast hog on a spit. An aura of white light flowed around the vetala's corpse which Agnes would later explain was clove magick, preserving the body.

The group, minus Bell, walked towards the invisible wall by the side of the manor, the corpse of the vetala floating alongside them. Agnes opened the wall, and the group made their way through the gardens. Dim lights from the manor windows blinked in the darkness, giving them light to guide them towards the second magickal barrier. Luna turned back to look at the manor and saw Lily and Belinda waving down at her from their dormitory room. She gave them a brief wave back before continuing to follow the group, her eyes not once leaving the floating vetala.

Once they reached the forests, they walked for about half an hour, then stopped. Augustus brought out his crystal wand, and a figure appeared from the darkness of the trees.

"Who goes there?" he demanded, holding his wand straight out before him.

"Ain't that a friendly way to welcome your sister from another mister!"

"Dahlia!" cried Luna, running towards the fairy. They hugged for a few moments as the others watched on. "What are you doing here?" she asked, finally letting go.

"Well, King Engogabal gave me orders to come along on your trip to vamp land. He said you'd be needing to use the fae tunnels."

"I'm perfectly capable of using them without my father's servant," retorted Augustus.

"I'm not here for you, I'm here for Luna Green. King's orders. If Luna goes with you, she will need a bodyguard."

"You're going to be my bodyguard?" asked Luna, surprised.

"Yeah, of course. You're pretty important, you know. Plus, it means I get to hang out with my fave gal. I wasn't going to say no, was I?" said the now pink-haired fairy. She nudged Luna in the side, and the two giggled.

"By the way, I prefer your hair pink," whispered Luna to the fairy.

"Are you quite finished?" said Augustus.

"Yes, we really need to press on," said Agnes. "Which one of you is going to open the fae tunnels?"

Dahlia made a mock bow. "Sir, the pleasure is all yours."

Augustus rolled his eyes as he continued to wave his clear crystal wand in the air. The familiar rush of wind hit them in the face as the swirling vortex of the fae tunnels appeared before them. Luna took one last look at the familiar scene they were leaving behind, before taking a step inside the wind tunnel.

Chapter 36

The world seemed to pause as they stood inside the fae tunnel. Not so much as a strand of hair blew out of place; once inside, everything was still and peaceful. Much like standing in a lift. Except there was no background music, only the heavy breathing of fellow anxious travellers. The immense power of the encircling wind only became apparent when you stepped inside or outside the floating vortex.

Thankfully, there was no smell of rotting flesh from the floating vetala. The clove twining seemed to do the trick. Luna hoped they didn't need to travel back with it. Its menacing death grin seemed to follow her wherever she moved, the colourless eyes staring into her soul.

"We're here," announced Frances Chavron.

The vampire waved his cane for Agnes to leave the tunnel first, followed by a reluctant Luna. Once the rest walked out, the fae tunnel minimised until it was nothing but a tiny dot, disappearing into oblivion. The night was cool, but not freezing like it had been back in Ireland, and a soft breeze pulled at Agnes' top bun. Her pale blue hair whipped gently, framing her long angular face.

Luna looked up at the sky. A beautiful sunrise was taking place, the red hues slowly disappearing behind hills in the foreground. Her eyes settled upon the hills, and that was when she saw the castle.

"Beautiful," said Dahlia in awe.

"Is that—"

"Bran Castle," finished Frances Chavron, answering Luna's question before she could ask it.

The group of six stood quietly for a few moments as they took in the scene before them. Luna couldn't help but think of all the Dracula films she had watched late at night with Belinda when they should have been asleep. They had kind of creeped her out, but the goth girl loved those films, and Luna felt her heart sink that Belinda wasn't here to witness the castle for herself.

"Did you know that the author, Bram Stoker, based his book on actual events?" added Frances.

The rest of them looked at him.

"Yes, it seems the author knew a lot more about us vampires than you'd think." Frances smiled, showing off a glint of a fang. "Though his Count Dracula is not the real one. The original Dracula was laid to rest six hundred years ago."

Augustus shrugged. "What an endearing story, but

I'm afraid we don't have time to reminisce."

"Damn, I wanted to hear the rest," whispered Dahlia to Luna.

Luna nodded in agreement as the group headed along a quiet street. Small bungalows lined the road and lights shone dimly from behind closed curtains. The group walked in the middle of the road, avoiding the parked cars. It felt so unreal to Luna that she had just travelled to a different country via fae tunnel in less than half an hour, when it would have taken them three hours to fly by plane, not to mention the waiting around and travelling to and from airports.

They continued walking in silence, Frances leading the way. Eventually, he turned onto an uphill path. Looming above them, at the top of the road, was an illuminated Bran Castle.

"Is that where they live?" asked Salvador, breaking the eerie silence. "I mean, isn't it a bit obvious?"

Frances halted, turning to him, "I do not understand your question?"

"He means vampires living in Count Dracula's castle is a bit obvious," Dahlia clarified. "Surely the humans must realise?"

"Exactly," Salvador continued. "Hundreds of tourists flock to this place daily."

Frances waved his cane in the air. "Quite the contrary, Mr Williams, as you shall soon see."

"Wait, didn't you say a local was going to meet us?"

asked Luna.

"Ah yes, Flavius should have met us by now," added Agnes.

"There must have been some complication. I'm sure Flavius will find us soon," said Frances. "It is just as well that I know my way."

"Maybe he didn't get the memo," grinned Dahlia.

The group continued to follow the winding path until they reached the front of the castle. Signs detailing the castle's history decorated the entrance, dampening the authenticity of the place. Luna liked to think they were travelling back in time, but the signs made it difficult not to acknowledge that they were most certainly in the modern day.

Instead of aiming for the entrance to the castle, Frances took a sharp right and continued to walk along the side of the castle wall, leaving the path behind. The group followed him along the grass-covered verge, Luna holding onto Dahlia all the while to avoid tripping over shrubs in the dark. Trees dotted their view as they continued to follow the vampire along the perimeter of the castle.

At last, he stopped outside a wooden doorway, set deep into the castle's brick. Vegetation grew around it, almost concealing its identity. The others watched on as Frances unscrewed the ruby from the tip of his cane and placed it inside a carved shape in the centre of the door. Luna watched in awe as the hexagon shaped stone twisted around until they could hear a hollow clicking sound.

Salvador and Augustus exchanged glances.

Moments later, the door slowly creaked open, and Frances gestured for them to enter, but none of them wanted to be the first, leaving Frances to do the honours. Agnes followed, reassuring the others. Dahlia stayed at the back behind Luna, her eyes scanning the darkness behind them in case they were being followed.

As the old door creaked closed after them, Luna jolted. The atmosphere was completely different. It was like they had just stepped into a scene from one of Belinda's horror films. The air was thick and musty, and grey mist swirled around their feet.

"Smells like old people," whispered Dahlia into Luna's ear.

Frances Chavron led the way through the mist, which sat low above the ground. Luna could just about make out gnarled ancient trees, creating the illusion of warped human shapes at first glance. A graveyard loomed before them, gravestones jutting out at all angles. As they made their way around them, Luna attempted to read their lettering, but it was futile, for the ancient headstones were veiled in thick moss.

Frances headed towards a dark, stone-grey building. It looked like a giant headstone, but Luna guessed it must be a mausoleum of some kind. Arched doors marked the entrance, and Frances led the way, leaving the others to follow him down the stone steps. Luna swore she saw the floating vetala move, as though it sensed it was in a realm of death.

A short while later, they entered a huge, dimly lit room, with lanterns hanging on either wall, creating shadows that seemed to dance around them.

"Cine esti?"

Luna shuddered, and so did the others, as a deep voice boomed from the darkness.

Frances held his cane aside, stopping the others from walking any further. "My lord, it is I, Frances Chavron."

Silence.

"De ce esti aici?"

"What is he saying?" whispered Agnes to Frances.

Frances held his hand up to shush her. "I need your help. I have brought powerful beings with me from Ireland."

The silence that followed was deafening, but then a snuffling sound came from the darkened corner.

"Vrajitoare!"

Frances coughed, clearing his throat. "Yes, my lord, I have brought a witch, but—"

A wheezing sound interrupted him.

"Celestian!"

Luna froze. Dahlia gripped onto her arm for reassurance.

Quietly at first, then louder, a shuffling sound drifted towards them from the dark corner, and slowly, a hunched over man-like creature emerged into the dim light, making some of them gasp. It shuffled closer, using a cane similar to Frances to aid its walking.

The being's skin was pale, but not as translucent as the vetala's, and deep lines were etched into the man's face, creating an immortal vision of what an elderly person past the age of six hundred would look like. His hair was pure white and extremely long, draping behind his back past his knees, and his forehead revealed a receding hairline, dotted with dark brown liver spots.

Frances bowed before him. "My lord, I have some startling news to share with you."

The old man tried to peer behind him, and Frances took a step aside, revealing the floating vetala.

"Vetala!" he hissed. His accent was prominent.

"We found it in the forests where the damaged portal lies," continued Frances. "In Araig. We think it was already dying when we came across it."

The old man shuffled closer, his long, dark grey robes trailing across the stone behind him. His eyes were almost milky white, like the vetala's, but Luna could see that his pupils were merely concealed by cataracts. He looked so old that it should have been impossible for him to exist at all.

"My lord Aurelius, I wish to introduce you to Agnes Guthrie, Salvador, Augustus, Dahlia and Luna Green."

The old man sniffed at the air. "Ah, Celestian."

"Yes, we brought her to show you that we are

protecting the last known Celestian. She attends Agnes Guthrie's school, in Ireland."

Luna was grateful Frances didn't mention her father, Jack, for he wanted to stay hidden.

"I am honoured," wheezed the old man. He bowed his head. "Bring the vetala closer," he instructed. His voice crackled between words.

Agnes manoeuvred the creature through the air, letting it come to a stop in front of the man.

He seemed to examine it, sniffing the surrounding air. "It was half-dead... before being struck by something..."

"Yes, we have werewolves at the manor. One of them encountered it, striking out in fear of being attacked. But my intuition tells me that the creature was already dying, for he found it during daylight," explained Frances.

The old man looked over at him. "Only one?"

"We are not sure, but I fear they are escaping from the damaged portal inside the Dead Forest in Araig. We brought it here to ask for your knowledge of the ancient creatures, so that we might use that knowledge to destroy them, and close their realm for good."

"You will need the ruby crystal... do you know of its whereabouts?" asked Aurelius.

Agnes Guthrie stepped forward. "We have been given clues, my lord, but they are riddles and not easily unravelled. The previous head teacher and founder of our school, Edward Blackhill, gave us these riddles to pass on. He is no longer with us in the living world. But I have been able to communicate with him by scrying."

"What is the riddle?"

"'By day they are visible, by night they are invisible'. At first, we thought the riddle had something to do with the vetalas only being invisible at night, but it would make little sense for the vetalas to have the ruby, otherwise they would have already used it to break through into our world and close their portal for good."

Count Aurelius held a bony index finger out towards the floating vetala, and stabbed his long sharp nail straight into the dead creature's temple. Luna recoiled at the squelching sound as his nail dug deeper into the creature's skull. Aurelius pulled his finger out and, to the others horror, placed it straight into his mouth. Two sharp incisors caught the flickering light as he licked his lips.

"This vetala isn't the only one who first escaped. I sense his travels through the portal; I can see around him…" The count paused. "He had already been captured, lured by something else in the forests."

Agnes turned to Salvador. "The Jonas Sisters."

"Have they all escaped?" asked an uncharacteristically anxious Augustus.

The count slowly shook his head. "Not all, but most of them were lured by some kind of dark magick… no, wait… blood. A child's blood."

Chapter 37

"I told you Clarissa was bait," said Agnes, pacing up and down.

Luna suddenly felt terrible for doubting the girl. Maybe Agnes was right. Maybe she was just a victim. But then… why would a random child with no magickal knowledge be talking to the figure in the oil painting? Or more to the point, why would the figure be talking to her?

Luna was about to mention this to the others, when Aurelius held his hands out towards the wall. One of the torches came loose, and Luna watched as it travelled down towards him, before being grasped by the count. He held the flame against the vetala, and Luna was instantly hit by a wave of heat as the dead creature lit up like a bonfire doused in petrol.

As the body continued to burn before them, Frances spoke to Aurelius in hushed tones. "How do we stop these creatures?"

Aurelius looked back at the burning vetala, then back

to Frances. "Fire, and lots of it."

"Is that it?" Salvador walked around the burning creature to face the vampires. "How do we do that without burning down our precious forests?"

"You must find the ruby, then all will become clear," Aurelius intoned.

"But we don't have the ruby," answered a frustrated Salvador.

"It is time I called on the others," continued Aurelius, ignoring Salvador's irate comment.

"Others?" Luna and Dahlia chorused. That was all they needed... more of these walking talking corpses, with a penchant for human blood.

If Aurelius heard them, he did not offer a response, instead shuffling back into the dark corner where he had emerged from. They could hear the sound of stone scraping against stone echoing around the small mausoleum, followed by the shuffling of feet.

"Oh no, please tell me that wasn't the sound of coffin lids opening?" remarked Dahlia.

Luna turned to stare at her in horror as Aurelius came back into view from the dark shadows. This time, he wasn't alone. Two more hunched figures shuffled behind him.

Frances Chavron bowed. "Gentlemen."

The two strangers nodded their heads in response, stopping before the group. Both of them looked as old and lifeless as Aurelius, the only difference being that the one on the right had dark grey hair, not white hair, and their robes were brown, not grey.

"May I introduce you to the elders, better known as the Architects," announced Frances to the others.

Aurelius spoke to the other two in their native tongue as Frances translated, telling the group that Aurelius was updating the Architects on the riddle and the reason for their visit. One of them looked down at the ashes on the ground were the vetala had once been and nodded his head in agreement with Aurelius. A few moments later, Aurelius turned his attention back to the rest of them.

"Regarding the missing crystal, our concern is that we may know where it is hiding."

"Well, that's glorious news, is it not?" said Agnes.

The vampire gave a slight nod of his head. "It is where the crystal may be that we are worried about."

Luna suddenly thought back to the vanishing lake, and how she had been the only one who could retrieve it. It all made sense now, why she was here. Only a guardian of the athame could claim the crystals.

"We think the ruby is with our master," said the old vampire on the count's left side.

Frances Chavron placed a hand over his mouth. "Surely not?"

"That doesn't sound good," mumbled Luna to Dahlia.

"May I ask who you are referring to?" enquired Augustus.

Frances turned to him. If it was possible for a vampire to drain blood from their own face, then he was the unliving proof, thought Luna.

"They refer to the one whose castle we are currently intruding."

Now it was Augustus' turn to waver.

"Count Dracula," whispered Luna.

"It seems Vlad Dracula may possess the ruby within his casket," said Aurelius.

"Is he a walking corpse like you?" asked Dahlia.

Thankfully, the three ancient vampires ignored the fairy's comment, if they had heard it at all.

"B-but how can we be certain this is true?" asked Agnes.

"Vlad is visible during the day, when people visit the castle. They pay to see his home; to connect with his persona. At night, he is invisible, as he lies hidden in his tomb," explained Aurelius.

"So, he doesn't even come out when it's dark?" asked Salvador.

The two Architects looked at one another. "We are here to prevent him from returning," they chorused.

"But isn't he like you?" asked Agnes.

Aurelius shook his head gravely. "Unfortunately, Dracula remains a cold-blooded killer who would not hesitate to rip each one of your throats open to justify his thirst for blood."

The vampire looked in Luna's direction, making her

shiver.

"Okay, so where is the King of Goth buried?" asked Dahlia.

The Architects turned in her direction.

Aurelius laughed. "If I were you, I would be the first to run."

"Oh yeah, gramps, and why's that?" scoffed Dahlia.

"Haven't you learnt anything from the book of the dead?"

Dahlia looked blankly at the ancient vampire and shrugged.

"Before humans, only darkness and light existed in all our realms. We represent the dark, and you fae make up the light. But what happens when dark and light collide?"

The dank room fell eerily silent. The sound of water dripping echoed in the background.

The count licked his dry lips. "We become One. There is nothing left of either."

"O-kay," said Dahlia. "But what has that got to do with me personally? We all know that if the damaged portal opens it will unleash the darkness from every evil realm, overcoming the light from the rest of the world and realms."

"Exactly, but what creatures are the epitome of light?" The count lifted a long bony finger towards the fairy. "One sip of fairy blood can make a vampire immensely powerful, so powerful that they can take out an entire army of light beings. Your blood would allow the dark to win any war instantly. There would be no need for the athame, or its hidden gems. Darkness would prevail."

Luna sensed Augustus back away from Frances Chavron.

Aurelius turned his attention to Luna. "And you, my dear Celestian, you are what they call the crème de la crème."

Chapter 38

"This is absurd!" retorted Salvador.

Everyone turned their attention to the warlock. "We speak of darkness and light when the real problem is how do we retrieve the ruby without waking Dracula?"

Aurelius turned to Luna. "I sense you are a guardian of the athame, am I right in believing so?"

Luna nodded gravely.

"Then I am afraid there is no other option. One sniff of her Celestian blood will be enough to awaken Dracula from his eternal slumber, but as the only guardian here, she is the only one who can retrieve the ruby."

"We should have brought another child," murmured Salvador. "Maybe one of the young witches."

Augustus snorted, "And what use would they be? Luna is the most powerful of all the children, and certainly more powerful than those pathetic witches."

"We cannot place our last existing Celestian in danger," retorted Salvador. "We are her guardians."

"We don't have time to go back and fetch another guardian."

Augustus and Salvador looked at Agnes, surprised to hear her speaking up for Aurelius' suggestion.

"The lady is right," said the count.

Agnes nodded to him. "Please tell us where we can find Vlad's tomb."

Count Aurelius nodded, before turning to his companions. "Trebuie sa securizam castelul."

"Secure the castle? Whatever for?" asked Frances.

"We do not want Count Dracula to escape."

The others watched open-mouthed as the three ancient vampires huddled together. A few moments later, Aurelius beckoned the others to follow them. Frances followed the three elders into the dark corner where they had emerged from earlier. Augustus held his crystal wand out before him, a white glow emanating from the crystal tip. Agnes followed suit, muttering an incantation under her breath.

Luna stayed close to Dahlia's side as they made their way through the darkness into the corner of the room, where the stone wall was now missing, having moved aside earlier to allow Aurelius and his fellow vampires to enter. Emerging from the mausoleum, the group found themselves in a narrow tunnel, requiring them to walk in a single line. Luna gagged at the overpowering stench of damp. Water dripped from the low ceiling, making the girl shiver. She wished more than anything that she was back at the manor, safely tucked up inside her bed.

Aurelius led the way through the long tunnel, finally coming to a stop before a wooden door. The sound of the iron handle being turned echoed around the claustrophobic tunnel, giving them hope that they would soon be free. Luna's heart pumped inside her ears as they entered yet another dark tunnel. So much for freedom.

This new tunnel led them down a steep flight of fractured stone steps, forcing them to focus all their concentration on not falling. As they continued to descend further and further down, Luna wondered if they would ever reach the bottom. Luna half turned to Dahlia, to find her face etched with frown lines. Luna swore she could see a glint of fear in the fairy's eyes. If Dahlia was feeling apprehensive, what hope did she have?

Finally, they reached the bottom of the stairs, and were faced with yet another door. This one looked to be made of steel.

"I am afraid I cannot open this door, for it is crafted from solid silver. Would one of you do the honours?" asked Aurelius.

"Silver?" whispered Luna.

"Silver kills vampires," whispered Dahlia in her ear.

"Like iron with us fairies."

Their group shuffled around as the Architects and Frances Chavron moved back. Augustus stepped forward, as did Agnes and Salvador. The three of them studied the door, each pushing it with no results.

"How can we open this if there is no handle?" asked Salvador.

"Light creatures made it after Dracula was 'killed' during a battle six hundred years ago, and it has since remained unopened, for we cannot open it ourselves. It was the only way to stop him from escaping. Only dark magick can open it."

"But none of us can use dark magick," said Agnes.

"Huh, we should have brought the green-haired witch after all," muttered Augustus.

Agnes ignored the fairy, and instead approached the door, aiming her wand directly at it.

"Aperta!"

The tip of her wand crackled into life as a light shot out from its tip, only to bounce back off the solid door.

"Revelare!"

Again, the spell bounced back with no effect.

"I'm afraid your spells are not of any use here," said Aurelius.

"Allow me to try," offered Augustus. He pointed his crystal wand towards the centre of the door. The crystal instantly lit up, and a white light shot out, crashing against the solid silver. For a moment, it looked as though the magick was working, the centre of the door seeming to soften as though it were melting. Augustus aimed his wand again, and again. But after a few attempts, he conceded defeat. The door would not budge.

Salvador paced back and forth, muttering under his breath.

"You are a warlock, surely you must know something of the dark arts?" grumbled Augustus, obviously annoyed with himself.

Salvador turned towards the door, holding out his signet ring. "Muestrate!" Again, a shot sparked out, but nothing happened.

"What was that?" asked Dahlia.

"I asked the door to reveal itself in Spanish, my native tongue," explained Salvador.

"Try Romanian," suggested Agnes.

"I'm afraid none of that will work. Language is not the answer," informed Aurelius.

The other two elders huddled behind him, whispering in his ear. Aurelius gestured to the one with dark grey hair and the Architect stepped forward, pointing a long bony finger at Luna.

"The child," he said, in a deep, crackled voice.

Luna looked horrified as her head turned this way and that. "Me?"

The elder nodded.

"Of course," said Agnes. "Luna can use her crystal."

She held out her hand towards Luna, beckoning for her to come forward.

Luna shuffled to the front, with Dahlia by her side. She glanced nervously at her friend and the fairy gave her a nod of encouragement. Turning back to the silver door, Luna studied it for a few seconds.

"What do I do now?" she asked.

Agnes joined her. "Hold your crystal and focus all of your intentions on the door. Imagine it melting away."

Luna half nodded, but if she was honest with herself, she wasn't sure this would work. She had been practising many different things with her crystal lately, but she had never achieved anything of this magnitude, not since the day at the vanishing lake.

"Clear your head," soothed Agnes.

Luna touched the crystal around her neck and gazed at the solid door before them, trying to remember the meditation method that Bell had taught her. She always struggled to clear her head; images of Amadan and the shadow walkers would always find their way into her subconscious, and ever since she had channelled the spirit of Jonas Schmidt, she had been too scared to go into the depths of her own magick.

"You can do this."

Luna felt the comforting hand of Dahlia on her left shoulder. Biting into her lower lip, Luna closed her eyes and imagined the door melting like wax. Again, unwanted images appeared behind her eyes. Something dark and foreboding entered her thoughts. It felt like a completely different energy than before. Was she picking up whatever was waiting for them on the other side of the door?

Luna tried to push these images away and focus solely on the door. Slowly opening her eyes, she stared at the solid silver. Without blinking, she envisioned the silver liquifying, pouring away like water gushing from a hosepipe. Then, like a volcano erupting, silver lava began to flow from the door's centre, cascading over the ground like a metallic waterfall.

"It's working!" cried Dahlia.

"Shh, you will put her off," scolded Agnes.

Luna wasn't sure if this was all in her mind's eye, but hearing Dahlia in the background seemed to strengthen her focus, and she watched as the centre of the door melted away completely. Her instincts told her to step back as she continued to focus, the silver liquid now forming a pool of metal upon the stone floor.

When the darkness of the room beyond the door appeared, Agnes clasped a hand over Luna's, directing her hands away from her crystal.

"You've done it my dear."

Tears ran down Luna's cheeks as she blinked a few times, clearing the grit from her eyes. She could just make out a dark gaping hole where the door had been. The sound of the others moving brought her senses back to reality.

"Can you see anything?" Salvador asked the three elders.

Aurelius and the two other vampires stepped far back, away from the melting door.

"I'm afraid we will not accompany you inside," Aurelius informed them.

Frances Chavron also edged away from the pool of silver on the ground. "I too am hesitant to enter."

Augustus shrugged. Then, crouching down, he stepped through the gaping hole, followed by Salvador.

"We should go too," said Agnes to Luna.

"But what if I don't want to? Haven't I done enough already?"

Agnes nodded her head gravely. "I wish it were that simple, my dear, but I am afraid this is just the beginning of our journey."

Dahlia placed an arm around the girl's shoulders. "Come on, you're not alone kid."

Reluctantly, Luna followed Agnes into the dark room beyond.

"I hope you're not thinking of locking us in here," said Dahlia, turning to the four vampires.

"We too want to stop this manifestation of vetalas, before it's too late," said Frances.

Dahlia frowned at him for a moment, before disappearing through the gap.

The air inside felt instantly claustrophobic, and there was a potent smell of stale flesh. Agnes and Augustus led the rest into the centre of the room, both their wands beaming rays of light. Dust particles danced in the still air as Augustus held his wand towards a large, oblong shape in the centre of the room.

"Whatever is it?" asked Agnes, as she joined his side. Both of their lights revealed the shape to be some sort of monument.

Augustus held his wand over the top of it, to reveal a script engraved into the stone.

"What does it say?" asked Agnes.

"It's in Romanian, but I can just about make out a name. Vlad Dracula." Augustus stumbled backwards. "I guess we've found him."

Salvador and Dahlia rushed over to join them. Luna hung back, glancing behind her into the darkness. She couldn't make out the vampires on the other side of the door, and their absence made her even more anxious than she already was. But, not wanting to remain behind, she promptly hurried over to join the others.

The slab of stone was at least six to seven feet long and adorned with sculpted images of armoured men holding swords above their heads.

"Is this a coffin?" asked Luna.

"I'm afraid so," answered Salvador.

Luna shivered. "Now what?"

Dahlia shrugged, her eyes betraying her terror. "I guess it's time for us to meet the most famous vampire of all time."

Chapter 39

"Shouldn't we have a stake?" asked Dahlia, as Salvador and Augustus pushed the top slab aside.

Augustus glared over at her as he continued to push the coffin's heavy lid. It opened slowly, the sound of ancient stone scraping away hundreds of years of grit and dust. As the gap became wide enough to reveal the body that lay inside, both men jumped back. Luna edged closer, peeking over Agnes' shoulder. She could just make out a torso, dressed in gilded armour. Her eyes focused on the being's arms, then its hands, laid with one over the other. A red formal coat, no doubt from the era when Vlad had died, was draped over his shoulders.

"He has preserved well. History dictates that the Turks beheaded him…"

Everyone turned to see Frances Chavron standing behind them.

"And was he beheaded?" asked Dahlia.

Frances shook his head. "No, but he was 'killed' in

battle. His people hid his body; no one knows they buried him here under the belly of the castle." Frances walked over to the tomb. "Today, they still search for his burial place." He paused, his expression reflective. "Vampires have been living for thousands, if not millions, of years, from when time began. That is the reason vetalas are the beasts they are. Vlad Dracula became known as 'the first' vampire, but there are many who preceded him. Indeed, the being who made him a vampire was ancient beyond comprehension."

Feeling brave, Luna moved closer to the stone tomb. Her eyes moved to the uppermost part of the coffin, where Dracula's head lay, and she was shocked to see his flesh still very much attached to his bones. His eyes were closed, and his long, dark hair rested upon a satin pillow, his facial hair partially covering a smooth, almost porcelain complexion.

"Dahlia's comment regarding a stake rings true to a certain extent. At the time of Vlad's 'death', it was tradition to bury the dead with a stake through their hearts," declared Frances.

Luna witnessed Dahlia shiver as she cautiously peered into the coffin.

"Where is his stake then?"

Frances moved closer to the body, and Luna could sense that he was afraid of getting too close to the infamous vampire.

"If you look to where his heart should be, you will

see a hole. His own people placed a stake through his heart, to prevent him from coming back. Or at least, that was their belief."

The others peered inside the coffin, and Luna watched the others examine the body from a safe distance. Looking back at the lifeless body, Luna tried to find where the stake had once been. It took her longer than she had expected, but she eventually identified a dark stain the size of a football, positioned over the ancient vampire's chest.

"Why is it gone?" asked a horrified Agnes.

"Someone removed it before sealing this tomb with a silver door. We are the first to enter in six hundred years."

"And hopefully the last," added Dahlia.

"Where do you think they hid the ruby?" asked Luna.

"It is said that Vlad Dracula owned the crystal, and had it encased within the handle of his kilij sword," said Frances.

"His what sword?" asked Dahlia.

"Kilij. It's a Turkish sword. Rumour has it they buried it alongside him."

"Okay… so they buried him with the stake missing and instead replaced it with a lethal weapon," remarked Dahlia snidely.

Agnes held up a hand to quieten the fairy. "We need to respect Vlad's resting place."

"How are we going to respect him and search for the

ruby at the same time?"

Luna stepped forward. "I guess I need to make that decision on behalf of my fellow guardians."

Agnes nodded to her, and the rest took a few steps back, leaving Luna alone by the count's lifeless body. She scanned her eyes across the ancient remains, unnerved by the body's uncanny similarity to a living person. Luna was hesitant to touch anything, but she needed to find the kilij. The obvious location of it would be on top of the body, or by its side, but there was no visible weapon in or around Vlad's body.

Using only her index finger and thumb, Luna nervously reached for the deep-red woven fabric surrounding the body. Her heart raced as she slowly pinched it between her fingers, slightly pulling at it, but the weight of Vlad's armour weighed it down.

Luna let go, exasperated. "This is no use, they must have hidden it underneath the body," she said, turning to the others.

Agnes took a few steps towards her. "We cannot move the body for fear of awakening the count."

"Then we have no choice but to use magick," announced Salvador.

The others turned to him, aghast.

Salvador shrugged. "What other choice do we have?"

"Salvador is right, if we use a levitation spell then we can lift him gently while Luna searches beneath the body," instructed Agnes.

"If you must," insisted Frances Chavron. "But make it quick. None of us want to be here any longer than we need to be."

Agnes nodded to Salvador, who stepped over to her side as Augustus and Dahlia stepped forward. Luna took a few steps away from the coffin, not taking her eyes from the ancient dead vampire. Agnes, Dahlia and Augustus held their wands straight out before them, while Salvador pointed his signet ring at the open casket.

"Ortum," all four chanted in Latin.

When nothing happened, they chanted again. Suddenly, Luna noticed something stir.

"He's moving!" she cried out.

Frances Chavron rushed to her side, confirming Luna's revelation. "Dracula is lifting, keep going."

The four continued to focus on the casket, muttering their chant over and over. Finally, Vlad's body came into view, rising above his coffin.

"Quick, Luna, search the casket," instructed Frances Chavron.

Luna jolted into action, moving towards the coffin. There was just enough space between the count and the base of the casket for her to look inside. Her heart pounded in her ears as she rummaged through the reams of red silk fabric. She didn't want to think about the count's body lying on it for centuries, wasting away.

"There's nothing under here," she cried, as she

frantically burrowed her fingers through the ancient cloth.

Frances edged closer, peering over the coffin's edge. "Keep trying."

Just then, Luna's hand caught on something metal. "Wait, I think there's a secret compartment." Her fingers felt around the base until her hand came into contact with some sort of handle. She pulled at it, but it wouldn't budge. "It's stuck," she cried.

"Try harder," urged Frances.

Using both hands, Luna tightened them around the small handle and pulled with all her strength. But it wouldn't open. She glanced desperately over her shoulder for support from the others, but they were entirely focused on keeping Vlad afloat.

"I think it's locked. What should I do?" She turned to Frances Chavron.

"Use your crystal, just like you did with the silver door."

Slipping her hands out from the casket, Luna clutched onto her crystal around her neck. She focused on the lock, seeing it open in her mind's eye.

"We can't keep this going for much longer," warned Agnes. "We need to hurry."

A bead of sweat formed above Luna's top lip. She wanted to wipe it away but remained focused on the locked compartment. A faint clicking sound drifted towards her ears, and she immediately reached into the casket and pulled at the handle of the compartment. To her relief, the base of the coffin opened up. Using two hands, Luna reached inside, pulling out a four-foot long curved sword.

"I found it!" she cried, holding it up for the others to see, but as she turned with it in her hands, something gripped onto the sword, pulling her back.

Frances Chavron fell backwards, his eyes wide open in sheer horror, and the other four dropped their arms, fear etched on their faces. Luna remained frozen in place, too terrified to turn around. She could feel the strength of the hands that were now gripping onto her shoulders, and as the smell of death wafted towards her nostrils, Luna struggled not to gag.

Vlad Dracula was awake.

Chapter 40

"Tradator!"

Luna wept as she stared at the others before her. Behind Luna, Vlad Dracula stood at least six feet tall. Fingers with long, curved nails gripped tighter into her flesh. He let her go with one hand and snatched the sword in the other, before placing it threateningly under her chin. A distinctive ruby glistened from its gold handle.

"Let her go, death breath!" Dahlia charged towards them but was stopped abruptly by a firm hand on her shoulder. She looked up to see Augustus, his eyes pleading with her to stop.

"Please, Dracula, the child is innocent," begged Frances Chavron. "We are the traitors, not the girl."

Vlad glared at the vampire, his eyes beaming red. "You awakened me and stole my treasure!" he boomed.

Agnes held both hands out towards him. "Please, let her go," she pleaded. "Let us explain why we are here."

Vlad sniffed the surrounding air. Luna stiffened as

she felt his breath come closer to her neck.

"Lumina," he breathed. His accent was thick.

Luna couldn't speak Romanian, but even she understood that he was saying something to do with light... perhaps that was her name in his native tongue?

To everyone's horror, the count held his head back, and a pair of large, curved fangs sprang out from his open mouth. As he brought his head down towards Luna's exposed neck, Agnes let out a piercing scream. Instantly, Augustus and Dahlia rushed towards them, both fairies shooting out magick with their crystal wands. Vlad staggered backwards, stunned by the sudden impact of the fairy magick. Luna released herself from his grip and ran towards Agnes' open arms, prompting the count to let out an anguished cry of fury.

Luna trembled in the arms of her headmistress, now fully exposed to the horror of Vlad Dracula's form. There was no doubt that this man had once been Vlad the Impaler. Long black hair fell over his shoulders, and his once piercing dark eyes gleamed an angry red, his sharp features partially hidden by his black goatee.

Vlad lifted his sword, the sharp curved end pointing towards them, ready to attack.

"STOP!"

Everyone, including Vlad Dracula, turned as the three elders appeared inside the crypt.

"Dracula, you must listen to us," said Aurelius. "We have given permission for these beings to wake you."

Luna knew this was a lie, but they all seemed to hold their breath as they waited for the count's reaction. He held his stance, his eyes glaring towards the three elders.

"You have all betrayed me," said Vlad.

Aurelius held both hands out towards him. "My lord, we have protected your resting place for centuries, and only now have we taken it upon ourselves to bring you back. We are under threat, my lord. The vetalas have returned."

This statement seemed to jolt the count out of his threatening stance, and he brought his sword down slowly.

"You dare to mention the vetalas in my presence?" he boomed.

Aurelius bowed his head. "Yes, my lord. We have been informed by those who stand before you that they are escaping from Nocte Viventem."

Vlad Dracula narrowed his eyes at the three men, while the rest of the group held their breath, awaiting the count's next move.

"You speak the truth?" he asked.

The three elders nodded their heads in unison. Vlad looked down at his sword, bringing it closer to his face to examine the glistening round ruby on its gold gilded handle.

"Is this what you seek?" he asked, turning to the group from Blackhill.

Luna nodded her head, but then twisted to look at the

others, in case their reaction was different to hers.

"Yes, my lord," said Agnes. "We are the guardians of the ancient athame, the protectors of the darker realms." She let go of Luna and took a step closer to the vampire. "We desperately need the ruby to stop the vetalas from continuing to enter our world."

Vlad glared at her, then turned to the elders. "You dared to let this happen!" he boomed.

The three vampires all bowed their heads. "We did not know, my lord. But I fear they will destroy our land and come for you too if we do not stop them."

This seemed to strike a chord with the count, and Luna noticed a look of fear flit across his face. Luna wanted to ask why someone as powerful as Vlad the Impaler would fear the vetalas, but she guessed this wasn't the time to speak out.

Vlad studied the ruby once more. Placing a hand over it, he twisted the crystal until it came loose. The ruby was bigger than Luna had expected, but then she remembered that the onyx crystal had been a similar size until they had placed it onto the athame.

"I do not want to part with this, for it was given to me by my ancestors." He held it out before him, palm open. "But I fear what may lie ahead if I do not. My people have suffered enough under the wrath of those creatures. They destroyed my land, feeding on our children!" Vlad regarded himself. "I fought them before, and won, but only once I had been transformed into the being you see before you."

"We would not have won against them, if not for your newfound power," stated Aurelius.

Vlad Dracula snapped his head towards the elder. "They fed on my son!"

Aurelius shied away. "Defeating such an enemy was no mean feat, my lord. Casualties are always to be expected, in any war. These creatures are the epitome of evil."

"Will you help us, my lord?" asked Frances Chavron.

Dracula settled his red irises on the vampire. "You are one of us?"

Frances nodded.

"Then you know what needs to be done."

"But—"

"Dracula cannot leave his tomb," said Aurelius.

"But why?" asked Dahlia. "He's awake now."

Vlad spun towards her, his red eyes gleaming. "I am so thirsty! Your blood is the essence I need to recover from this endless sleep."

Dahlia stepped back.

"But I do not want to return, nor do I wish to feed on the souls who are trying to save my people."

Luna had not expected to hear those words from an infamous killer.

Vlad held out the ruby to the group. "I give it with my blessing, but believe me, I will not hesitate to rip every one of your throats open if you tarry here any longer. My thirst grows with every minute that passes."

Agnes gently nudged Luna, urging her to collect the ruby from him. Shaking, Luna accepted the crystal from the count's outstretched hand. Once she had grasped it, she quickly backed away from him, returning to the others.

"I am so sorry, my lords."

Everyone in the room spun around as a dishevelled middle-aged man burst into the room.

"I did not realise the time," the man panted.

"Flavius," uttered Frances.

The man stopped dead as he took in the strangers' faces all staring back at him, and as his head drifted slowly towards the open casket, he recoiled in horror. But as Flavius opened his mouth to scream, something whooshed straight past them with unimaginable speed. When the dust settled, it was their turn to recoil. Lying, draped across Vlad Dracula's arms, was a dead Flavius. His dead eyes stared lifelessly back at them, his throat having been torn open to reveal a river of dark liquid.

Dropping the body, Vlad wiped the blood from his mouth, and returned to his crypt. Once he had climbed inside it, he turned to them one last time. "Go. Now!"

Luna and the others did not need any more persuasion, and they all fled out of the enclosed tomb, their eyes not daring to meet the gaze of the dead man who lay motionless on the stone floor in a pool of blood.

"Shouldn't we bring him too?" said Luna as they all

raced out.

"If you value your life, then no," replied Frances pushing her towards the exit.

Turning back towards the gaping hole that had once been a door, Luna and the two fairies melted the pool of solid silver that had amassed on the floor, using it to cover the gap, sealing in Count Dracula for good.

Feeling accomplished, they made their way back to the fae tunnels. Luna clung to the ruby, holding it tight to her chest, her heart finally full of hope.

Chapter 41

A sense of foreboding hung in the air as the group arrived back at the manor, minus Dahlia, who had taken a fae tunnel back to Illuminos. Luna was told to go straight to her bed, but after her recent adventure to Transylvania, she knew she would never sleep. Nor would she forget the senseless killing of an innocent man.

Before she could head upstairs, Agnes Guthrie took the ruby from her.

"Shouldn't we be placing it back into the athame?" asked Luna.

"My dear, the other children are asleep. We'll do it first thing in the morning, so the others can be part of it," explained Agnes.

"B-but who knows how many vetalas have come through already. We need to close the portal, so no more can escape."

"Child, you are tired, and must rest. We have a big day tomorrow."

With that, Agnes Guthrie walked away, heading towards her office. Salvador and Augustus bid them all goodnight as they parted ways. But when Luna thought she was alone, she sensed someone watching her. Spinning around, she saw Frances Chavron still standing there.

His amber eyes seemed to bore into hers. "You are right, Luna. We should deal with this straight away." He hastened in the direction Agnes had gone. "I will speak to Agnes, but in the meantime, go to your room until further notice."

Luna watched him disappear down the dark hallway after Mrs Guthrie, before reluctantly heading up the staircase towards her own room. She doubted he would manage to change her mind, but if he did, she supposed someone would notify her.

Luna expected Belinda to be fast asleep when she reached their room, but the witch was standing at the window between their beds.

"Still no sign of Poe?"

Belinda turned from the window to face her. Her eyes were red and swollen from crying.

"Nothing. I can't even sense him telepathically."

Luna joined her, looking out into the darkness of the night.

"You don't think something bad has happened to him, do you?" sniffed Belinda.

Luna placed a hand on the girl's forearm. "No, I think

he's just got lost," she soothed. But inside, Luna was angry. They had the ruby; if the escaped vetala had got to Poe, then they should be closing the Nocte Viventem portal over for good. But instead of voicing this to Belinda, she beckoned her away from the window. None of the other children knew about their journey to Transylvania and telling Belinda about finding the ruby would only make her feel worse. No, she needed the girl to get some sleep. Tomorrow morning, Mrs Guthrie would announce it to the others. But as Luna turned away from the window, Belinda grabbed her arm.

"Wait!" she hissed. "There's somebody out there."

Luna spun around to look out into the darkness. She was about to say she couldn't see anything when a light bobbed up and down within the gardens.

"There!" pointed Belinda.

Luna pressed her face closer to the window, and that's when she saw another light moving behind the first one, as though someone was trying to catch up.

"What the…"

Beyond the invisible barrier they could just make out more tiny dots of lights at the perimeter of the forest.

"We need to alert the teachers," said Belinda.

Luna's head was spinning. Surely Mrs Guthrie wasn't going into the woods to close the portal without them?

"Come on," beckoned Belinda, who was already halfway out of the room.

Luna shook her head and hurried after the young witch. But just as they reached the dim hallway, they almost collided into Lily.

"I was just coming to get you two!" she cried.

"What happened?" asked Belinda.

"I was following Clarissa again, and we were right to suspect her of something."

"What did you see?" asked Luna.

"She went back to the painting and was talking to it again. But this time, I got closer. She was talking to a woman inside the painting."

"I knew it!" snapped Luna. "Do you know who it was?"

"Well, at first I could only make out a shadow, but as the figure came closer to the edge of the painting, I saw a middle-aged woman, with ginger hair."

"Never mind that, what were they saying?" asked Belinda.

"The older woman was telling Clarissa that it was time to meet up with the others, and that everything was going as planned."

Luna quickly thought of the lights outside. "We must hurry," she called out. "Wake the others. It seems the Sisters of Jonas have found what they have been looking for."

Belinda nodded, following Lily down the corridor. As they banged on the other children's doors, Luna hurried down the staircase to look for a teacher. But as she approached the dim corridor leading to Mrs Guthrie's office, she stopped dead. The forest painting had been slashed down the middle.

"Mrs Guthrie," she called, as she hurried towards her office. The door was slightly ajar and Luna barged through, letting out a shrill cry as she took in the scene before her. The headmistress was lying sprawled on the floor, her limbs twisted, and a hooded figure was hovering above her.

As the figure turned, Lily appeared beside Luna, letting out an audible gasp. It was her. The woman from the painting.

Chapter 42

"Ah, the famous Luna Green," said the woman. The hood of her cloak had fallen down to reveal a plump middle-aged face, and steel-grey eyes glared at the two girls from under a fringe of shocking ginger hair.

"Who are you?" asked Luna, her friend's presence giving her courage.

"I think you know who I am, Miss Green," the woman smirked.

"Winnie," Luna whispered.

"All this time you've been hiding inside the painting," Lily breathed, her eyes wide.

The older woman cackled. "Good hiding place, don't you think? Although I must admit, it did surprise me when you sensed me the day you arrived, Celestian. Your powers are truly extraordinary."

Luna shook her head. She had so many questions for this woman, but right now, Agnes was lying injured on the floor. She needed to help her.

"What have you done to her?" Luna demanded, edging closer to the headmistress.

The woman pulled out a wand. "Stay back!" she hissed.

"What do you want?" Lily exclaimed, determined not to let the witch scare her.

Winnie laughed again. "Isn't it obvious?" Her cold eyes slid towards the painting of Edward Blackhill. Luna followed her gaze. The painting was missing! But then Luna realised it was lying face down on the floor. Someone had thrown the painting off the wall, exposing the safe. And worst of all, the safe was wide open.

Luna's eyes widened in horror at her sudden realisation.

"The athame!"

"Oh yes, I got the complete package. Ruby too," chuckled Winnie.

Luna instinctively reached for her crystal around her neck.

"Uh uh," tutted Winnie, pointing her wand menacingly at her. "You are too late. Your friends Frances Chavron and Clarissa are already heading to the Dead Forest as we speak. They have the athame, and the ruby. Oh, and seeing as the onyx crystal is already on the dagger, we can always reverse the spell and open the Damnatorum portal again."

"You can't!" shouted Lily. "You don't have the grimoire."

Winnie laughed. "Oh, that old thing. Been in my family for years. I used a spell from the grimoire to hide inside the painting. Thankfully for me, my stay there felt like days, not years. But, after I teleported inside the painting, the grimoire did not travel with me. I do not know what happened to it, nor where it could be." She turned towards the window. "I should go, you know. I've got people to catch up with." She turned back to face them. "But feel free to search for the grimoire. It will save me the time and effort. I will get it back, mark my words."

"Are you one of the Sisters of Jonas?" asked Lily, stalling the witch.

Winnie chuckled again. "My dear, I'm the one who founded the coven. After all, my older brother is the principal reason for its origins."

"Wait, you're Jonas Schmidt's sister?"

"Got it in one."

"That's the reason you took the job here as a nurse, so you could spy on Mr Blackhill, then continue to spy on us after he died," gasped Luna.

"Oh, Edward didn't just die, dear. He was murdered."

Luna stumbled backwards. "It was you?"

Winnie shook her frizzy ginger hair. "Not guilty. But whoever did deserves a gold medal."

Luna's head was spinning. "You said the grimoire belonged to your family?"

"Had it for centuries. You know the story of Elizabeth Drake? Well, my ancestors murdered her for the grimoire. I still don't understand why she was chosen in the first place. Pathetic girl."

"She killed all her fellow villagers and cursed their land!"

Winnie clapped her wand against her other hand. "Well, this has been fun, but like I said, lots of things to do—"

"Put down your wand!"

Luna and Lily both startled as Augustus and Salvador burst into the office, but before anyone could react, Winnie spun her wand around her head, disappearing in front of them.

"What the—"

"She must have teleported, no doubt she's on her way to the wall."

Salvador rushed over to the window while Luna bent down to check Agnes, thankful that she could feel a pulse.

"Looks like Winnie stunned her. She'll be fine in a few moments," said Augustus, kneeling down beside Luna.

"What happened?" Bell Tilly ran into the room, gasping in horror as she noticed Agnes on the floor.

"We don't have time," said Luna, getting to her feet. "They have the athame and the ruby."

"Who?" said Salvador, turning from the window.

"Frances Chavron and Clarissa, that's who!" cried Lily.

"They're taking the athame to the Sisters of Jonas. They're going to open the portals, both of them," Luna explained, her tone urgent.

Augustus and Bell looked like a pair of deer in headlights.

"I knew we shouldn't have trusted that vampire scum," snarled Salvador. "But Agnes wouldn't hear of it."

"Frances Chavron must have used a glamour spell on Mrs Guthrie and the rest of you once we returned from Transylvania, making you agree to leave the ruby in the safe, instead of closing the portal as soon as we got back to the manor," explained Luna. "I was so angry and confused that we went to all of the trouble of travelling to Transylvania and risking our lives only to come back and be told to go to our beds. It all makes sense now."

"I remember thinking it seemed preposterous to leave the ruby until morning. But then I forgot all about it when we parted ways," murmured Augustus.

"Wait, does Frances know the password to get out of the barrier?" asked Bell.

"No doubt he does. He's been in the forests with us plenty of times," answered Salvador, staring ahead. His olive skin slowly drained of colour. "He was talking to me a few nights ago, asking how secure the greenhouse door was that leads to the gardens... he asked me to repeat the incantation for both that and the forest barrier." Salvador shot his head around to face the others. "He must have used his vampire glamour on me, and has somehow copied my voice for the spell."

"Come on, we need to go after them!" growled Augustus.

Bell chose to stay with Agnes until she recovered, while Luna and Lily ran after Augustus and Salvador to join the rest of the children and teachers in the foyer. Most of the children still looked half asleep, and when Luna told them what had happened, none of them seemed shocked that Frances Chavron had been part of the plan to steal the athame. They had all been suspicious of him, right from the start. Only his son, Sebastian Chavron, looked bewildered.

Not having time to ask him questions about his father, Luna hurried after the teachers into the gardens, followed by the rest of the children.

"The wall is down!" shouted Salvador, who was first to reach it.

It felt strange to Luna as the group made their way through the gardens to the edge of the forest without having to use magick to pass through.

"Call your animal guides!" yelled Hattie Bordeaux.

The children, excluding Belinda, silently called upon their guides, and as the large group disappeared inside the dark forest, animal sounds echoed through the trees, forming their own unique war cry.

Chapter 43

Sounds of whoops and cheers drifted towards them from the trees up ahead. The witches were not far away.

Luna sat astride Theodore, her ankle making running difficult, as Hugo swung from the overhead branches, Magnus sprinting along the forest floor below him. The Edgar twins had changed into their wolf forms and ran ahead of the group – they could just make out Leonard's white fur in the distance. Luna would later discover that the two wolves who had accompanied the Edgar twins when the children had first been introduced to their animal guides were in fact ghost wolves. They guided the twins into their transformation, before intertwining with them to make one. She watched them disappear ahead, while Tamara's eagle swooped silently between the treetops, his large wingspan ominous above them. Luna searched for Belinda in the group, and when she finally found her, she could sense the witch's fear and sadness emanating from her aura.

Soon, the atmosphere changed, and Luna knew they

were entering the Dead Forest. The trees poked out through the darkness like misshapen creatures, and the children's feet crunched loudly over the dead foliage. Suddenly, the twins halted, and when the group reached them, they found the werewolves sniffing the air.

"We're near the portal," whispered Salvador to the other teachers.

Archie Brutt nodded and slid quietly into the shadows of the dead trees. His tall lanky frame disappeared, encompassed by the inkiness. Suddenly, a tiny ball of light appeared. As the group crept towards it, Luna disembarked Theodore, following on foot. Drawing closer, she could just make out the source of light. It appeared to be emanating from their maths teacher's open palm.

Using his source of light, Archie peered through the darkness. After a few seconds, the teacher cupped both hands together, extinguishing the light, allowing the darkness to swallow them once more.

"They're here," he whispered.

Salvador and Augustus pushed through to join him. For a few moments, they seemed to watch something, when suddenly, a dark figure rushed out from the right, attacking them.

"Vetala!" shouted Archie.

The Edgar twins instantly leapt for the creature, and the largest of the animal guides pushed forwards, each of them trying to help fight the creature as Augustus and

Salvador assaulted the vetala with magick. Terrified, Luna stood back from the fray, desperate to do something to help. Grasping onto her crystal, she concentrated. Seconds later, a bright white light emanated from her entire body. The rush of energy began in the soles of her feet, racing up through the rest of her body and pressing its way along her arms. Luna threw both her hands out instinctively, and a beam of bright white light shot forth.

At first, the beam struck a tree, splitting it in half. The other children, aware of what she was doing, quickly moved aside, calling their animal guides back to them as Luna aimed her hands at the vetala. Salvador, Augustus and the two werewolf twins were still battling the creature, and as Luna fired another beam, it only narrowly missed them, fortunately firing at its actual target.

The vetala squealed with pain and Salvador jumped to his feet, kicking at the creature that now writhed on the ground. Augustus aimed his crystal wand at it, shooting it with a blast of magick.

"Luna, hurry!" he called out, his magick momentarily pinning the creature down.

Luna ran over to join him, releasing another beam of light at the writhing creature. As the light hit it, an explosion of orange flames erupted, enveloping the vetala's disgusting body in a ball of fire and ash.

Moments later, Hattie raced over, throwing a hex

over the fire and drowning the flames. As the fire died down, they discovered that there was nothing left of the vetala but a heap of ashes.

"Is everyone okay?" asked Salvador, his eyes searching the group, checking that everyone was present.

"Archie!"

The group turned to find Augustus kneeling by the teacher's side.

"He's been bitten," he cried.

Salvador and Hattie rushed over.

"Do you have anything we can give him?" Salvador asked Hattie.

Hattie rummaged through her pouch of ingredients. "I can try to take away his pain, but I won't be able to heal the bite."

Luna pushed her way through the group to see what was going on, slumping beside the injured teacher.

"Where is the bite?" she asked.

"My side," said Archie through gritted teeth, gesturing to his injury.

Luna held out her hands and placed them gently on his left side. A bright light glowed from her palms. She held them there until it dimmed out.

"What are you doing?" asked Salvador.

"She's healing him," said Augustus.

Archie rubbed his injured side, his fingers frantically trying to find the wound. He looked up at Luna in awe.

"I-it's gone," he stammered. "How did you know what to do?"

Luna shrugged. "I didn't. It just seemed natural."

Augustus and Salvador helped Archie back onto his feet.

"Can you walk?" asked Salvador.

"I think so." He held up his torn shirt to reveal a small red mark, but no open wound.

"Come on, we can't waste any more time. The coven will have already opened the portal," demanded Augustus.

As the group carried on their way, Hattie held Luna back.

"Well done, child. You have come such a long way since you arrived at the manor. But I'm afraid I must be honest with you. Though you may have healed Mr Brutt's wound, the curse will remain."

"You mean, he will turn into one of them?" said Luna, aghast.

Hattie Bordeaux nodded her head gravely. "I'm afraid so."

Luna held onto Theodore for support as Hattie walked on to catch up with the others. She instinctively looked down at her ankle. Another walking time bomb, she thought. How long would it be until she too turned into something evil?

Theodore bent his head down and nuzzled into her neck. "We will overcome this, Luna."

Luna froze. Slowly, she looked up at the unicorn. "Did you just speak to me?"

Theodore seemed to nod his head.

"But your mouth didn't open? Or did it, and I just can't see because it's dark?"

The unicorn let out a low grunting sound. "We're communicating telepathically."

"Wow, Belinda was right after all." Luna hung her head. Poor Belinda, and poor Poe.

She was about to ask Theodore a question when the group stalled.

Voices sounded up ahead.

Salvador held a hand out behind him, warning the others to keep quiet, before crouching down silently. The others followed suit. Luna spotted what he was seeing. A group of people were standing before the elm tree, chanting, their hands joined to form a circle. The Sisters of Jonas were casting a spell to open the Nocte Viventem portal.

Luna spotted Frances Chavron, who was not part of the circle, holding onto something as he made his way into the centre of the ring of witches.

"He's holding the athame!" whispered Salvador.

"We need to stop him," hissed Augustus. "He will place the ruby on its blade and open the portal."

"Luna, get over here, we need your power," urged Salvador.

Luna joined them at the edge of the tree line. She

could hear the chanting becoming louder, and she instantly recognised Winnie, swaying back and forth to the rhythmless tune. Suddenly, a swirling mass of wind appeared before the coven, like a mini tornado sucking inwards.

"The portal is opening!" shouted Salvador over the rising wind.

Without any more delay, Luna gathered her energy together, lifting herself up off the ground as she aimed her hands at the coven. Screams of panic and surprise filled the air as her energy crashed against them, knocking the witches off their feet. Frances Chavron was thrown back hard against the nearest tree and he slumped to the ground, dropping the athame at his feet. Salvador, Augustus and the Edgar twins charged in, pushing and biting as they made their way into the circle. The children charged after them, their animal guides snapping and clawing at the witches. Luna slumped to her knees, feeling weak. She had already used up most of her energy.

Theodore licked her face, urging her to get back up. "The moon will appear shortly."

Using his mane, Luna pushed herself back up onto her feet. The portal whisked faster in the centre of the circle; screams of disembodied voices whistling through the air. Luna could just make out a grotesque white torso emerging from the portal. Panicking, she limped towards the others, who had already chased away most of the coven. Winnie was the only one who remained. Glancing at the children, the witch rushed towards Frances, bending down to retrieve the athame. Luna could just make out the two crystals already placed inside the blade. The rest of them gathered in a line, each with their animal guides, waiting for whatever was going to come through the portal.

"Drop it, Winnie!" shouted Salvador. "You won't win."

Winnie walked over to the portal and smiled over at the creatures that were now piling through. "I think I already have," she said. "All I need now is to retrieve the grimoire and I will be the Queen of the Dark Worlds!"

Frances Chavron seemed to shake himself awake, his eyes widening in horror as he witnessed the terror that was emerging from the damaged portal. Before anyone else could move, he jumped to his feet and ran towards Winnie. Her face was a mask of shock as the vampire shoved her backwards into the portal. A long scream echoed from somewhere within as Winnie was sucked into the darkness, plunging her into an eternal torture.

Frances Chavron quickly picked up the athame that she had dropped and made for the treeline.

"Get him!" screamed Augustus.

But it was too late. More vetalas had materialised from the gaping mouth of the portal, leaving completely outnumbered.

Chapter 44

Luna didn't know what to do. Should she chase after Frances Chavron, or stay and fight the vetalas?

Her internal battle lasted only a few seconds. There was no escaping the hoard of creatures making their way through the portal. She needed to help defeat them. Taking her stance, Luna moved forwards with the teachers closing in behind her. The other children stepped back, watching as their teachers threw hexes and spells at the creatures. Most bounced straight off them, leaving no damage at all.

Suddenly, a burst of magick soared over their heads, hitting a few of the creatures. When Salvador and the rest quickly turned to see whose magick it was, they were relieved to see Agnes Guthrie fully restored, alongside Bell Tilly. The two witches cast endless enchantments at the vetalas, Agnes aiming her wand while Bell's runes swirled around the creatures, hitting them with counter hexes before zooming back to land on their master's hand. Tamara stepped towards them, aiming her wand at the vetalas in an effort to help. But it was no use; the hoards were still advancing.

"It's time to use your guide's ultimate power!" shouted Agnes over the commotion.

The children glanced at one another in confusion, looking on in shock as Hugo jumped forward, much to Magnus' horror.

"No Hugo!" he screamed.

But the orangutan ignored his master and continued to move closer to the nearest bloodsucker. Instantly, as he reached the vetala, he changed shape, his long limbs stretching out as the rest of his body expanded to massive proportions. Before their eyes, the friendly orangutan had turned into what looked like a mammoth orange gorilla. His large teeth snapped as he pounded the earth with both knuckles, before charging at the vetala, knocking it to the floor.

The rest of the animals followed suit, morphing into deadlier versions of their former selves. Inky the bat now resembled a pterodactyl, gnashing its sharp teeth at its enemy, and Prince, Tamara's eagle, became a giant griffin. Together, they flew above the vetalas, swooping down and ripping into the flesh of their grim bodies, before spitting out the chunks of meat like chewing gum.

The vetalas scattered everywhere, disappearing into the darkness of the trees as Evan's python, Mr Binks, became an enormous serpent, its tongue forking in and out, seeking its prey as it slid menacingly through the dead foliage. Isaac's boar, Boris, had doubled in size, and proceeded to charge at the vetalas, knocking them over like a line of skittles with his deadly oversized tusks, while Lucas Kane's now giant lemur, Lemmy, hissed and scratched at the creatures, snapping them in half whenever they got too close. Meanwhile, Angelica's tiny ginger cat was now a giant sabre-toothed tiger, and Angelica watched in awe as her lazy feline raced after the fleeing vetalas.

The children didn't know what to do; they had never witnessed this before, nor been told that their animal guides were capable of such a feat. The only animal that was missing was Poe, but no one had time to reflect on this as they chased after their guides, who were now running through the Dead Forest on a mad killing spree.

Luna had stayed behind with Theodore, the only guide who had failed to change form. The two of them stood before the portal as it continued to spin its vortex. Thankfully, the influx of vetalas seemed to have slowed for now.

"How can we stop this?" shouted Luna. "We don't have the athame or the ruby!"

"Belinda went straight after him when he escaped." Luna turned to see Augustus standing behind her.

"She'll get hurt," cried Luna. "And I'm too weak to do anything."

Augustus held his crystal wand out as a wave of new arrivals made their way through the portal, killing one after another, and Theodore galloped towards them, spearing them with his horn. Suddenly, the ground felt like it was opening up as a vibration of stomping feet surrounded them. Vetalas ran towards them, jumping out of the trees as they were pursued by all the transformed animal guides.

"They've rounded them up, to bring them back here," said Augustus over the racket.

"But how can we get them back through the portal?" shouted Luna.

A body suddenly flew through the air, landing in a heap in front of them.

"Frances," hissed Augustus.

The Edgar twins, still in their wolf forms, gagged as they tried to remove the taste of vampire from their mouths. As the madness continued all around them. Frances Chavron cowered where he lay.

"Where is the athame?" demanded Augustus.

Salvador emerged from behind the trees, followed by the rest of the teachers, and immediately ran over to Frances, crushing his boot down onto his chest, pinning him down.

"Hand it over!"

Frances scowled up at the warlock, trying to crawl away, but Salvador just bent down and picked him up by the scruff of his fancy coat collar.

As the guides continued to fight the vetalas, trying to keep them all inside an enclosed area, a white glow from above shed light down onto them. Luna levitated into mid-air.

"The moon!" shouted Agnes, pointing up to the sky.

As Luna's body convulsed, her arms shot straight out at each side, her eyes turning white as they rolled back into her head. Like a light switch being turned on, Luna's body vibrated as a bright white light enveloped her. The brightness affected the vetalas, and they screamed in agony, their bodies sizzling as they tried to seek refuge in the shadows of the trees. But the animals and their masters stopped them, herding them back into the circle of light.

Luna looked like some sort of saint, with her worshipers below her, looking up in awe. The creatures writhed in agony as their bodies sparked into flames, each one disappearing in a mound of dust.

"They're dying!" cried Bell, with tears in her eyes.

The commotion of the dying vetalas almost gave Frances Chavron the chance to escape, but Salvador wasn't giving up that easily. He had never trusted the vampire from the start, and there was no way he was going to let him get away with the athame after letting the rest of them do all the hard work in retrieving the ruby. Especially Luna Green.

Salvador reached down to grab Frances once more, but again, the vampire wriggled free. But just as he got to his feet, ready to make his getaway, a huge orange hairy arm grabbed him around the waist and lifted him up high.

Frances screamed as he came face to face with an orange gorilla baring huge incisors.

"Hugo!" shouted Magnus.

Salvador went through the vampire's coat pockets and sighed with relief as he discovered the athame in an inside pocket. Hugo dropped the vampire, and Salvador quickly noted that they had indeed attached the onyx and the ruby to the blade.

"Here." Salvador looked up as Archie Brutt handed him a pocket-knife. Accepting it, he twisted the tip of the knife into the ruby, turning both ways until finally it came loose. Suddenly, he heard a cry, and saw to his horror that Frances Chavron held Archie Brutt by the neck. His fangs were extended, ready to bite down on the teacher's exposed skin.

"No!" shouted Salvador. He held the ruby in one hand while the other grasped the athame, his hands gesturing surrender.

"No, Salvador, don't do it," said Archie through gritted teeth.

Frances Chavron lowered his head, his sharp fangs ready to bite into Archie's artery. Hugo took a step towards them.

"Drop the athame and ruby and tell the monkey to step back!" Frances demanded.

Salvador looked on helplessly, but just as he was about to drop the athame and the ruby, he watched Archie Brutt twist his body around and push the vampire towards the open portal.

"Do it now!" he summoned over his shoulder.

As Salvador hesitated, Augustus grabbed the two magickal objects from his grip, and without further delay, placed the ruby back in its rightful place on the athame's blade.

"NO!" screamed Salvador, watching helplessly as his dear old friend was sucked inside the portal along with the vampire. The vortex spun backwards, diminishing into thin air, until it was only a dot on the horizon, eventually vanishing completely.

Salvador fell to his knees, pounding at the dry earth. "Why?" he asked the emptiness before him. "Why?"

Chapter 45

The walk back to the manor had never been so exhausting. Everyone had expended all their energy during the battle, and Archie's sacrifice had hit them all hard. Not only that, but Belinda was still missing.

Luna had been reluctant to leave the Dead Forest without her friend, especially in the knowledge that the Sisters of Jonas were still out there, but after a lengthily search, there had been no sign of the young witch. Concerned for the other children, who all looked as though they might fall over any second, Agnes had insisted that they all return to the manor, sending the Edgar twins out to search for Belinda.

Drained of energy, the children trudged after their teachers, while Salvador shadowed the group from behind, his blank gaze fixed on the ground.

"Do you think he'll be okay?" Bell whispered to Agnes.

The head teacher shrugged sympathetically. "I hope

so. Only time will tell."

"Why did he do it?" asked Luna, trying to distract herself from Belinda's disappearance.

"He was already dying. The bite of the vetala would have soon transformed him into one of them," explained Agnes. "He saved us all by taking that piece of—," Agnes paused, composing herself. "Archie Brutt is a hero, and for that, he will be greatly honoured. Not just by all of us, but also by the light creatures."

A sound of feet coming towards them startled the group into stillness.

"Who goes there?" Agnes called.

A familiar face came into view. "It's just us."

"Dahlia," cried Luna. She rushed towards the fairy, grabbing her in a bear hug.

"Whoa," laughed the fairy, as she embraced her back. "Are we too late?"

Augustus snorted. "As always." He brushed past Dahlia and headed towards his father, King Engogabal. His brother, Cassieus, appeared from behind. The three of them embraced.

"We heard the vetalas had escaped, and were just on our way to help," said the king. "We didn't want to use the fae tunnels for fear that it would give us away."

"Too late," sniffed Salvador. "We kicked their asses back to where they came from."

The fairies stared after the warlock as he pushed past them, heading in the manor's direction.

Augustus shrugged as his brother gave him a look of bewilderment. "I'll explain it all later." He turned back to his father. "We left no prisoners. The volume of ash debris near the portal is proof of that."

"Is the athame safe?" asked the king.

"Yes, we have ensured that everything is as it should be," explained Agnes.

"Well, almost everything."

The group came to a sudden halt behind Augustus, as the tall fairy pointed towards the manor.

"Now will you change the magick password?"

Chapter 46

The mood in the manor was sombre. Even after another resounding victory, everyone was in a contemplative mood over Archie Brutt's decision to stop Frances Chavron from escaping. Salvador had disappeared into his office, while the rest regrouped inside the dining hall, exhausted from the events of the past few hours. Jeannie Gibbs, along with Murdoch, Aengus and Gobbins, bustled around the hall, serving warm drinks and sandwiches.

Luna sat next to Magnus, both of them reflecting on what they had witnessed, trying to cheer each other up in light of Belinda's continued absence.

"Who would have thought Hugo could be such a monster," Magnus pondered.

Luna looked over at the orangutan who, to Jeannie Gibbs dismay, was stealing sandwiches from her plate as she served them to the teachers. The hoglin batted Hugo's hairy hand away, before continuing her round of condolences.

Luna laughed weakly. "Yeah, no one prepared us for that. I guess we still have a lot of learning to do." She paused. "It's strange that they didn't change back when the shadow walkers attacked... maybe they are still learning their skills too."

As Luna's eyes skimmed the room, she noticed Sebastian Chavron sitting on his own in the far corner. In all the excitement, she had forgotten about him. Excusing herself from Magnus, she made her way over to the younger vampire.

"Is it okay to sit here?" she asked.

Sebastian nodded his head solemnly without looking up. Luna took the chair next to him.

"I'm so sorry for your loss," she said sincerely, placing a reassuring hand over his. His icy hand sent shivers down her spine.

He looked up, tears streaming down his cheeks. "I didn't know," sniffled Sebastian. "I didn't know my father was a traitor. He was so excited when we were invited here... he despised those foul creatures, how could he help them?"

His eyes were full of anger and Luna shifted nervously in her chair, not sure what to say. Noticing her anxiety, Sebastian's gaze softened.

"I am so sorry Luna. My dad made me spy on you, saying you were not to be trusted."

Luna thought back to the night when she took the death potion, and the mysterious footsteps they heard outside their room.

"I understand now those were lies. And I wish things could be different. But my father made sure that my future here at Blackhill is non-existent."

"But where are you going to go?" she asked.

"I'm leaving first thing in the morning. A coach is coming for me to take me back to France."

"Who will look after you?"

"You do know I am one hundred and fifty years old, right?"

The two of them looked at one another, and Luna smiled shyly. "We will miss you, Sebastian. I hope you can come back and visit."

Sebastian smiled back at her as Luna got to her feet, his fangs protruding slightly, making Luna shiver.

"Thank you Luna Green, and I truly hope you find your mother."

Just then, Agnes Guthrie tapped her glass, and a gentle ringing echoed through the hall, drawing everyone's attention.

"Now that you are all fed and rested, it is time we searched the grounds. Belinda is still missing, and I am anxious for us to find her as soon as possible. She could be in danger."

Chairs scraped back as everyone hurried to their feet, bodies scattering in different directions. Luna and Magnus remained together, meeting Lily in the hallway as they left the manor to search the gardens, with permission to pass through the enchanted wall.

It was still dark outside as the three of them scanned the darkness for their friend.

"BELINDA!" Lily yelled, her voice echoing around the gardens.

Luna glanced over to the gate, sensing the new barrier that the fae had created, their strong enchantment ensuring that no unwanted visitors could get in or out. Suddenly, a low thumping sound drew her attention to the sky.

"Guys, do you hear that?"

Lily and Magnus both stopped to listen.

Thump. Thump.

All three looked up at the sky as something small came plunging downwards, stepping apart as the creature landed on the grass between them.

"Poe!" cried Luna, ducking down to pick up the raven.

"Is he—" Lily murmured.

"No, he's still alive." Luna could feel his tiny heartbeat pumping against her hand. She checked him over, stopping as she noticed that something was attached to one of his wings. Carefully, Luna unwrapped a piece of parchment. As she unfolded it, something fell out.

"What's that?" said Magnus as he bent down to pick it up. "Ew, it feels like hair," he said, almost dropping it.

Luna took it from his grasp and held it up against the dim light. It was indeed a strand of hair, but it was the colour that gave it away.

"Belinda," whispered Luna, as she studied the bright green strand.

Lily gasped, placing a hand over her mouth.

"Does the parchment say anything?" asked Magnus.

Luna unfolded it, noticing the scribbled writing. Holding it up, she lit up her hand with some of her waning energy and read aloud:

Dear whoever finds this,

You think because you have the athame you can stop us. But I like to think we have something equally important.

We have the witch, and unless she helps us find the missing grimoire, or the next crystal, she will no longer be of use to us.

Give us what we want, or next time, it won't be her pet that we injure. No. Next time, it will be her head we throw over the wall.

Quickly now. Time is ticking.
The Sisters of Jonas.

The End

Acknowledgments

I would like to thank once again everyone in Cranthorpe Millner, and especially my editor Victoria Richards – it was a long slog, but we got there eventually!

Thank you to my biggest supporter, my mum, and to the rest of the family for encouraging me since my early storytelling years. A magnitude of laughter and tears have been shed, witnessing the loss of many loved ones along the way, whose support I shall always cherish.

But most importantly, I would like to thank all my readers. I'd love to connect with you all on:

Facebook: @ClaireHastieAuthor

Instagram: @claire_hastie_author

Twitter: @clairehastie12.

BV - #0012 - 280622 - C0 - 197/132/22 - PB - 9781803780610 - Matt Lamination